David Warby is a film editor, songw[...] with his wife and son. He is a glutton [...] himself in the third person when writi[...] debut novel.

DAVID WARBY

VIKING WEREWOLF

Copyright © David Warby 2024

Cover photography by Vlastas at Depositphotos.
Viking Werewolf logo by Llewellyn van Eeden.
Map by David Cousens.

David Warby asserts the moral right to be identified as the author of this work.

ISBN: 9798325253119

This novel is entirely a work of fiction. The names, characters, and incidents portrayed in it are the work of the author's imagination. Any resemblance to actual persons, living or dead, events or localities is entirely coincidental.

Set in Fournier MT Std.
Cover font: Cinzel.

All rights reserved. No part of this publication may be reproduced, stored in a retrieval system, or transmitted, in any form or by any means, electronic, mechanical, photocopying, recording or otherwise, without the prior permission of the author.

For Ethan

ACKNOWLEDGMENTS

Many thanks to my 'bookclub' buddy, Ben Mears, who coached and coaxed me all the way from the starting pistol to the finish line. And to Rebecca Rouillard, my other beta reader—my heartfelt thanks. I hope you enjoyed the brownies.

Enormous gratitude goes to my alpha reader, Tamzin, whose keen eye and loving support helped bring this book into focus. It only took ten years. No biggie.

Further thanks must be given to my brothers Paul and Joshua (both writers in their own right), Ethan, Althea, David Cousens, Rob Jones, Llewellyn van Eeden, Bevan Gauld, Alex Smiley, and the good people of Lofotr Viking Museum. Each of you has breathed life into this project in one way or another.

CONTENTS

1	The Cave	1
2	An Unwelcome Rumour	5
3	Loved Ones	10
4	Valknut	21
5	The Ritual	26
6	Red Meadow	36
7	The Alpha	41
8	Teeth Of Iron	49
9	Aftermath	55
10	The Oracle	60
11	Prisoner	70
12	A Long Distance	76
13	Half-Blood	86
14	Requiem	92
15	The Daywalker	96
16	Traitor	105
17	Strange New World	111
18	Blood In The Streets	122
19	Half A Warning	136
20	The Brotherhood	140
21	Freya's Tale	148

22	All Hail The King	155
23	The World Tree	163
24	Klo Island	169
25	Sister Slaves	184
26	The Viking Way	190
27	The Battle Of Klo Mountain	196
28	The Darkness Below	205
29	A Shared Joy	215
30	Red Dawn	220
31	The Norns Of Fate	228
32	Deadfall	236
33	A Rushed Reunion	242
34	The Tipping Point	250
35	Ragnarök	257
36	The Offering	268
37	The Beastly Boys	273
38	Jörmungandr	279
39	The Wolf Victorious	289
40	Marigolds	299

Heimdall's Balcony
Serpent's Tail
Mount Varda
Alpha's Cave
Two Mile Hill
Seven Pits
Crescent Beach
Runolodda
Red Meadow
Dark Woods
Gudrun's Cottage
Hvalvik (Whale Bay)
Harbour
Klo Island

THE CAVE

932 A.D.

Scion held fast to the icy spear.

As the youngest, and with the most to prove, the boy fought hard to hide his shivering. But he need not have worried. The older huntsmen gazed fixedly ahead, grim in their thick furs, as they crept toward the yawning jaws of a bear cave.

Beyond the cave, a pine forest swept into the distance where mountains rose like jagged teeth. Scion gazed up at the low winter clouds, crumbling in the predawn light, turning the white earth to pink. After three weeks of incessant snow, even the promise of sunlight appealed. The promise of meat, even more so.

Ever since Scion's people had settled in these lands, the woods had teemed with elk, reindeer, rabbit, and fox. An abundant hunting ground for the remote village. Yet this year had been different. Something—an unusually voracious beast—had slaughtered the game at an astonishing rate, leaving little but macerated bones and crushed antlers in its wake. To make matters worse, the barley harvest had been a meagre affair, not enough for the village of Runolodda to survive until spring.

So, with his people frustrated and on the brink of starvation, Chief Lennärt had dispatched twelve men and a select handful of the more *cunning* boys in a last-ditch attempt to gather what they could before the cold set in for the season. Whether or not this particular bear in this particular cave was to blame for the recent killing spree was a matter for debate, but regardless, the meat would go a long way to filling the pot.

Scion smiled at a memory: His father stooping to ruffle his fin-shaven hair. *'Better to catch a bear snoring than roaring, lad'.*

Then they crowded in. The other memories. Unbidden and unwelcome.

A frozen lake. Thin ice. Screams.

His goatskin cloak billowed open with a sudden gust of wind, snapping him back to the present, making him curse.

Too loud, Scion realised, gritting his teeth.

Vali, the big man to his right, cuffed him firmly across the head. The boy nodded, submitting. *Sorry*, he mouthed. Vali grunted, turning his broad shoulders back to the cave. *Firm yet fair. That's the Vali I know.*

Vali, when not fixated on the hunt, came across as a warm soul with a sharp mind and a free laugh. His skill with the bow was legendary. Last winter, when Scion's parents had passed, Vali had taken the boy in as his apprentice at the tender age of six and provided him with the closest thing to family he now had.

Drengr and Manning, an inseparable pair of lumbering oafs with braided beards and matching purple trousers, exchanged a sly grin. A good head-cuffing never failed to amuse them.

'The runt should be knotting necklaces with the women-folk,' whispered Drengr. 'Not soiling himself under our quarry's nose.'

Manning snorted at this, sizing Scion up with a sneer. He was about to cast out a barb of his own when Vali's fierce glare bored into him. The pair shrank back, their gaze dropping to their boots in unison. They swiftly regained a keen interest in the cave.

Drengr, thought Scion. *More like dunga: useless fellow.*

'The next fool to make a sound—' began Vali.

But his words drowned in a deafening roar that sent a flock of ravens, perched above the cave mouth, exploding into the sky. All eyes jerked toward the sound. Scion stopped dead in his tracks, his stance wide, adjusting his grip.

That was no bear.

In the stillness that followed, Vali stepped back. The others followed suit, wide-eyed and shock-pale, straining to make out any detail in the inky hollow.

All was quiet.

Then, a low rumble.

Scion smelt it before he saw it.

An enormous, slavering brown bear burst from the cave, its great paws spraying up snow as it barrelled through the group. Men cried out, panicked, leaping clear. Manning, the bumbling oaf, yelled and hurled his spear blindly, missing the bear by a few feet. In the jostle, Scion was slammed onto his back, though he used the momentum to swing over onto his feet, ready to confront the danger.

The bear faltered, hurtling only a few more paces before buckling under its own weight. It crashed awkwardly onto its belly, leaving a slick streak of blood in the snow as it slid hard into a boulder. It shuddered for a brief moment. Then lay lifeless in a crumpled heap. Its head, throat, and shoulders were raked with deep gashes. A long tongue lolled from its bloody mouth, its eyes vacant. Slowly rising to their feet, the huntsmen gathered to the spectacle.

Drengr wiped a sweaty palm on his bright purple trousers before lifting a flap of bear flesh with his axe. 'What in Thor's name could do that?'

'Silence,' hissed Vali, his gaze fixed on the cave. He lowered his spear to the ground and snatched an arrow to his bow.

A hush.

Then—

Thunder growled from the darkness.

Men bunched closer, forming a bristling spear wall.

Scion squinted into the gloom.

There.

Movement.

A Shadow within the shadow.

Then, like spider legs curling around a door frame, long-fingered claws came into view, dripping thick red blood as the beast stepped into the light.

Scion gaped.

The Creature stood like a man on clawed feet, ten feet tall and covered in thick tawny hair. Its overlong arms were spread wide and low. Its back was hunched, coiled. Too many teeth flashed from the blood-smeared jaws of its enormous wolf-like head.

Vali was about to shout a command when it charged.

AN UNWELCOME RUMOUR

TWENTY YEARS LATER

Drengr stared blankly at the high ceiling of a colossal stone hall.

He flinched when the tall, thin man in the grey cloak twisted his ear.

'Hurry now, worm,' the tall man leered. 'Don't make this difficult for me, or I'll sure as shite make it difficult for you.'

Drengr shuffled ahead on grimy bare feet, oblivious to the string of drool dangling from his mouth, his once-bright purple trousers now faded rags over his scrawny legs. He blinked at the hundred or so warriors mingling about. Some played dice at the many tables. Others conversed or cleaned weapons, paying him little attention. A few caught sight of the old scar on his scalp, where the skull sank partially on the left side.

Klo Hall was an immense cave lined with guttering torches along roughly sculpted walls. Twin stairways, chiselled into the rock face, rose at the far end on either side, framing a high wooden dais that led up to a throne.

The tall man halted Drengr at the dais and forced him down with a cruel kick to the back of the knees. 'Kneel, worm!'

King Ødger seemed to notice them for the first time. He was a stout man draped in finery, a red suede cape cascading down the steps. He wiped wine from his walrus moustache and stared down at the tall man and the dribbling fool.

'This had better be good, Ulrick. I can smell this *wretch* from here,' he muttered.

The tall man touched the brooch at his breast—the Klo salute. 'He *is* that, my King. And mad as a bat. Yet, I've bent my ear to his babbling for some weeks now. This man knows something of our . . . past trouble.'

'Well?' pressed Ødger.

'He begs near the docks most days, blithering to himself, saying the same two words over and over: *Wolf-men* and *Runolodda*.'

At this, Drengr grew agitated. 'Knotting necklaces! Knotting necklaces!' he raved, then broke into a cackle, spittle dripping to the stone floor.

King Ødger frowned.

'Wolf-men? But that's impossible. My father was the last of that kind.'

'Perhaps not, my King,' said Ulrick. 'Look.'

Without any resistance, he lifted Drengr's tattered tunic to reveal the thin torso, raked with four thick scars equidistant apart.

Ødger winced. 'It's more likely he was mauled by a bear.' Though doubt had crept into his voice. Many summers ago, King Ari, Ødger's father, had returned from a voyage with a strange wound to his shoulder, an enormous bite mark oozing darkly. In addition, his back had borne similar lacerations to what the dribbling fool had suffered. Stranger still is what happened the following full moon in this very hall.

'My King. If I may say so, your father's affliction—'

'My father is dead, Ulrick. And the sickness has died with him.' King Ødger scowled at the beggar for a moment. 'If there *are* others . . .' he mused.

Ødger stood to fill his horn once more with wine. 'Is he bitten?'

'No,' assured Ulrick.

Ødger descended the creaking dais to take a closer look at Drengr. 'Where is this *Runolodda*?'

Terror surged through Drengr, his eyes darting everywhere and nowhere. The word had conjured memories that slid and collided through his broken mind.

He let out a pleading moan.

'North, my King,' replied Ulrick. 'Somewhere along the river Hreim. I hear they're a small farming community that occasionally sell swine in Hvalvik.'

Ødger sipped the dark wine and sighed.

'Gorm!' he bellowed. 'Come!'

A hush settled across the expansive cavern.

A broad man in a black fur cloak rose at the far end of the hall, the light casting him in silhouette. He advanced. All eyes averted as the clop of Gorm's heavy boots echoed in the stillness.

Interesting, noted Ødger. *Do they fear Gorm more than their own king? I must keep an eye on this one.*

Ulrick hid his delight. This was precisely how he had hoped the day would unfold. There was nothing he enjoyed more than bloodshed, and if Gorm was to be involved there would be plenty of it. As a Jarl of the Klo, Gorm had led many a merciless raid along the Northland coast and as far afield as Caledonia and

Almany, earning respect for his strategic mind and alarming brutality.

'My King.' Gorm's voice rumbled, deep and guttural.

It was hard not to be intimidated by the man. Torchlight glinted off his chain armour. A groomed beard tapered away from his shaved scalp. His blizzard-cold eyes gleamed a pale blue. Yet, most unsettling was how his palm never left the handle of a great double-edged battle-axe in his belt. Solid brawn, Gorm stood in contrast to Ulrick's lithe and sinuous build. If Ulrick was a blade, then Gorm was a hammer.

Ødger continued to inspect the beggar, not deigning to look Gorm's way. 'How many slaves were captured in the last raid, General?'

Gorm spoke plainly. 'Thirty Saxons, my King.'

'Burn them all. They may carry the Wolf's Curse. I will not have it poison my merchandise.'

Gorm frowned. 'The slaves will be inspected before sale. It would be unwise to—'

'Oh, unwise, is it?' Ødger snapped back his cloak. 'Are you familiar with the sagas, Gorm? They warn of Fenrir the Wolf, Doom of the gods, Slayer of all mankind.'

'I am familiar,' said Gorm, holding a steely expression.

'And yet it seems you fail to grasp that the saga has come to life,' sneered the King, glancing at his courtiers for their laughter and approval.

Gorm stared icily at Ødger. Sagas amused the idle, and only fools interpreted folklore literally.

Ødger smiled. 'You see my point.' He leaned in close enough for Gorm to smell the bitter wine on his breath. 'Muster a crew. Eradicate this threat. Discreetly. I will not have a handful of skin-changers interrupting trade. Understood?'

'It will be as you command, my King.'

'Excellent,' smiled Ødger, wringing his hands. 'Now. More wine!'

As Gorm turned away he caught Ulrick's expression.

The tall man grinned like a goblin.

LOVED ONES

They ran naked, bare feet thundering down the woodland slope toward the cliff's edge.

White-haired Tyr, the group's most competitive member, held the lead, with Birger and Scion fiercely contesting for second place. Olle trailed somewhere behind, out of breath but determined to keep up as best his wobbling belly would allow.

They whooped and crowed in the crisp autumn air, revelling in the sheer joy of a friendship shared since childhood. They had been dubbed *The Beastly Boys* after cornering a lone wolf in the forest and returning to the village wearing its bloody pelt, crudely ripped up and divided between themselves. The *Boys* had paraded through the muddy streets, draped in gore, beaming ear to ear. They had only been ten summers old.

Now at the age of twenty and some, they boasted sinewy muscle and oiled beards. Men in their prime. All but Olle, whose paunch hinted at a fondness for too much ale.

Tyr's snow-white hair—uncommonly satin smooth for a man—whipped about, stinging his eyes. He reached the edge of the precipice at full speed, threw his chin up, and leaped. In an instant, he took in the grandeur of his surroundings. The wide and steaming spring thirty feet below, ringed with trees. The turquoise sky. The smell of pine on the breeze. Tyr's thoughts frequently revolved around axe designs, the comparative draw weight of various bows, or where to find a better whetstone for his many blades. But as he plunged into the warm water, his mind reeled with how to avoid the enormous Birger landing on his head.

Birger the Bear, as he was known, had always been large. One of his earliest memories was of sitting in the soot of his father's forge, sparks flying while he watched metal hammered into sickles and ploughs. Knud the Blacksmith would howl with laughter to see Birger playing as a toddler with heavy iron ingots and steel offcuts like they were straw dolls.

Birger the Bear clapped a meaty palm onto Scion's chest, pushing him back with a laugh. They vaulted forward, slapping each other in mid-plummet, narrowly avoiding Tyr, who had covered his snowy head with his elbows.

Scion surfaced for air and smoothed back his fin-like strip of hair, the exposed scalp now tattooed with runes on either side.

'Ha! You sly cheat, Birger!' he grinned. 'I *had* you, by Odin! Admit it!'

'I'll admit that you're quick for a squirrel. But size always matters, or haven't you heard, wee man?' Birger the Bear laughed, soaking up the hot water.

'Brothers. Up there!' exclaimed Tyr.

Scion peered up the rockface that loomed like the prow of a great ship. Olle emerged from the clifftop forest and hurtled clumsily toward the pointed tip of the overhang. Even from this distance, the effort showed on his flushed, frowning face.

'Run, Olle, you glorious beast!' shouted Birger.

'Shut up!' huffed Olle, his faraway voice barely audible.

'What say you, brothers?' murmured Scion conspiratorially. 'Feet first this time?'

'Nay. Belly,' said Tyr flatly, flicking his long white fringe to the side.

'Always the belly,' agreed Birger the Bear, clicking his thick neck.

Always the jokester. Always the merrymaker. Olle was a man of simple pleasures: ale, song, feasting, and farming. Although the latter was mostly at the insistence of his equally rotund parents. Not the brightest candle on the shelf, Olle was still the most loyal friend the Beastly Boys could have asked for.

As Olle neared the drop-off something moved in his peripheral.

'Chilly day, isn't it?' chimed a soft voice.

'Aargh!' The last thing Olle saw before tripping and vanishing over the edge was a young woman in a blue dress propped behind a boulder and sunning her slender legs.

He plunged to the pool with little dignity and landed on his belly.

The others cheered.

'Oh ho! Impressive form, Olle! You *must* teach us your technique,' teased Scion. But his grin fell away when he caught movement up top.

The young woman was lying on her stomach, chin in her hands, blonde hair tied back, peering down. The Beastly Boys promptly had their nudity brought to mind.

'My, my,' she called. 'Fish in a stew. With carrots, I see. Can a woman not have a quiet afternoon without all this rushing about? I've never witnessed such a stampede.'

'Our apologies, Lady Astrid,' hollered Scion, fussing with his *fin*. 'We didn't see you there. Would you care to join us?'

Would you care to join us? Shut up, fool! What are you saying?

Tyr stifled a chuckle.

'Scion. Leader of the pack,' replied Astrid smoothly. 'A kind offer, but alas I have duties to attend to.'

Alas? thought Scion, his mouth drying up. *Well, that's something isn't it?*

Astrid: daughter of Chief Erik and Lady Freya. Astrid: hair like sunlight, eyes like starlight. The woman's gaze unravelled Scion more than he could hide and he kept tripping over himself in her presence.

'Duties?' he managed. 'Oh, aye. The Full Moon Ritual. That's tonight, is it?' Even from this distance, he noted her sudden unease. Had he said something wrong?

'Yes,' she said stiffly. 'And Thora will not appreciate it if her apprentice is late. Again.' They nodded, each forming a mental picture of the wizened Witch of Runolodda. The old woman had terrified them since childhood, and it would not do for Astrid to disappoint her. Again.

'Apologies,' said Astrid, 'but I must say my farewells. The Bitten will need . . . tending.'

Scion understood. They all did. Those many years ago, he had survived what was now referred to as *The Battle of the Bear Cave*. The Creature—now named the Alpha, and living among them—had bitten six of the hunters, injuring many others. Thank the gods the sun had risen when it did.

The elders called it a Ritual, though Astrid saw it as little more than guard duty—locking their infected kinsfolk behind bars until daybreak, only to repeat the charade at the next Full Moon.

She rose to her feet, brushing yellow leaves from her frock. 'Perhaps next time one of you will ascertain the water's depth before diving headfirst into a rock.' It was a genuine rebuke, though it carried a playful undertone.

'Goodbye for now, fellows. It has been . . . educational.'

Ascertain, mulled Scion as Astrid skipped away. *That's a word to bear in mind.*

He turned to see his friends grinning from ear to ear.

'*Would you care to join us*, 'ey?' quipped Tyr.

'Shut up,' mumbled Scion, as they burst into peals of laughter.

*

Astrid approached her horse, tethered to a tree and cropping a thistle.

'There you are, boy. Miss me?' She leaped fluidly onto his back to stroke his spotted mane.

'Come, Hermod' she urged, gently nudging his flank. 'Let's head back.'

Astrid had helped with the birth of Hermod, instantly falling in love with what she called his *freckles*—dozens of brown spots peppered all over his pale coat. She had claimed the foal for herself, ignoring her mother's objection that there were far more handsome horses to be had. And the pair had been inseparable ever since.

They cut across a dappled glade strewn with spruce needles and dotted with brown-capped mushrooms. Astrid paused to pocket a few sprigs of mugwort for her teacher, Thora the Witch, to grind into a tincture. Astrid loved the woods. It was her refuge from *duty*, that burden of leadership imposed upon a Chieftain's family.

Set the example.

Show strength and good judgement.

Always.

To a great extent, her rank ostracised her from the other young women who were free to simply *be* young women. Free to choose a path other than the one thrust upon them.

Astrid found nothing more unbearable than a cage.

That is why, as she envisioned the prisons to be used in tonight's Ritual, her mood darkened. Of course, she understood the logic. Runolodda would not be safe if Wolf-men roamed free beneath a Full Moon. Still, the idea of locking them away—even for a single night—gnawed at her heart.

Astrid turned Hermod onto the worn trail that led up to a high ridge. Here, the trees thinned and eventually parted to offer a view like no other. The village lay nestled in the valley before her, with pig pens to the south, and barley fields to the north. There began the Serpent's Tail, a winding path that led up into the mountains.

The village dwellings were squat, thatched, and huddled around the Great Hall—a grand longhouse ornamented by fine carvings and a pair of elegant rafters that crossed like horns above the gable. A tall timber fence encircled Runolodda, safeguarding the few dozen families from predators.

A tree-lined track stretched eastward from the village, climbing for two miles through an obscured pass to a large open field at the foot of Mount Varda. The field was named Red Meadow for its blush of bright poppies that extended to a drop-off down to Crescent Beach and the glittering ocean beyond.

A thin plume of smoke spiralled from the Great Hall, interrupting her reverie.

Oh, dear. They've lit the evening fire already. Can it be that late?

She spurred Hermod on with a click of her tongue.

Cold eyes watched them speed off down the slope.

*

Chief Erik sat atop a loaded cart beside the Great Hall, and sighed.

'Is this entirely necessary, Greybeards?'

Fiske and Selby, a pair of grizzled old goatherds, stood squared off and scowling. Each clutched a shield and an oversized axe, clearly too heavy for their reedy arms.

'Of course it is!' yelled Fiske. 'I caught this *vulture* butchering one of my goats!'

'Rubbish, it was *my* goat!' screeched Selby.

'Mine!'

'Your eyesight is worse than your breath!'

'Don't you start on my breath!'

'Why not? It's your best feature!'

'Hey!'

A crowd began to form. Men and women trotted from their log-walled homes, all grins, abandoning their crafts and cooking pots. A small girl carried her chicken, determined not to let it miss out. This was free entertainment, after all.

'What's all this, husband?'

Chief Erik revolved in his seat. His wife carried a bread basket, a dusting of flour down her embroidered mint-green dress.

'Freya,' he smiled. 'They're at it again.'

Freya rolled her eyes. 'Another neighbourly duel to the death, I see.'

'If I wasn't Chief I'd crack their stubborn old skulls together and be done with it.'

Fiske swung his axe wildly, the steel biting into Selby's shield. 'Chew on that, you thieving cockroach!' he wailed, making a futile effort to dislodge the blade.

'You first!' Selby hoisted his axe with considerable effort but the backswing yanked him off balance. He landed on his bony buttocks in a puddle, dragging Fiske down with him.

'Ooh, my back!' squealed Selby.

'My knee!' howled Fiske. 'You twisted my bloody knee!'

The crowd thundered their applause.

Freya drew in a breath and lowered the basket to tie back her tousled brown hair. 'Leave it to me, my love. Obviously, this requires a woman's intervention.'

Erik shook his head and chuckled. 'Hard to believe those two were once berserkers.'

With the matinee over, the crowd trickled away, leaving the old men slumped in the mud. As Freya approached, they perked up, taking a short break from snarling at one another.

'Lady Freya,' piped Fiske.

'Come now, Greybeards,' purred Freya, bending low. 'Surely there's an easier way to settle this misunderstanding?'

They swallowed hard at the sight of her ample cleavage.

'I suppose . . .' whispered Fiske, matching the level of her voice.

'Er—as you say, Lady Freya,' gulped Selby.

'I suggest we learn to share,' she said, passing Fiske a loaf of bread. 'I'm sure Selby would be happy to host you this evening. Perhaps a barrel of ale from my personal stores would do well to wash down a plate or two of roasted goat?'

The elderly duo exchanged a shrewd look.

'A whole barrel, 'ey?' grinned Fiske.

'When winter approaches,' continued Freya, 'Fiske can return the favour. Selby in the spring. And so on. You'll set a fine example of neighbourly fellowship to the village. They look to both of you for wisdom, you know?'

Selby wiped his drippy nose. 'Never eat yellow snow, I

always say.'

'Bathe once a week. And don't forget the cheeks,' offered Fiske, casting light upon the obvious.

Freya spread her hands and bowed.

'There you go. Now hop to it, gentlemen. That ale won't drink itself.'

Fiske sprang to his feet, rubbing his knee. 'Whatever you say, Lady Freya!'

'I'll fetch the drinking horns!' exclaimed Selby.

They hobbled off, arms over shoulders, singing in separate keys. Freya returned to her husband and hoisted the bread basket into the cart.

'Nicely done,' smiled Erik.

'If those two can't learn to share, they'll be mucking out the longhouse cesspit until they can.'

'Ha! Watching you work your feminine wiles like that makes me want to—' He stopped short as Astrid rounded the Hall, leading Hermod by the bit.

'Want to *what*, father?' she smirked. 'Sing her praises?'

Erik smiled. 'Exactly, Daughter. You stole the words from my lips.' His face fell when Freya advanced like a thundercloud. Turning his back to his wife, he snuck Astrid a mock grimace. She kept a straight face.

'Where have you been?' demanded Freya.

'Only out for a ride with Hermod. The poor soul is so restless in the paddock.'

'You left this at home,' scolded Freya, handing Astrid a dagger sheathed in its leather scabbard.

Astrid repressed a groan. 'Oh. Yes. Sorry, Mother.'

'What is our rule, Astrid?'

'To wear it without fail. But, Mother, it's only—'

'*What* is our rule?'

Astrid clenched her jaw. She held her mother's stare for a moment, then snatched the dagger and tucked it under her belt.

'Yes, Mother.'

Freya raised an eyebrow at Erik, hoping for more than she got—a crooked smile and a shrug. She made a clumsy attempt to lighten her tone.

'Well? Hitch the horse, Daughter. We don't have all day.'

Astrid turned away, taciturn, busying herself with the harness.

Freya rubbed her eyes.

They endured an awkward silence while Astrid finished up, then clambered aboard. Setting off, Hermod pulled the cart through the wide streets, passing the blacksmith's forge and the poky marketplace, where children chased a pig through the stalls, annoying an elderly woman at her loom. Smoke curled through vents in the thatched rooftops. Horses brayed in the stables, the sweet richness of straw on the breeze.

Astrid glanced nonchalantly at the young folk heading to the Hall for mead and merriment, and wondered if Scion was among them.

'Looking for anyone in particular?' Erik stared straight ahead as the cart rumbled on.

'No,' blushed Astrid, fussing with the silver brooch of her dress. 'Just taking in the sunset.'

'Ah.'

Astrid watched the ground roll by.

Would you care to join us? Scion had asked. The idea of swimming beside his naked body had sent a heat through her belly. Despite growing up in the same village, the pair had barely shared more than passing pleasantries so the invitation had come as a surprise. A rather welcome surprise. If only her life consisted of more than curfews and commitments . . .

Erik waved up to the guard wall and the main gates creaked open. Across the threshold, the path spilled out onto a stretch of flat gravel that soon rose into a forested mountain. There was a pass—unimaginatively named Two-Mile-Hill—that climbed through the rugged terrain to Red Meadow, the site of the Full Moon Ritual.

As the cart rattled along, Freya peered back at the rusting sky while she listened to Astrid and Erik swap stories and tell jokes—a welcome distraction from the emotionally draining ritual to follow. Astrid was always so carefree around her father. So open. Whereas Freya's own relationship with their daughter usually felt like the pressure before a storm. She wished it was not so. Wished she could bridle her need to fuss. To worry. Freya knew that she frustrated her strong, independent daughter. Nevertheless, she knew to remain vigilant.

Particularly since Astrid was the Alpha's daughter.

And little was known about half-bloods.

VALKNUT

The Great Hall throbbed with laughter.

A whole deer roasted on a spit over the central firepit, smoke rising to the rafters, dancers dancing, bards bellowing, horns of ale and mead sloshing across the tables.

The Beastly Boys made merry in the thick of it.

Olle hovered by the fire, tearing off strips of meat and draining cup after cup of stout.

A busty young lass sat on Tyr's lap, stroking his silky white hair and looking terribly bored as he waxed lyrical on the merits and demerits of various sword hilts.

Scion had just placed a wager on Birger the Bear.

—And immediately regretted it.

Birger had never lost an arm wrestle. He had taken on six or seven contenders in as many minutes, slamming their fists down with a roar, unstoppable as a rockslide. But then Torsten had risen to the challenge, and Birger's complexion now shifted from red to purple under the strain.

'Put your back into it, by Thor!' yelled Scion above the clamour.

Birger's father, Knud the Blacksmith, had money on this too. His voice, worn down from years of coughing in a smoky forge, came out a comically thin rasp.

'Come on, lad! You're a hammer! You're a hammer!'

Sweat poured off Birger the Bear.

Torsten wasn't exactly a dark horse. He sat thick-muscled, bull-necked, and sausage-fingered. A little younger than the Beastly Boys, he worked as a logger, keeping to himself, shy with the ladies, and reserved with the men. He seldom dropped by the Hall, but tonight he had something planned. Something out of character.

And then, as though the goddess of love had read his thoughts, in walked Tove. She wore a simple orange strap dress over a wool tunic, though for Torsten it was as though the sun had risen.

He melted.

For years he had admired Tove from afar. Tove the Poet. Tove the Songbird. Tove the Devout—Keeper of the Sacred Flame. How did one talk to such a creature? Conversation was never Torsten's strong point so tonight he would attempt a different approach.

Birger the Bear noticed Torsten's faraway look and pressed home the advantage, heaving down on his bulging forearm.

'Yes! Yes! Yes!' screamed Scion.

'You have him, son!' croaked Knud.

It was like watching a tree fall slowly but surely through honey.

'Argh!' At last, Torsten's knuckles were pinned to the table. He shifted his gaze back and forth, hoping Tove had not witnessed his defeat.

'A fine contest!' blared Birger, slapping Torsten on the shoulder. 'It seems the Norns allowed me to win this one.

Perhaps next time, 'ey?'

Torsten smiled weakly. 'Perhaps. Aye.' He tried to depart in peace, but Olle—accompanied by a group of Birger's admirers—shimmied onto the bench. Olle squeezed his bulging belly into place and thumped a keg down with a clatter.

'Sköl,' slurred Olle, and thrust a mead horn into Torsten's unresisting hand.

'Sköl!' chorused the group.

'And it would seem that the Norns wish you to stay for another drink,' grinned Birger.

Torsten sighed. It would be impolite to refuse. He sipped halfheartedly, hoping for another glimpse of Tove.

Scion returned from collecting his winnings and, finding the table full, cast around for an empty seat. He spotted Vali, alone in a corner, engrossed in digging a large knife into the tabletop.

He has that look again. Always stewing over a puzzle.

Everyone respected Vali. Not only did he lead the hunts—for he was certainly the most skilled of huntsmen—but he was also the eyes and ears of Runolodda, always alert and watching for potential threats to the village. And when something felt amiss, he was a dog with a bone, gnawing at the problem until it was resolved.

Scion threaded through the crowd and took a seat across from his adopted father.

'The woodlice bothering you, sir? I'll have a word with the proprietor.'

Vali flickered a smile and looked up. He was getting on in years with an ash-grey beard and creases in his leathery face that aged him all the more.

'Scion, my lad. Good hunting today?'

'Swimming, actually. Some old huntsman has already claimed all the game.'

'Ha!' bawled Vali as they clasped wrists.

'What's that you're etching?' asked Scion.

Vali lowered his voice. 'Remember the stranger who passed through last week? The tall, thin fellow in the grey cloak? Went by the name of *Ulrick*.'

'Of course. Not too many visitors this far North.'

Vali bit into a wedge of cheese. 'Exactly. Said he was a jeweller from Hvalvik in search of new materials.'

'What of it?'

'He wore a golden ring,' said Vali, sweeping aside a few wood shavings. 'It bore this symbol.'

Scion leaned forward. The carving was of three interlocking triangles. It put him in mind of arrowheads flying in formation.

'What is it?'

'That, my lad, is the Valknut—a symbol of Death. A rather strange talisman for a tradesman, wouldn't you say?'

'Could be a family heirloom. Might be he was simply ignorant of its meaning.'

'Perhaps,' replied Vali with a wave of his hand. 'Still, there was something shifty about his bearing, like a fox among the fowls. Gave me the shivers, truth be told.'

Scion raised an eyebrow at that. 'The unflappable Vali spooked by a lanky pedlar? Well, now I've heard it all!'

'Ha!' barked Vali. He held Scion's stare for a few heartbeats. 'You're probably right, lad. Family heirloom,' he mused, his eyes glazing over. 'How's Astrid?'

Scion frowned. 'Astrid? I don't know. Why would I know? Preparing for the ritual, I suppose.'

'Come now, lad. It's me. You look at her the way Torsten looks at Tove.'

'No, I don't,' lied Scion.

In truth, it seemed impossible to put Astrid from his mind.

Beneath her obvious outward beauty lay a wisdom and grace that belied her youth. And captivated Scion. He opened his mouth to speak when Tove's voice cut through the hubbub, singing a rousing melody.

> *The sea has her secrets that no man can fathom*
> *Still there be wonders that call out to me*
> *The ships in the shadows sink into the chasm*
> *Yet there is no grave that can keep you from me*

She poured her heart and soul into every note, her pure voice surging like a river, stirring everyone to join in. And then, quite unexpectedly, shy Torsten sat himself beside her and began to beat out a rhythm on a deerskin drum. That set the hall clapping and dancing. Tove smiled at him then, surprised though not displeased. Or so he hoped. Blushing, Torsten sang along for all he was worth.

'Ah, young Torsten's made a bold move!' laughed Vali.

'Indeed,' said Scion, wondering if he should resurrect their conversation.

> *I drank up the honey, you picked all the berries*
> *Odin has blessed us, to him we'll be true*
> *From morning 'till sunset when I shall be buried*
> *There's no other life that will keep me from you*

Vali burped. 'Let's hope Olle left us some o' that venison, 'ey?'

He rose from the table and wove his way to the fire pit. Scion sighed, glancing around at the drunken revelry. He held his drink halfway to his lips for a moment, staring at the ominous carving.

No, not arrowheads, he brooded.

Teeth.

THE RITUAL

Stars sparkled in the inky sky.

Thora the Witch watched as Erik's cart trundled into the meadow. A cold bite on the breeze compelled the old woman to hug her many-coloured mantle tighter and tie the strings of her hood, mercifully lined with a soft ermine pelt to keep her balding scalp warm.

'Mm. Greetings, child,' said Thora, as Astrid leaped from the cart.

Thora's young apprentice had crafted an almost exact replica of her own colourful necklace—a repeating pattern of jade and turquoise beads. The Witch found the obvious mimicry amusing, yet held her tongue.

'Greetings, Thora,' replied Astrid, offering an arm to lean on.

Nobody knew quite how old Thora was. She was certainly among the first settlers to Runolodda, that raggedy band who had had enough of the raiding life, all of whom were now long in the grave. She had aided in the birth of almost everyone in the village, including Vali. Her sweeping knowledge of plant names and properties made her a discerning herbalist and trusted medicine-woman. Even in her dotage, Thora's skill grew—owing to an innate curiosity for all living things and an appetite for bold experimentation. And though she was no seer, she fulfilled the role of village Vǫlva.

The Witch.

She led Astrid to the torch-lit foot of Mount Varda, a wall of grey slate that loomed like a sentinel over the meadow and the dark forest beyond. Here, six men and six women crouched low, testing the locking mechanisms on a row of hinged iron grates. Each grate covered a pit—three paces wide and twenty feet deep. The sound of clanging metal rippled on the wind.

A number of the women had noticed Astrid's arrival. They strode over to empty the cart and distribute the contents—bread, smoked meats, and white ceremonial robes.

'Your parents are well, mm?' asked Thora, shuffling along the length of the pits.

'They keep a brave face, considering what tonight holds.' One of the men, soon to be locked away for the night, paused in his work and shot Astrid a withering look. She averted her gaze, mortified by her own indiscretion. 'And how do you feel of late, Thora?' she rallied. 'You're thinner each time we meet.'

'Bah! Eating only slows me down, child. Mm. Much to do. Much to do. Especially tonight. There is ground to cover before midnight. Mm.'

Midnight. The hour of The Change.

'Of course . . .' Astrid hated this part. 'Shall we ready the sacrifice?'

'Aye. Mm. Manning brought it along.' Thora waved a gnarled finger, the skin thin as dry paper. 'It's there beside the standing stone.'

Astrid glanced back at Manning as he finished checking the locks. He would be lowered into a pit tonight. Would become a beast. How did he tolerate the matter with such composure? She glanced at the other infected ones. Since their encounter with the Alpha, none had ever fallen ill or suffered a wound for too long. Their Wolf-blood produced a healing property, made all the more potent when in their Wolf form. There was, Astrid supposed, an upside to their situation.

'Come, child,' chided Thora, snapping Astrid from her musing. 'The night wears on.'

'Right away,' said Astrid, departing with a polite nod.

Thora rubbed her eyes.

She recalled those days, some twenty winters past, when the Alpha had first appeared. The old woman could still smell the bloodshed, hear the wailing of the injured.

And she remembered the bite marks.

At first, some believed that Fenrir, the Great Wolf of Ragnarök, had broken his chains and risen from the abyss. Others supposed that one of Fenrir's offspring—Skoll, who chases the sun, or Hati, who chases the moon—had fallen to the earth.

But six of the surviving huntsmen learned the power of the curse for themselves. For when the moon grew full once more they changed in an instant. Their rational minds were stripped away. Their hearts succumbed to an all-consuming rage. Their bodies writhed and mutated. They could resist these effects no more than kindling can resist a flame, and the moon held sway over body and mind from midnight until dawn.

Hence, the people of Runolodda saw the Alpha in a new light. This was no monster, but a tragic figure deserving of their mercy and their fellowship. For as daybreak revealed its hidden human form, so too did time reveal the Alpha's character—a loyal friend, a dependable labourer, and a born leader.

This is wisdom, thought Thora. *To look beyond the outer appearance, beneath the skin, and into the true nature of a soul.*

She meditated on that notion, and for a moment contemplated walking to the meadow's edge to watch the moonlight dance on the waves below. But her ancient knees ached, so she chose instead to hobble back to the torchlight.

She would have seen the ship.

*

It towered above the breakers.

The massive dragon-head prow curved up like a cobra poised to strike.

The moon framed its tall sail, which bore the Valknut—insignia of the Klo.

The wind whipped Gorm's cloak like a tattered flag.

He gave the signal.

Men dropped over the rails to the dark swash below and pushed quietly up the beach. Horses were led down a gangplank, their hooves barely making a sound.

The small bay was as Ulrick had described. A steep slope cast its shadow over a crescent of white sand, hemmed in by enormous boulders to the right and a rugged coastal path to the left. Gorm understood the problem. The quickest way up to the meadow would be to navigate the slope directly in front of him. But the path looked treacherous and the bright moonlight would give away their position as soon as they crept over the top.

Gorm heaved the battle-axe over his shoulder.

Best to traverse the shoreline to the left. They could make their way up to the trees and double back through the forest to the meadow. Arduous, but apparently a short enough distance to make it before midnight.

Gorm slid down an oar and waded through the frigid shallows. He found his lieutenant going man to man, inspecting shields, checking weapons.

Ulrick had done well.

His ruse as travelling jeweller had certainly borne fruit—spending a night in Runolodda with a rather talkative wench—bedding her, plying her with drink until the secrets spilled out. Vague snippets, really, but enough to confirm the presence of Wolf-bloods in the village.

Of the resident Alpha.

Of their monthly Ritual.

Gorm donned a heavy iron helmet and signalled to move out. He would soon see for himself.

*

Moonlight flooded the sky.

Erik and Freya slipped into their white robes, lit their torches, and strode barefoot across the sweet-smelling meadow to meet the others. There were now seven men and seven women—the number of completion—encircling the sacrifice. A sedated wolf lay trussed to a smooth stone pedestal. It took shallow breaths. Its eyes fluttered open and shut. Astrid squirmed behind Thora, who hovered vulture-like over the beast.

There came a hush.

Then the Witch began to chant, her voice bizarrely rich and low for such an old woman. The others joined in, releasing a relentless drone across the meadow.

They sang the song of endings.

Of burnt-out stars and fallen trees.

Of splintered shields and forgotten battlefields.

Of broken ships on ocean floors.

Thora raised a ceremonial dagger. The razor edge glinted in the torchlight.

Astrid braced herself.

The Ritual moves through three phases.

First, we disown the Wolf within us.

Thora brought the blade down with surprising force, as though the act could somehow dispel all that is dark and violent and ugly from the world. Her thin arms shuddered and the wolf twisted once, twice, without so much as a whimper. It was over so quickly that Astrid was caught off-guard. She fumbled with her bowl for a moment then thrust it into position to catch the blood.

She swallowed bile.

Obviously, she had witnessed sacrifices before—on the eve of harvest, or to bless a womb—but those animals were always cooked and eaten. This wolf would simply be dumped into the fire like deadwood. Despised, condemned, destroyed.

A message to Odin that we are not in league with his enemy.

We do not serve Fenrir.

*

Scion was drowning.

He flailed, screaming bubbles, beating his fists against the ice.

He saw shapes move above him. Heard the bite of axes on the frozen surface.

The cold would soon pull him down, down, towards the black deep.

Mother . . . Father . . . I tried . . . I'm sorry . . .

The shapes began to blur.

The dark crept in.

He heard a far-off noise like a rushing wind, growing louder and louder, rising to a fever pitch until it filled the whole world.

'Scion?'

He jerked awake.

The hall still buzzed with music and laughter, though the crowd had started to thin. Vali rested his hand on Scion's back.

'Shall we call it a night, lad? An old man like me should be in bed at this hour.'

Scion stretched his back. 'Sorry. I must have . . . Aye, let's head—' he paused to shake off the dizziness. 'Let's head on home.'

He wobbled to his feet, bumping the table with his knee, cups clattering to the floor.

'Ouch.'

Throwing an arm over Vali's shoulder he took slow, deliberate steps, passing Olle who slept on a bench, hugging a snoring piglet to his belly.

'Good night!' shouted Scion, to nobody in particular, as Vali led him out into the bracing air.

They shuffled down the street and passed a few dwellings before their own homestead came into view. Vali cleared his throat. 'You know, lad . . . We all know you tried,' he said. 'Remember, you were only a boy.'

'Whassat?' slurred Scion.

Vali paused at the threshold and nudged the door open. 'Nothing, lad. To bed with you now.' They stepped inside, shutting out the darkness behind them.

In the distance, points of light flickered at the foot of Mount Varda.

*

Thora slashed her palm.

They were now gathered in pairs before the pits—seven wives with their husbands—ready to do their duty, ready to protect the village once more. Shields and weapons lay in neat piles beside the pits.

Astrid caught the Witch's blood and stirred it into the wolf's with a woven cow's tail.

The Ritual moves into its second phase: we stand in solidarity with the accursed.

Astrid stepped up to the first couple, Manning and his wife Sif, who shivered beneath her thin white robe. They gave Astrid a small nod and raised their palms to the moon. Astrid lifted her gory paintbrush and wrote the number *seven* on each of their palms.

'We cannot choose our blood,' she intoned.

'We cannot choose our blood,' they repeated, the warm stickiness running down their wrists.

'We can only choose our loyalty,' she said.

'We can only choose our loyalty.'

At that, Astrid moved on down the line to face the second couple, repeating the steps, but this time painting a *six* on their hands.

Erik watched his daughter work. For years she had painted his palm, had beheld the moon's effect. He knew how much she despised all of this. The confinement, the transformation, the piercing howls that lasted until daybreak. And yet, as with all her many responsibilities, Astrid set her jaw and pressed forward. He loved her for that. He loved her for a great many things.

Freya tugged at Erik's elbow, stretching her fingers to the moon.

He came to his senses. 'Oh. Aye. Sorry.'

Astrid hid a smile as she smeared their palms.

One.
'We cannot choose our blood,' she said.
'We cannot choose our blood,' they echoed.
But if we could, I'd choose you every time, thought Erik.

*

Ulrick crashed through the trees.

The crew kept pace—trained soldiers more than raiders, disciplined and fit. The path stretched further than anticipated, and the forest canopy blocked out most of the moonlight. Spreading roots had cracked a few toes and twisted a few ankles, yet they forged on regardless.

It would not do to disappoint Gorm.

*

The third phase: We cripple the Moon's sway.

Manning removed his robe and stood naked while Sif unlatched the grating. The old scars left by claw marks and bites covered most of his body. He unspooled the rope—held by a stake driven into the ground—and lowered himself in. Manning had done this for twenty years now, yet to descend like a bucket into a well still felt humiliating.

His feet touched sludge.

'Made it,' he called up.

The rope slithered back up. 'Good luck, my love,' called Sif.

Manning grunted. It always smelt like wet dog and mildew down here. He saw Sif heave the grate shut and lock it. Apparently, he had tried to scale the slick walls at some point, as the lacerated stone suggested. But Knud was a skilled blacksmith and his heavy grates had never been breached. Still, Thora had instructed that grease be poured down the walls as an extra precaution. This, as Manning noted with disgust, only added to the pit's foul stench.

Thora inspected the lock for herself. Only then did the next couple proceed.

Down they went, one by one into the rot and shadow, the clang of iron echoing beneath the stars.

Six.

Five.

Four.

Three.

Two—

Astrid heard a rustling sound from across the meadow.

Freya noticed her daughter's pinched brow and followed the line of her gaze.

A fox dashed from the treeline, saw the firelight, and darted about nervously before scampering off down Two-Mile-Hill.

Thora squinted over Erik's shoulder.

He too looked back.

And then came the storm.

RED MEADOW

They poured from the woods like a flash flood.

Erik gaped at the swarm of sprinting, shouting men, their swords raised and glinting. There must have been thirty or more of them, charging at an alarming speed. He spun around in a half-crouch, reaching desperately for his axe and shield. Had he sharpened the blade this morning?

Freya was already screaming for the women to take up arms, though the enemy roar drowned out her voice. She saw Astrid backing towards the last open pit, her wild eyes flitting back and forth.

'Astrid! Behind you!' yelled Freya, snatching up a sword and breaking into a run.

Astrid felt her heel slip over the edge just as Freya grabbed her sleeve, pulling her back, an arrow singing past her ear.

'Victory or Valhalla!' Erik charged the line, his battle cry taken up by the women, their hearts thundering like hoofbeats.

Enemies collided to the sound of ringing steel.

Erik chopped the nearest shield with such force that it split in two. But the raider recovered quickly, whipping his blade at

Erik's exposed torso. The sharp point missed by a hair as Erik sidestepped, twisting his hips to deliver a deadly swipe to the neck. The next man closed in quickly and Erik was knocked hard onto his back, almost losing his axe. He hefted his shield in time to deflect a savage overhead blow and kicked out blindly. There was a satisfying crack as his assailant's knee caved backward, the man crying out in agony. By the time Erik staggered back to his feet, Sif had slit the man's throat. They shared a nod and plunged back into the fray.

Thora hunched over the first pit, feverishly working a key into the lock.

'What's happening?' cried Manning from below.

'What do you think? We're under atta—'

A spear tore into Thora's back and out through her ribcage, punching her from her feet. The key sailed from her grasp and landed in the dirt. The old Witch lay in a spreading pool of blood, coughed once, and exhaled a long, final breath.

Astrid saw it happen. 'No!' she cried in horror.

Freya propelled her towards the cart. 'Move, Daughter! We have to move!' She ducked the swish of a broadsword, stabbing her attacker in the groin. The man's shriek split the night.

'Hurry now!' she yelled, virtually dragging Astrid forward.

And then—a distinctive shape moved across her field of vision.

Time slowed.

Through the blur of blood and steel, a face came into focus.

Gorm.

He sat astride a great black warhorse, his merciless cold gaze crawling across the chaos.

Terror seized Freya's heart.

No, it cannot be.

Gorm's battle-axe cleaved through the air, smashing a woman's shield to splinters and throwing her high into the air. She landed headlong, her neck snapping like a brittle twig.

Freya reached the cart and frantically unhitched Hermod. The horse was terrified—trembling, pawing, his muzzle peeled back. Yet there was no time for soothing. She pressed the reins into Astrid's hand. 'Ride! Make for the river. Head downstream until you find a cottage. Tell her I sent you.'

'Tell who? Mother, what are you talking about?'

'Do it now, girl!'

Astrid screwed up her eyes. Would this be their final exchange? The last time she saw her mother? Her father? The thought shattered her glass composure and she choked back the urge to sob.

Unexpectedly, an old memory came rushing back to Freya—the whole family together in bed as she sang lullabies to her little girl and stroked her golden hair, those adoring blue eyes fluttering closed in the warm firelight.

'All will be well, my love. You'll see. Simply stay out of sight and follow the river. Trust your mother now, alright?' She pressed Astrid to her chest, kissing her forehead, then tore away before the tears came.

Astrid saddled quickly and sped off across the meadow, raising cries of alarm.

'After her, you fools!' yelled Ulrick as he blocked an attack. 'She'll warn the villagers!'

But instead of descending Two-Mile-Hill, Astrid veered around the melee, spurring Hermod toward the treeline. She cried aloud as two horsemen on the edge of sight gave chase. Ulrick cursed beneath his breath. He had not supposed these peasants capable of any cunning. He certainly had not expected their women-folk to fight with such ferocity either.

Erik cut a swathe through the raiders, his blade biting flesh more by chance than by skill. Though his luck could not hold forever. He saw Sif take an arrow to the shoulder and cry out. A rider wheeled his mount and swung a pole-handled hammer through a second woman's skull. It shattered in a spray of teeth and blood, splashing Erik's face with red gore. He wiped his eyes, and immediately felt a burning pain in his side. A raider wrenched the sword free and Erik slumped to his knees with a groan, his shield clattering to the ground.

The raider kicked Erik's jaw with a roar.

There was a sharp crack.

Then everything went black.

*

Astrid ducked at the final moment.

A spear flashed through the air and lodged into a pine tree. She dared a glance over her shoulder. The enemy's horses rumbled down the path, no less than twenty paces behind.

'Fly, Hermod!' she cried. 'Fly for the river, boy!'

Without slowing, the nearest horseman tore the spear free, ripping off a chunk of bark as he rode. He kicked his mount for a burst of speed, flipped his grip, and took aim once more.

Hermod was three summers old, a colt in his prime. Astrid had named him after Odin's messenger—Hermod the Swift, Hermod the Furious. And in that moment, with the enemy descending upon them, he embodied his namesake and ratcheted up into a full gallop.

'Yes, boy!' cried Astrid.

They pulled away from their pursuers, blurred hooves kicking up dry leaves and dust down the faded trail. The pines clustered more densely, the path snaking, and the raiders lost their clear line of sight.

'Curse it!' cried the second horseman. 'She's a slippery eel, this one!'

It was dark in the thicket, though Astrid knew these woods intimately. Up ahead, a partially fallen tree had lodged in the branches of another. She kept low in the saddle, ducking beneath the thick rotten trunk. Without looking back, she heard the thud and cry of a rider abruptly struck from his mount.

That should slow them down.

The second horseman yanked on the reins. 'Fool! Open yer bloody eyes!'

'No time for this,' croaked the first, cradling broken ribs as he regained his feet. 'Go. I'll . . . I'll be along . . . soon enough.' His breath came ragged, his jaw clenched.

'You had *better* be,' spat his comrade, launching ahead.

Astrid pressed the advantage. She banked left, shinnied up a gradient, and bolted down the other side. Pine needles whipped her cheeks though she paid them no mind.

She knew what to do.

The cliff's edge came into view. Was it only earlier today that she had basked here in the sunshine while four naked men streaked by? *Would you care to join us?* Scion had asked . . .

She reined Hermod in and slipped from the saddle.

'Run, boy! Lead them on a merry chase, you hear?'

She slapped his freckled rump and, in a flash, Hermod was up the slope and back on the trail. Astrid blinked down at the hot spring. The river ran beyond the trees below and there was no time to wait. She took a deep breath.

And leaped.

THE ALPHA

Scion's bladder ached.

Shadows flickered up the timber walls and along the rafters, dancing across the thatch ceiling with the curling wisps of smoke. He stumbled from bed and threw another log on the dwindling fire, stoking it with the toe of his boot. In the dim glow he could see Vali passed out on his bench, wrapped in wool like a snoring lamb. Even so, Scion snuck past with care. The old man had a tendency to lurch awake at the sound of a pin drop, knife in hand.

Their cow stood awake, pondering whatever cows pondered in the dead of night. Scion slid in wet manure, cursing as he shouldered open the door. The bracing cold sobered him up somewhat, though his head still ached as he untied his trousers.

Ascertain. That's the word Astrid had used, wasn't it? I 'ascertain' myself to be drunk? No, that doesn't sound quite right. I wish to ascertain . . . er . . . oh, let it be. Stick to what you do best, Scion: making a fool of yourself over a goddess.

Eyes closed, he let his water flow, not caring that it splashed over his boots.

An owl hooted in the distance.

Then came a sound like a muffled thunderclap.

Scion opened a bleary eye to see thick black smoke rise on the distant meadow.

'By the god's blood . . .' he gasped.

The pits were on fire.

*

Manning screamed as he burned.

An archer took aim to put him out of his misery.

'What are you doing?' bellowed Ulrick, slapping the longbow aside. 'You'd waste an arrow on this worm? Leave the flames to their dinner and go collect weapons with the others. The tide won't wait for the likes of us.'

The greased pit had erupted in a blinding fireball. The raiders now took turns to ignite the others, laughing and whooping like a pack of mad dogs. The Bitten refused to beg for mercy, glaring instead at their tormentors who shot arrow after flaming arrow into their prisons. The sole survivors of the massacre, Erik, Freya, and Sif knelt with their wrists bound behind their backs, forced to watch. They clung to their composure until Manning finally fell silent, at which point Sif toppled to her side and let out a long and harrowing wail.

Gorm stood stoically from a distance and observed all.

He had disagreed with the purpose of this mission from the start. Why destroy a potential weapon? Certainly, Wolf-men were wild and ungovernable creatures, yet there was always a way. They could be smuggled into an enemy camp, or sent into battle ahead of the ranks. Anything seemed preferable to roasting them in a hole in the ground. King Ødger lacked imagination, ambition. The sluggard would rather feast with his harlots and bootlicking courtiers than strengthen his own sword arm on the training floor. Ødger seemed content to send out raiding parties, sure enough, but Gorm wanted more.

Gorm was a conqueror.

He would have to persuade the weak fool somehow.

Smoke crawled up Mount Varda.

Ulrick sidled up to Erik and savagely yanked back his hair. 'What are you doing out of your kennel, 'ey? You've been a very naughty boy, haven't ya? Killing our men like that. What came over you, puppy dog?' Ulrick scooped a glob of blood from Erik's nose and licked it off his finger. 'You know, I killed one of *your* men recently too. An old friend, I believe, from years ago. Drengr was his name. Strange chap. Sunken skull. Not all there, if you catch my meaning.' He leaned closer to Erik's ear, his voice dripping with malice. 'Took a long time to die, he did. And the pitiful squeals!' Ulrick clapped his ears in mockery. 'Eek! Eek! Eek! Bore a hole in my head, it did!'

Erik turned a cold eye on him, but Ulrick gazed into the distance as if recalling a fond memory. 'Ah, well. Nobody lives forever. Speaking of which—' he twisted Erik's hair in his fist and dragged him towards the open pit.

'Hold!' boomed a voice. Ulrick spun on his heel, hiding a spike of annoyance. Gorm approached and cocked his head at Erik. 'This one comes with us.'

Ulrick gave Gorm a long stare. Then the joke landed and he barked a laugh.

But there was no joke in Gorm's dull gaze.

Ulrick shifted nervously. 'But the King said to—'

'I know what Ødger said, Ulrick. Have this peasant swaddled in chains and secured to the mast.' He gestured for Ulrick to notice the number *One* painted on Erik's palm.

Confusion marked Ulrick's expression. 'You wish to keep the *Alpha* alive?'

Gorm nodded. He understood Ulrick's dark motives for manipulating King Ødger into attacking Runolodda. Ulrick possessed an insatiable bloodlust—a fire Gorm warmed to in those he led—yet it was the mention of Wolf-men that had piqued Gorm's own interest.

'You and I shall speak on the return voyage,' said Gorm, laying a hand on Ulrick's shoulder. 'Trust me, old friend.'

Ulrick felt a flush of pride. To be taken into Gorm's confidence, to be publicly named his friend—well, these were high honours indeed.

'Then we'd better hurry,' grinned Ulrick. 'Midnight won't wait for the likes of us.'

*

'Open the gates this instant!' yelled Scion.

The watchman twitched nervously on the rampart. 'Not tonight! It's the full moon, for Thor's sake!'

'Did you not hear me? Red Meadow is on fire!'

'Look, if the pits are burning then what's to stop the Bitten from reaching us? They'll lose their minds soon enough and come tearing through our homes!'

'Do as he says!' roared Vali, drawing closer with a mob of groggy villagers in his wake.

Knud seemed to have rolled out of bed still wearing his leather blacksmith's apron. 'You can shut the gates behind us, you dolt!'

The watchman hesitated, then gave in. 'Fine. But don't come running back with *them* in tow! We've women and children in here!'

Vali clutched Scion's arm. 'The fire—An accident, do you suppose? An attack?'

Scion shook free and strode purposefully for the stables. 'Only one way to find out.'

'The pass is treacherous by night, lad,' said Vali, falling in step beside him. 'We don't want to hobble the horses.'

'Our kin could be in danger up there! We can't stand by and do *nothing*!'

Vali rounded on Scion, blocking his path. 'And if the Bitten are running loose? What then?'

The high gates creaked open. Scion drew in a deep breath.

'Then we save whoever we can.'

*

The wind had picked up.

The raiders descended the switchback trail from Red Meadow to Crescent Bay below, yet even as they reached the first bend one of them slipped and tumbled down the near-vertical slope, screaming, his limbs flailing with every bone-shattering thud. From then on, everyone took far greater care.

Eventually, Freya felt the beach sand crunch beneath her bare feet. Passing the fallen man's pulverised corpse, she spat, earning herself a cuff to the back of the head. Erik and Sif—the arrow still protruding from her shoulder—shuffled on ahead, led like cattle to the longship, up the gangplank, and onto the wide deck.

It was cluttered with nets, furs, blankets, barrels of drinking water, and crates of food. Men either took up oars at the rowing benches or coaxed the horses to sit on the floorboards. A short, hairy man took Freya to the stern and shoved her down alongside Sif, pale as sour milk, her back resting against a stack of crates. Then, without warning or pity, the hairy man tugged Sif's arrow free.

He waited, expecting a scream.

But Sif only stared at the sky, allowing warm tears to streak her grubby face. The hairy man blinked at her, then grumbled something incoherent as he snatched up a torch to slowly heat the flat of his axe. Freya tried to hold Sif's hand but Hairyman slapped her wrist away.

'Back!' He ordered, then cleaned the wound with salt water, fulfilling his duty to keep the *merchandise* from spoiling. Lastly, he sealed it with the red-hot blade. Sif's back arched, eyes widened, and she passed out. Hairyman huffed, satisfied, and marched off to join his crewmen who were in the process of carefully and *thoroughly* chaining Erik to the central mast.

'Swiftly now,' barked Gorm. 'The hour is upon us.'

Erik spat blood. A broad iron collar was fastened around his neck, shackles around his wrists and ankles. He tried not to shiver, but his thin ceremonial robe offered little warmth against the cocoon of thick, cold chain.

Gorm ran his fingers over the locks and grunted with satisfaction. 'Weigh anchors! Deploy the sail!' he barked.

The canvas dropped, snapped, and billowed in the salt wind, the dark fabric emblazoned with a bone-white Valknut, adopted symbol of the Klo. The white-on-black contrast was designed to catch the eye. And chill the spine.

It certainly did both.

'Row!' yelled Ulrick. 'Njord blows too softly into our sails tonight!'

Oarsmen heaved against the current and the ship creaked beyond the shallows and out to the wine-dark swell toward the waiting moon.

Ulrick's gaze crawled over to Freya.

Now here is some pretty plunder, he grinned.

Swaggering down the length of the deck, he ruffled Erik's hair as he passed—a master with his new favourite hound. As he approached Freya, she drew up her knees and threw a protective arm around Sif.

'Hello, my dear,' leered Ulrick. 'Would you care to dance?'

Freya glared up at him.

'Ha! Such poor manners. What did I expect from a pig-herder's wife? Tell me, my sweet, have we met before? You're a touch familiar.' Freya turned as though bored, hiding her face in her hair. Ulrick got down on his haunches, his breath close and foul. 'You're trembling like a sparrow, my sweet. Something troubling you, Little Sparrow?'

She lashed a stinging slap across his cheek.

'Leave us be, snake! I've had enough of your bile tonight.'

Ulrick's face hardened. He drew himself up to his full height and cracked his knuckles. 'Oh, I think you can take some more, Little Sparrow.'

With that, he dragged her screaming behind the crates and forced her to the floor with surprising strength, despite his lanky frame. Freya squirmed and bucked but her limbs were pinned under his weight.

Erik heard her cries and thrashed against his restraints. 'Freya! No!'

He felt Gorm swivel his jaw back around. 'Eyes front . . . *Alpha*. And hold your pitiful bleating. This is the way of war.'

Erik shut his eyes and roared up at the Moon.

Gorm tensed. *It's happening*, he thought, taking a tentative step back.

Midnight.

In an instant, the horses reared up, neighing together in panic. Gorm spun around, saw them spring and kick as though on fire, knocking aside men who tried desperately to grab hold of the whipping reins. Then, in a heartbeat, the horses broke away and vaulted over the ship's rail into the sea.

Gorm staggered forward.

The crew stared dumbfounded. There was nothing they could do. The horses struggled frantically, the hissing surf swallowing them up. Down they went, until there was no sound at all but the creak of the rigging.

The air shifted.

A low growl filled the night.

Gorm whirled on Erik, spear at the ready. The crew unhooked their shields, darting their heads this way and that, unsure from which direction the sound came. It seemed to fly around the decking like a restless spirit.

Erik began to shake.

Gorm braced himself for The Change. Swallowing, he tried to reassure himself that the chains would hold. But then he grasped the reality of the situation.

His prisoner was laughing.

'So, you think that *I* am the Alpha?' chuckled Erik. 'No, Gorm. But I'm sure she is eager to meet you.'

With a yell, Ulrick came flying over the crates, knocking the hairy man from his feet and crashing into a water barrel.

All eyes turned slowly to the stern.

Freya loomed head and shoulders above them all—a snarling Wolf-woman, hackles raised, claws out, teeth like sallow daggers. She released a guttural howl that shook the air. And then—

The Alpha pounced.

TEETH OF IRON

The full moon cast a baleful glow across the sea.

Freya launched herself at the nearest raiders, smashed through their painted shields, sent them sprawling across the floor. One man found himself suddenly alone and far too close to the beast. Desperately, he snapped his spear forward. But the Wolf-woman sidestepped, hooked her left claw clean through his abdomen, then twisted her hips with a right-handed swipe across his temple, shredding off most of his face. His skull hit the deck with a sickening splat.

Ulrick backed up, turned, and shoved his way through the dumbstruck crew to Gorm's side. 'What do we do? There's nowhere to run!'

'No, there is not,' said Gorm, his deep voice flat and steady. 'Though we have faced similar danger and lived. Remember the escaped lion on the voyage back from Almany? We do as we did then. Get to the stern. I'll take the prow.'

Almany, thought Ulrick. *Aye, it worked but we lost half the crew!*

Yet what else could be done?

In spite of the cold, Ulrick felt sweat sting his eyes. He fidgeted with the gold ring on his forefinger. 'Alright. But first I'll need to slip past the creature.'

'Be quick about it,' urged Gorm.

Wiping his brow, Ulrick turned to face the threat. He took a deep breath, tossed aside his grey cloak, and edged forward.

Sif woke beneath a pile of netting. The first thing she saw was Freya biting a man's head clean off. Then, another tried to hack the Wolf-woman's knees from behind, his surprise attack undone when a five-daggered claw stabbed into his chest and out through his back. Sif stared in awe at the violence of the battle, the fluid poetry of her friend's savagery.

She retreated further into her hiding place when a strange movement snagged on her periphery. Something out of place. The one called Ulrick prowled past the crew and back towards the stern. Sif peered over to the broad man, Gorm, who had shifted his focus back to Erik. Clearly, they had a scheme brewing, though Sif could not guess what.

Gorm dug out the keys from a fold in his black leather vest and gave Erik a dead-eyed stare.

'Oh, Gorm,' chuckled Erik. 'Caught off guard, were you? Ambushes will do that, you know. Or had you not heard? *This is the way of war.*'

Gorm exhaled slowly and rubbed his fingertips over his stubbled scalp. 'The way of war . . . aye. Though the way is seldom clear, as every victor knows.'

He released the first lock.

'To *survive*, one must read a battle moment by moment and adapt accordingly. Clouds will change their shape again and again until they cover the entire sky. Adaptability, you see? Contingencies upon contingencies.'

He released the second lock.

'But that is mere survival. Now, to *conquer*? Ah, to conquer one must be willing to embrace a two-fold truth. On the one hand, surrender is never an option. One must win the race at all costs, whether it be a sprint or a marathon. The victor possesses an iron will, you see—to run faster and further than his foes ever would.'

He released the third lock.

Chains fell to the floor like a python uncoiled. Erik felt the wind whip his thin robe.

'And on the other hand?' he asked, swallowing.

'On the other hand—' said Gorm, checking the length of chain that joined the shackle around Erik's neck to the mast. '—Nothing can outrun death.' He broke Erik's nose with a single devastating punch, then hoisted him over his head like a sheaf of wheat. 'That is the way of war,' he stated levelly, and hurled Erik into the sea.

Sif gasped. Unseen, she shot out a hand to stop what could not be stopped.

Erik thrashed in the frigid dark, gripped by terror as the heavy chain dragged him under. A jagged rock, invisible in the pitch black, struck his head.

He was dead before the breath could escape his lungs.

Above, the ship sailed on and the chain went taut to drag him by the neck across the seabed, the air from his open mouth bubbling in his wake like a stream of teardrops.

It was the breaking point for Sif. The night had robbed her of her husband, her future, and now her beloved leaders would fall too—Erik to the deep and Freya to the sword. Freya, who had physically helped Knud the Blacksmith build the seven pits for the Ritual in only four weeks. Freya, who had sat with Sif and Manning in silence for three days and three nights when a fever took their firstborn. Freya, who had ruled for years alongside

Erik with compassion and wisdom.

Freya, whose feral eyes held no trace of recognition as they locked with Sif as she cowered in the netting. The Wolf-woman snarled at her, stepping closer, everyone her enemy tonight. Sif closed her eyes. So, this is how her days would end; slain by her close friend on a ship of blood.

Surely tonight, I shall join Manning in Valhalla.

The notion brought a welcome peace. She opened her eyes and surrendered to the inevitable, as Freya raised a claw to strike.

But the blow never came.

An archer had reached his bow and shot Freya in the hip, the iron point sinking deep, making her flinch. She whirled on the man, who paled as she came bounding over the deck. And before he could nock another shaft, she leaped. Clawed feet crushed him to the floor and Freya slashed his throat open with a vicious swipe.

Sif came back to herself. No, she could not abandon Freya to these barbarians. She would turn despair to anger, if not for herself then at least for those who had fallen tonight. And for those who might yet fall. She spotted a bow beside a crate and crawled for it with a newfound reserve of strength.

Gorm had reached the prow.

He hefted the iron anchor over his shoulder. Its chain was long enough for what he had in mind. He only hoped that Ulrick had reached the secondary anchor on the opposite end of the ship.

Ulrick had. The iron was not as heavy as the timber-and-stone anchors used in the early days—yet sleeker, finer, sharper. Ulrick knew how much Gorm enjoyed a display of wealth. Not for vanity's sake but rather as a show of power. Ulrick dragged the anchor toward the hulking beast. His lips curled up in a hideous grin.

Freya snapped her jaws at the crew. They circled her warily, searching for an opening, though her reach equaled that of a spear and her reactions were viper-quick. A bare-chested archer had the presence of mind to attack from a safer distance. He drew back and sighted. Before he could shoot, an arrow from the shadows tore through his armpit and struck his heart. He collapsed instantly, spluttering blood, his own arrow flying wide.

'Yes!' hissed Sif as she took aim once more from her hiding spot. Her second shaft deflected harmlessly off a raised shield, its bearer glancing around in surprise. As she snatched for a third arrow, her eyes locked once more with Freya's. There was still nothing there but animal hate.

Ulrick saw his moment.

Rushing up from behind Freya, he launched into the air with the stern anchor raised like a pickaxe, and threw his entire weight into the swing. The sharp hook sank deep into her shoulder. Freya howled in pain and clawed the air blindly, missing Ulrick by a hair. He hit the ground in a roll and whirled to face her, unsheathing his sword in one fluid motion.

'Have at me, Little Sparrow!' he bellowed, backing toward the central mast where Gorm stood waiting.

Freya pawed at the anchor, blood running down her arm, soaking the coarse, thick hair. She wheeled on Ulrick and hurtled towards him, claws reaching. But at the last moment, with his throat only inches away, the chain caught on its bolt, pulled tight, and jerked her from her feet, the hook punching out through her shoulder blade. She thrashed on the deck, scoring the wood and shrieking.

Gorm had timed things perfectly.

Drawing up beside Ulrick, he loomed over the writhing Wolf-woman, the prow anchor in both fists. Then, as though chopping firewood, he swung it down into Freya's thigh, shattering the femur with a great crack.

'Two divisions!' he bellowed. 'Pull the lines!' And soon there were men on both chains in a tug-of-war. Freya roared in torment, caught in the middle. It was a fiendish trap, since to advance or retreat meant the iron teeth would only drive deeper into her flesh.

The short, hairy laughed. 'We have her now, by Thor!'

At that moment, Sif's arrow flew with all the luck of Loki. It took the hairy man in the neck, lacerating the artery, showering a length of chain with slick blood. Fingers slipped, the line went slack, and men toppled over one another as the tension vanished. Freya seized the opportunity to rip the first anchor from her shoulder. She roared in pain as it came free and clattered to the deck.

'Oi! Over there!' yelled a red-haired crewman.

Sif had been spotted at last. She fumbled frantically for another arrow as the redhead came running, a sharp axe held high overhead for a kill stroke. She rolled clear and the edge bit the rail. She snatched a glance at Freya, who tugged the second anchor from her ruined leg.

'Curse it! She's free!' roared Gorm, 'All hands! Attack!' and the crew rushed forward.

Freya managed to narrowly dodge a thrown spear, limped to the side, holding her shoulder in a massive claw. She growled, low and deep. There was more fight in her yet.

Sif tried to rise but was kicked onto her back. As the axe came down once more she saw her old friend rage into a storm of blades.

Sif smiled.

It was the last thing she ever saw.

AFTERMATH

Golden waves settled beneath the stern eye of the rising sun.

Without a helmsman, the ship had turned in the wind and run aground, carried to Crescent Beach by the powerful tide.

Scion was first to reach the shipwreck, followed quickly by Birger the Bear, Tyr, Olle, and a shivering band of villagers. It had seemed an eternity waiting for the current to carry the Klo ship ashore, the copper clouds bruising gradually into grey.

Scion's hands balled into fists. If only their own ships had been anchored *here* instead of five miles inland along the river. Granted, they were much smaller crafts used only for fishing and would never have caught up to the Klo warship. And yet, Scion would have tried. He shook off his frustration and hurried through the freezing surf.

The ship now slanted at an angle, the deck displayed like an easel. The mast had snapped and dipped into the swell, a once proud beast hiding its head in shame. Bodies littered the deck and began to wash up on the beach, where Vali led the villagers in a sweep.

'Bring any survivors to me! We will deal with these vermin in the old way!'

A grey-haired woman approached, the sleeves of her lavender woollen dress pulled up above her thick forearms. 'Don't forget our *own*, Vali. They may yet live,' she said, though her voice carried doubt.

'Of course, Hedda,' he said, observing her five stout daughters edge down the rocky slope with slings full of linen bandages and vinegar.

'We'll need help carrying the wounded back up, of course, if —*when*—we find them,' said Hedda, waving for the girls to pick up the pace. 'There's a cart up on Red meadow. We can do more for them back at the Great Hall.'

Vali nodded and Hedda scuttled off, barking orders.

Hidden, Gorm listened from behind a lone skerry, his feet not quite reaching the sandbank as he bobbed in the water. In order to keep his head above the surface, he had been forced to relinquish his cloak and armour to the greedy sea. The bitterly cold waves lapped against his back and he felt his fingers begin to numb as he clung to the pitted rock, the sharp limpets slicing his palms.

Curse these swineherds. If I had my axe I'd finish them off once and for all.

He pressed up against the rock and shook out his left hand, hoping to get the blood flowing again. It was then that he noticed the wound.

Teeth marks in his wrist, wide and deep.

Gorm felt a wave of nausea as both the physical pain and the dreadful implications began to sink in. When had this happened? He remembered lunging into the fray. There had been a frenzy of claws and blades . . . and then the ship had hit a rock, shuddered, and he had been thrown flat on his back—

He took another long look at the bite.

Wounds don't lie.

There could be no doubt. He would become one of the accursed Wolf-kind. The thought sent a shiver down his spine. What would the excitable King Ødger make of him now? Would he decree banishment? Execution? Regardless, Gorm needed to report back. Probably best to take the coastal path again, head through the woods and follow the river to the harbour. He could take a cargo ship back to the island.

Adapt and overcome, thought Gorm. *There are always contingencies.*

He was about to swim away when a voice carried across the water.

'It's Freya!' shouted Scion from the lopsided ship, 'She's alive!'

A corpse pinned her to the deck. Scion heaved him aside, grunting at the man's weight.

'By Thor's beard . . .' exclaimed Birger the Bear, pulling up short beside them.

Freya was human once more; naked, her skin almost blue with cold. Her right shoulder drooped unnaturally low and her left thigh had healed crookedly. There was no denying it would need to be reset. Other than an arrow that protruded from her calf, all lacerations to her skin now showed as nothing but thin, clotted incisions.

Scion covered her with his own cloak. 'Quickly, Birger. Let's move her to dry ground.'

Birger raised her head and recoiled. His hand came away wet with blood. 'Her hair is soaked,' he whispered.

'Might not be hers.' Scion took her legs carefully, and together they carried her to the beach where Hedda and her burly daughters bustled about.

'Any sign of Astrid?' asked Scion, laying Freya at Hedda's feet.

'No, not yet,' she said directly. Hedda was a hard woman, yet not uncaring—in her own way. 'Chin up, son. She's a tough lass. Resourceful too.'

He nodded, clenching his teeth.

'Now stand aside,' she demanded, with a flutter of her fingers. 'There'll be time for fretting when the work is done.' She clapped once and her daughters immediately went to work, rubbing warmth into Freya's limbs until Birger could tear floorboards from the wreckage for a makeshift stretcher.

Gorm watched from his hiding place.

So, the Wolf-woman lived. He spat into the salty water. This fight was far from over. He took a deep breath and sank out of sight.

Tyr and Olle waded around the shipwreck, the icy water coming up to their armpits in places. So far, there was nothing among the debris but a few decimated raiders.

'So much death,' whispered Olle, shaking from more than just the cold. 'The Bitten, massacred. Their wives . . .'

'Aye,' said Tyr, his tone as calm as he could keep it. 'They fought hard against so many. They will feast as fallen heroes in Valhalla tonight.'

'None could have survived this attack. None but the Alpha.'

'Just keep looking, Olle. I didn't see Erik or Sif among the dead. Nor Astrid.'

'Perhaps they fell overboard, or were taken by the undertow?'

'Perhaps,' said Tyr, rounding the upturned keel, 'but we mustn't give up until—' Something caught his eye.

'What is it?' asked Olle from behind.

A body bobbed in the water, knocking against the ship's barnacled underbelly.

'Oh,' whispered Olle, spotting what appeared to be long dark hair trailing on the surface. 'Tyr . . . could that be Sif?'

'Wait here,' said Tyr, taking a closer look. Not hair, no. Seaweed had draped over a head and tangled in something metallic.

A chain.

Tyr wiped away the algae, recoiled with a gasp, and sprawled backwards into the foam.

A crab gorged on Erik's lifeless, milky eyes.

THE ORACLE

They called her the Oracle.

Gudrun was scarcely five summers old when she saw Yggdrasil the World Tree in the first of her *seeing dreams*. The Giant Ash had been engulfed in flame with her mother and father perched in the upper branches, weeping over the devastation that spread to the horizon. The following night a fire took the family's crop. Gudrun had held her mother's hand while the field burned, the absurdity of shivering in the heat causing her to giggle.

It was the first time she had ever seen her father weep.

Years passed and her reputation as Seer grew.

In one memorable dream, the goddess Idunn, whose apples give long life to the gods, caught the potter's son stealing her enchanted fruit. So, she planted a serpent in his belly as punishment. Gudrun had woken to learn that the potter's son was indeed ill, complaining bitterly of stomach cramps. She removed apples from his diet and the boy recovered.

In another, she saw a water spirit present her husband with a jewelled treasure. Days later he found a bracelet of crimson garnets in the river. She dreamt of barren women flying as eagles to their young. They were soon found to be with child. She dreamt of trappers drowning in snow. They learnt to listen when she warned of an avalanche. She dreamt of a horse bolting from an adder. The owner was told where to find it.

Thora had recognized her talent and trained her for a short while, but Gudrun's know-all attitude so irritated the Witch that the apprenticeship was quickly *dissolved*.

When Gudrun was older, and her son had grown, a terrifying vision came to her one bitter winter's night. She saw Fenrir the Great Wolf free itself of its shackles and rise from the depths of the earth to draw a shadow over Runolodda like a shroud. She saw men morph into wolves with claws for hands and teeth sharp as steel. She saw a wave of blood, high as mountains, crash through the valley, the people tumbling, drowning in a maelstrom of death and destruction.

She had woken in a pool of sweat.

There was no denying it. She had seen Ragnarök, the End of Days.

Then the cries had rung out. Hunters returned from a bear cave with terrible wounds, and a bedraggled young woman they blamed for the carnage. Her name was Freya and she appeared malnourished and feral.

That night around the fire, Gudrun heard the full tale—how Freya had emerged from the depths of the earth. Her wolf-like appearance. The attack. The destruction.

Gudrun had approached the elders, told them of her vision, warned them of the imminent danger. This woman was undoubtedly Fenrir the Wolf, harbinger of Ragnarök.

With Freya caged, Chief Lennärt deliberated and debated for weeks, until the full moon rose again. The village would have been massacred had it not been for the brave actions of Gudrun's own son, Erik. That night—allegedly due to Freya's warning—he took the Bitten one by one and locked them in the cage alongside her. At midnight, they transformed and howled and thrashed in their prison, fulfilling part of Gudrun's vision.

She was not about to see the rest of it come to pass.

She called for the Bitten, along with their *Alpha*, to be put to death at once. Chief Lennärt, too weak and too indecisive, named Erik his successor and retreated from the whole affair. Gudrun had begged Erik to rid the village of this curse. Freya was an abomination—Fenrir himself, masquerading as a damsel in distress. A Wolf in sheep's clothing, more like. But Erik would not heed his mother's warning. Where Gudrun saw a villain, he saw a victim. Freya was to be invited into the village, to be made a part of the community, and shown empathy rather than judgement. The Bitten could not be held accountable for their condition any more than she could.

Gudrun had spat at that. How could her own son be so blind? He had been seduced, and in so doing had invited death into their midst.

She would not stand for it.

Gudrun had left by morning, leaving nothing behind but a decorated battle horn, wrapped in a bundle at Erik's door. He had understood the significance of such a parting gift. Were the *wave of blood* to flood the valley, were Ragnarök to begin in earnest, Erik needed only to blow the horn and Gudrun would come to his side. Of course, it was a purely metaphorical gesture, yet she knew he would grasp its meaning. For all his foolishness, she was still Erik's mother and would fight to her final breath to keep him from harm.

Perhaps her absence would draw him back to her.

Gudrun had built a cottage in the woods beside the river Hreim. Traders from Runolodda would drop in from time to time with news of the village. She had learned that soon after her departure, Erik had wed Freya, raising her to rule alongside him—the Chief and the Alpha. Could Erik not see the enemy's schemes? And then, less than a year later, news arrived of her granddaughter's birth. Astrid was her name. A half-blood. Half belonged to the Wolf, yet half belonged to humanity, by Thor! Belonged to Erik. Belonged to her—Gudrun the Grandmother. She often wondered what to feel about that and what Astrid's purpose might be. But Gudrun was old now, and the years had eaten away at her curiosity. It would fall to Erik to decide the fate of Runolodda.

Gudrun opened her eyes and gazed sleepily around her cottage. Light played through the window, carrying birdsong and the fragrance of pine. She rolled over, nestling deeper into her blanket. Over the last four weeks she had dreamed of nothing at all.

Until last night.

Sleep had shown her a field, and in the centre, Odin the Gallows God, hanging by the neck from a tree. Then the face was no longer Odin's, but Erik's. Gudrun had cried out, but before she could reach her son, the ocean swallowed everything.

Gudrun had found herself drowning.

She swam up, broke the surface, the waves flattening to become planks of solid wood. She lay on her belly aboard a great ship and looked up to see an enormous woman, her mouth stretched abnormally wide, displaying ragged teeth. Gudrun recognised her as Odin's wife, Jord the Giantess, whose mother is the Night. Jord barged through a pack of black wolves, each wearing a gold collar as they swarmed, gnashing and biting, red eyes full of hate.

And high above this battle, three pale women crept from behind the Full Moon like spiders. These were the Norns who spin the webs of Fate. Each slung a thread around Jord and lifted her away, the wolves snapping at her feet, howling, straining to reach. But the Norns bore the Giantess away, lowering her as a breeze would lower a feather, gently onto a white shore.

There came a rush of wind.

Then silence.

Gudrun had breathed in fresh air.

The breeze blew warm, filled with the strong scent of wildflowers. Gleaming in gold, a sundial stood before her, its height reaching to her waist. She glanced around to find herself at the heart of an immense white lily, its petals stretching far and wide. She could feel the silky softness beneath her bare feet, and basked in the heavenly sunlight.

Before long, a Great Wolf appeared in the distance, and Gudrun tensed as it crept closer, closer. There was nowhere to run. Hiding as best she could behind the golden sundial, she could do nothing but hold her breath and wait. The Wolf drew up beside the lily, and with a swift motion, sank its teeth into one of the delicate petals before running off, laughing as it went.

In an instant, the flower turned from white to red, as though every petal bled.

The air twisted.

The sun began to move rapidly across the sky. Mesmerised, Gudrun watched the shadow move around the sundial, marking the accelerated passage of time. And with each passing hour, the red petals grew darker and darker, until by the seventh hour they were completely black.

There was a flicker and the sun vanished, replaced by a twinkling night sky. A half-moon shone down, large and bright. It remained there for a moment, then flickered like a candle, instantly becoming a young woman in a blue dress, floating large against the expanse. Her golden hair shimmered like the northern lights and Gudrun knew in her heart that this was Astrid, her granddaughter, shining as a goddess in the dark.

The enormous petals quivered as Astrid burned brighter, and a creeping dread ran up Gudrun's neck. She clung to the sundial and fought the terror. The night soon flooded with a light so intense that she had to shield her eyes. With a sudden, jarring motion, the petals beneath her feet thickened and hardened, growing rough underfoot. The air turned musty and sharp, and Gudrun forced her eyes open. The petals were no longer petals at all, but the claws of a gigantic, hairy creature.

Gudrun cried out.

Clung to the sundial.

And the claws clenched shut.

It had been a cruel night.

Awake, Gudrun sat in her cottage and tried to shut out the images. 'It was only a dream,' she said aloud, trying to reassure herself. Yet, she knew better. There was a quality to the *seeing dreams* that set them apart from the others.

She washed her leathery face in a bowl and bundled up in layers of assorted pelts over a threadbare tunic, donning her thick, shaggy boots. Dressed and warm, she stared at the floor for some time, wringing her wrinkled hands. Absently, she began to run her fingers over the feathers and shells that decorated the weapon in her lap—a blowpipe of hollowed moose bone. She would take some fresh air. An interpretation for this bewildering dream would only come through meditation and reflection.

At least, she hoped so.

Was Erik dead?

Was Freya unleashed?

Could Astrid bring forth the Great Wolf?

Had these things passed or were they yet to come?

'They call me the Oracle,' she whispered to herself, rubbing her weary eyes. Gudrun doused the firepit and glanced around for her blow darts.

Then she was through the door and into the woods.

*

Astrid felt parched and utterly drained.

It had taken hours to run from the hot spring to the river, stopping only once to strip off her wet clothes. They had been wrung out and wrapped in moss to absorb the moisture, beaten against rocks and swung overhead—anything short of a fire to dry them out. Her pursuers could be nearby so it was best not to draw their attention. They had likely caught up with Hermod and realised Astrid's cunning ruse, then backtracked. She knew the forest better than they, but an advantage like that did not guarantee evasion.

By the time she finally caught sight of the river she was shivering in her damp dress, had a blistering headache, and her bone-dry tongue stuck to the roof of her mouth. Astrid slipped from the trees and moved lightly across the wide bank, suddenly conspicuous under the bright blue sky. Here, the river Hreim flowed ankle-deep over a wide silty bed that crunched between her toes. She stooped to take a long, satisfying drink, and splashed the sweat and dirt from her face.

Her colourful necklace slipped from her tunic and dangled in the rippling water. Out of respect for her teacher, Astrid had meticulously duplicated Thora's design—a series of jade and turquoise beads arranged in a recurring pattern—and wondered if the old woman had noticed.

She tucked it back into her dress and slowly exhaled.

Mother. Father. May Odin guide me safely back to you.

Annoyingly, Freya had always handled Astrid like a glass goblet. But last night's attack had begun to make sense of all the fussing. Perhaps Freya knew of these raiders. The maternal rules Astrid wore like a tight arm ring may have always been meant as a shield.

Astrid stood, the crisp water numbing her bare feet.

Had she already overshot the cottage Freya mentioned? Hopefully not, for it could very well be the last warm shelter for miles in any direction. Astrid had never come this far south before. The river ran from the far Northern mountains, past Runolodda, and all the way to the port of Hvalvik, where it spilled into the Silver Sea—approximately five full days on foot. With any luck, the horsemen had given up the chase and returned to their horde.

But luck was not on her side today.

Even as Astrid cast about for a makeshift water bottle, they spotted her.

'There she is! Hyah!' came the cry, as the riders burst from the trees.

Turning to run, Astrid saw one of them still cradling his broken ribs. They came crashing across the shallow water, hoofbeats splashing up a glittering spray. Against all hope, Astrid sprinted, her heart thumping against her ribs. But in seconds, the horses came up snorting, blocking her path, circling her like a stray sheep, and Astrid felt bile burn her tightening throat.

The first rider dropped from his saddle and used a leather sleeve to wipe snot from his moustache. 'Slippery eel,' he seethed. 'Think you're so clever, do ya? You made me miss my ship! And I *never* miss my ship.'

His injured comrade was not in the mood. 'Be quick about it, Sveinn. It's a long ride back to port.'

'So? If she's gonna run all night and keep me from me beauty sleep, she deserves ta lose her feet, don't ya reckon?'

'Then go ahead and do it! I can barely breathe!'

This was Astrid's chance. She slid the dagger from her belt and whipped it forward. But the rider pivoted smoothly, snatching her wrist in an iron grip.

'Give me that!' he growled, 'Think you're so quick, too, 'ey?' He seized the dagger and swiped for her face. Astrid threw up a protective arm, and the blade sliced her palm instead. Screaming, she toppled backward into the shallows. Before she could regain her footing, the man locked an arm around her neck, scrunching her hair with his free hand, her agonised cry cut short as he thrust her head under the water.

'Give it up, witch!' he roared, driving a knee into her spine.

Astrid would die here today. She knew this for a certainty. Drowned in water scarcely deep enough to submerse her entire head. The mountains leaned back, as indifferent as the gods, while she struggled for her life. Birds soared overhead. Trees whispered. Light tip-toed on the water. Only her killers would bear witness to her final moments.

Her vision blurred.

She gulped water.

Images swam past her mind's eye. Old Thora the Witch, the spear piercing her back. Her parents, fighting tooth and nail to keep her safe. Fire and blood and the ringing of swords. Darkness pressed in on the edges of sight and she realised that her murderer was technically correct—she *was* a witch. The new Witch of Runolodda. Or at least she *would* have been, if the Norns of Fate had not chosen this day to be her last.

Her body went limp.

'Finally,' said the injured horseman, wincing. 'Can we get going now? Please?'

Sveinn lifted Astrid's head and pressed the dagger to her throat. She wasn't breathing. 'This one's been a real pain in the neck,' he grinned. 'Get it?'

He flinched.

At first he thought a wasp had stung his neck. Then his eyes widened in panic, and he clutched his throat.

'Sveinn? What is it?' asked the injured man.

But Sveinn was already foaming at the mouth. He dropped the dagger, shook violently, and splashed face down in the river. Another twitch, then he was still.

The injured man frantically whipped an arrow to his bow, guiding the nervous steed with his knees. He squinted in the sunlight and a movement in the trees caught his eye. Yet before he could fire, a poisoned dart flew into his jaw. He toppled from the saddle, spooking the horse, and Gudrun came hurtling across the sandbank. She raised the blowpipe to her lips and fired a second dart for good measure, hitting his leg, though his limbs had already stopped thrashing by the time she reached Astrid.

At least the girl lay face up.

She was not breathing, the coloration of her skin closely matching the pale blue of her dress.

'Stay with me, lass,' said Gudrun, kneeling beside her. She clasped her fingers together, held her breath, and pounded down on Astrid's belly. The girl coughed and sputtered water, taking in huge drafts of air. 'There you are, my dear. There you are. You're alright now.'

Astrid half opened her eyes.

'Who the f——?' she murmured.

And fell unconscious.

PRISONER

The Great Hall had never felt so sombre.

The slain were arranged along the walls for their families to view. Or in some cases, to identify. Sif's body had been recovered from the sea and laid opposite Thora, who lay wrapped in her multi-coloured mantle. The old Witch stared unseeing up at the rafters.

Grief filled the dimly lit room like a haze. Children wailed and pawed at their dead mothers. These were innocent women, cut down by a cowardly foe, whose motives were as obscure as their methods were cruel. The charred remains of the Wolf-men had yet to be gathered up, though by now their fate had been relayed to everyone in the village. Chief Erik, too—they whispered—was dead.

Scion and Birger, aided by Olle and Tyr, carried Freya's stretcher into the gloom and lifted her upon a table, prepared with a covering of soft straw and cowhide.

Hedda took immediate control.

'Bring it closer to the fire! We need light and warmth for the Lady. Tyr, I shall need two strong splints and half a dozen leather straps. Belts will do. Birger, fetch me pincers from the forge and heat them in the firepit.' The men nodded and set off. 'More vinegar, please girls!' she added, 'and a sharp knife! We'll need to re-open these wounds to clean them out.'

Her daughters set to work.

Hedda put her grey hair into a bun and rolled up her sleeves.

'Let's hope you stay asleep through this,' she whispered to Freya, though the likelihood of that remained slim.

Scion came alongside and carefully handed her a razor-sharp seax. 'I trust you know what you're doing, Hedda.'

'I've seen Thora work her healing before. Now, hold the Lady's ankle, lad. We must—' she broke off as a large man burst into the hall.

'Where is she?' demanded the bull-necked Torsten. 'Where's my mother?'

He staggered, drunk with anguish, knocking men aside, banging into tables. Then he saw her. Was struck dumb. Mourners averted their gaze, allowing Torsten to lumber forward and curl himself slowly and reverentially over his mother's cold body, his broad shoulders shuddering as he sobbed openly.

Hedda could not help but stare.

Was this not the arm-wrestling logger who only last night had challenged Birger the Bear? She would not have thought a powerful man like he could show such tenderness. People were a puzzle to Hedda. Each possessed their own universe of ideas and feelings—mysteries beyond her grasp—and it always surprised her when they spilled out.

Best to focus on the task at hand.

Broken bodies were easier to comprehend than broken hearts.

*

It was over.

Mercifully, Freya had lost consciousness mid-surgery, her screams still ringing in Scion's ears as he stepped out into the daylight. Thanks to Hedda, the bones were set straight, and Freya's Wolf-blood would accelerate the recovery tenfold. If all went as expected, she would return to full health in only a few days.

The Beastly Boys stood assembled beside the doorway, deep in conversation.

'What did I miss?' asked Scion, joining the huddle.

Red flecks of spatter dotted Tyr's snow-white hair, though he paid them no mind. 'One of the raiders was found alive,' he said.

'What? Where?'

'He's been taken to the stables,' said Olle, his hands folded and resting on his paunch. 'Vali wants him kept breathing. Says he needs information.'

'As do I,' growled Scion, turning to go.

'Wait.' Birger the Bear produced a gold ring from his pocket. 'You boys seen this before?'

'Where'd you get it?' asked Scion, running his fingers over the intertwined triangular grooves of the engraved Valknut.

'From one of the bodies on the beach. Each of them wore one, including the prisoner in the stables.'

'Their spy had one too,' said Scion. 'It's the sigil on their sail.'

'This is an oath ring,' said Birger. 'Most likely a gift from a King to his most loyal subjects. These are no mere raiders. This is an army.'

'So there would be more of them out there,' muttered Tyr.

'How many, is the question,' said Olle.

'Well,' said Scion, 'Let's go find out.'

*

For a pair of old men their knuckles were hard as hailstones.

It was difficult to say how long the beating had lasted. The prisoner had been driven to his knees, his outstretched arms tied to a crossbeam, and battered until every muscle ached and his vision swam. At one point, his interrogators had paused to argue about a goat—some quarrel over who ate what, and how much—and then, having reached an impasse, decided to take their frustrations out on their prisoner.

'He's never going to talk,' wheezed Fiske.

'We haven't asked him anything yet,' said Selby.

'Have we not?'

'No.'

A brief moment of reflection.

'Ah, well,' shrugged Fiske, driving a fist into the man's ribs. The horses snorted below, but up here in the stable's hay-stacked loft, the prisoner could do nothing but bite the tight gag between his teeth.

Then, in answer to an unspoken prayer, a voice carried up through the floorboards. 'That's enough, fellows,' called Vali. 'Time for a breather.'

Selby rolled his eyes. He turned to leave, then snuck in one more jab for good measure. The prisoner's head snapped back, then flopped forward. He let out a groan. Fiske grinned at Selby, wagged a finger, and clambered down the ladder.

The prisoner heard voices from below.

'I don't care! I'll ask him again!'

'He'll tell you what he told us, Scion. That she was thrown overboard.'

The voice quavered. 'Astrid has *drowned*?'

'I doubt he speaks true. Think about it, where's Hermod?'

'Her horse? I . . . I've not seen him, as a matter of fact. Taken by the raiders, perhaps?'

'Up on the meadow, there are tracks leading into the woods. Three horses. One set starts where the cart stood. I believe Astrid escaped. What happened after that—'

'—Only the tracks will tell. Vali, you're sharp as a splinter. Do we know any more about these raiders?'

'Not yet, but our captive can't hold out forever.'

The prisoner heard a creak on the ladder and braced himself for another beating. But it was a woman's head that poked up through the hatch. She kept her eyes down as she set a bowl of water on the landing and climbed up. She was quite beautiful, noted the prisoner. Hair like wheat, a vibrant orange dress hugging her shapely body. A sweet tangerine.

But this was not the time for flirting.

'Hello,' he whispered.

She remained silent and began dabbing his cuts and bruises with a wet rag.

'I'm not who they think I am, you know?' whispered the prisoner. 'I'm not one of those . . . brutes.' She pressed his swollen eye a little too hard, causing him to wince. 'They were heading North and I paid to join the voyage. That's all. I knew nothing of this raid. Please, I was only a passenger. You must believe m—'

'You wore their sigil,' said Tove.

The prisoner glanced down at the pale band of skin on his finger. 'Oh, the ring? Aye, I'm their jeweller. I wear it now and then, but only to exhibit my craftsmanship to potential customers. I swear by the gods.'

Tove wrung the rag out. She looked into his eyes for a moment and was about to say something, but shook her head instead, wetting the cloth once more.

The prisoner cocked his head to the side. 'I've seen you before. You're the singer, are you not? Aye, I've visited your Great Hall before, not too long ago in fact. You have a lovely voice, if you don't mind me saying. What is your name?'

Tove stood. 'Finished.'

She made to leave when the prisoner whispered, his words meant solely for her. 'I'm not who they say I am. I swear by Odin. I swear by Thor. I swear by all the gods of Asgard.'

She stood still, unsure, her back to the man. Then she slapped the rag over her shoulder and slipped back down the hatch.

Ulrick grinned like a goblin.

A LONG DISTANCE

Flames crackled in the firepit.

Astrid snuggled beneath a thick bearskin and felt the cold melt from her bones. The gamey aroma of rabbit stew filled the air and caused her mouth to water. The cottage was cosy, if not a little cluttered. The low thatch ceiling was strung with salted venison, pelts, dried flowers, and herbs. A loom leaned beside the doorway. Rows of shelves lined the wattle-and-daub walls, packed full of bottles and pots of varying colours and sizes.

The old woman entered. She had draped Astrid's clothes over a fish-drying rack outside, and now eyed her visitor with something between wariness and compassion.

'Feeling better?'

'Yes, thank you. You've been very kind . . . Grandmother,' said Astrid, trying out the word.

Astrid had heard of Gudrun—her father's mother, who had left the village one day for reasons unclear. Over the years, Astrid had made the occasional effort to ask after her, but the only answer her parents ever gave was that *Gudi* lived too far away, and that hopefully she would return someday.

And yet, here she was, her cottage a day or so's journey from Runolodda.

The old woman stepped closer, allowing a thin smile beneath her furrowed brow. 'Your hand. Has the pain subsided at all, my dear?' Gudrun had washed and bandaged the deep cut on Astrid's palm, sewing it closed with silk thread.

'It stings somewhat, though the stitches are holding, thank you.'

Gudrun's gaze softened. 'You remind me of Erik. It's the nose, I think.'

Astrid thought of her father's hooked nose and felt mildly insulted. 'Oh?'

'Your father's father was also named Erik, did you know? I used to call them Erik the Sipper, and Erik the Nipper. Heh.' She peered into the pot and gave it a stir.

'Your husband—Grandfather—is he about?' asked Astrid.

'Oh, no. I'm afraid he died ages ago, my dear. Silly bugger went for a piss in the woods and got himself mauled by a bear. Heh heh, reckless Eriks, the both of 'em.'

Astrid picked at the fur blanket. 'And you've lived here for, what, twenty years?'

Gudrun sighed. She knew what the girl insinuated.

'You're wondering why I kept to myself. Why I never looked in on you.' The silence grew uncomfortable, and Gudrun had to look away from those questing blue eyes. 'Honestly, my dear, I was afraid.'

'Afraid of what?'

Gudrun wrung her hands, not looking up. A cloud had settled in the room.

Astrid toed across the floor to sit beside the old woman.

'Afraid of what, Grandmother?' The question was a caress.

Gudrun folded her arms and leant forward, rocking back and

forth, her chin drawn in and her eyes shut tight. She missed this. Company. And now, having only just met her granddaughter, how could she say what needed to be said without pushing her away?

The rift with Erik was . . . complicated.

Her visions were . . . upsetting.

Not to mention that Astrid—the half-blooded *half-moon*—could be dangerous.

'Come,' she said at length. 'First we eat. You must be famished. And then, I wish to hear more of this attack on the village. Anything else you can remember. Agreed?'

Astrid sighed. Obviously, the trembling woman before her was not ready to face old ghosts. There would be time to talk another day.

'Agreed.' She gazed at the floor while Gudrun fussed with the crockery. She accepted a steaming bowl with a half-smile and they ate in silence, staring into the flames.

At least they were together.

*

Scion led his horse from the stables and deftly mounted.

'Are you sure you won't join us, Vali? We could do with your eagle eyes on the trail.'

Vali reached up to stroke the mane and gave a wry smile. 'And all those years of teaching you to track? Wasted my breath, did I? No, lad. Those cretins will be back and I must aid in fortifying the village. Lady Freya will need all the help she can get, and I intend to be there for her.'

'I understand,' said Scion. 'I imagine you have a strategy in mind?'

'That will be up to Lady Freya. She is the sole ruler now.'

Scion exhaled. Freya slept, thanks to a concoction of opium and hemlock found in Thora's house. But would a grieving widow, wounded as she was, be up to the task? Vali may have to play a more pivotal role in the days to come.

'Fair enough,' he said at last. 'Be well, old man. May Thor protect you and may Odin keep you.'

'Until we meet again, lad,' said Vali.

They clasped wrists, exchanged a curt nod, then Scion turned to kick his horse ahead.

Passing the market, he saw many a downcast face, heard many an angry word. They were a hardy bunch and tough as leather, but could Runolodda prevail against an army whose sigil signified Death? To defeat an enemy of equal strength demands courage. A stronger foe, cunning. They would need both. Scion instinctively rested a hand on the hilt of his axe. The sooner he returned with Astrid the better.

He came to the forge just as Knud the Blacksmith and his son, Birger the Bear, emerged from the smoky shadows.

'Aye, of course you can go,' croaked Knud, his voice little more than a wheeze. 'You boys will only be gone a few days anyway. The village is already well-armed, trust me. I spend all day sharpening old swords, not forging new ones.'

'And armour? There are many who will want something crafted, Father. If you need me to stay, just say the word.'

Knud bit his lip. He would never tell his son, but he much preferred to smith alone. Working the forge was Knud's greatest joy in life, and ever since Birger had been old enough to swing a hammer, the lad had been underfoot. Still, Birger worked with such enthusiasm that the idea of relegating him to engraving away from the overcrowded forge would devastate the young man.

'I'll be fine, son. There are plenty of men to work the bellows for me.'

Birger breathed an inner sigh of relief. He would never tell his father, but smithing was not his idea of stimulating work. Engraving was the only task he relished. Clobbering steel was, to be blunt, deathly boring. His was a mind for art and stories, especially old ones of the gods and the elves and the giants. He had memorised every tale he'd ever heard and chewed them over and over each night before falling asleep.

Birger shrugged, and threw a leg over his own mount. 'I shall be back in the forge before you know it, Father. I promise.'

They shared a strained smile at the image.

'Right then,' rasped Knud. 'Off you piss.'

And with that, Birger and Scion set off.

Tyr and Olle waited for them at the gates. Their horses were packed and ready for the journey ahead, though Olle was already dipping into his saddlebag for a snack.

'All set?' asked Tyr.

'All set,' said Scion, waving up to the watchman. The timber gates creaked open.

'You may need this,' said Tyr, holding out a necklace of jade and turquoise beads.

'Astrid's necklace. But how—'

'Not Astrid's. Thora's. But aye, they're identical.'

'So?' asked Olle, at times a little slow on the uptake.

'With any luck, we find a traveller who's seen it. They could point us in the right direction.'

Scion held it up to the light, the refracted colours dancing and flickering across his face. 'Clever thinking, Tyr. Thank you.'

He pocketed the necklace and turned his horse to face them. 'My thanks to you all, friends. I can't say what we may encounter out there, but there's none I'd rather have at my shoulder. You are men of honour, each one.'

'Say no more,' said Birger the Bear. 'As the skalds wrote:

it's an easy road to a good friend, no matter how long the journey.'

Tyr clapped a palm on Birger's shoulder. 'Well said, Birger. Extremely sappy for a blacksmith, but still, well said.'

They all laughed.

'Heh. Look at us,' said Olle, dusting crumbs from his beard. 'Vikings on a quest.'

'Come,' said Scion. 'We have many miles to cover and the sun is midway.'

'Indeed,' said Tyr, kicking his horse into a gallop. 'Try to keep up, brothers!'

Hooves thundered on the hard earth as they rode out.

And the gate slammed shut behind them.

*

Night fell and Scion's knuckles whitened on the reins.

'Curse it!' he grumbled. 'It's too dark to track any further.'

'We'll need to stop. Make camp.' said Tyr. 'I'll get a fire going.'

It had been a frustrating day. At first, the tracks had been easy enough to follow. Three horses, one trail, heading south. Yet the hoofprints had abruptly doubled back near the hot spring, heading north toward the village. Eventually, the spoors split— one set continuing north, while two peeled off, heading south once more.

It was thought that the raiders must have given up, leaving Astrid to escape back to Runolodda. However, a few hours later, when Scion finally caught up to Hermod, Astrid was nowhere to be seen. He grew agitated. Either she had been captured, or she had given her captors the slip and gone on foot. Either way, she remained in danger.

They followed the two horse tracks deep into the forest, and finally found a single footprint as the sun began to set. A woman's print.

So, not captured then. Not yet, at least.

'She must be past the gorge by now,' said Scion, squinting to tie his horse in the pale moonlight.

'But that will take her through bear territory,' said Tyr, 'We tend to avoid it. Astrid knows that.'

Olle poured a measure of mead and passed it around. 'We'd better ration the drink. This will be a lengthier trip than expected, I reckon.'

Birger plopped himself down against a large willow and sighed. 'Who's for some smoked bacon?'

'Mead?' asked Scion sharply. 'Smoked bacon? Taking this seriously, are we, brothers?'

The camp fell silent.

Tyr snapped twigs into a pile.

Birger coughed. 'She'll be alright, Scion. We'll find her.'

'You know that for a certainty, do you?' Scion placed his palms on his head and closed his eyes. 'Such a waste of a day, doubling back like that . . .'

'I wouldn't say that,' said Tyr. 'At least we know she's given herself a head start.'

'Eh? How's that?' asked Olle, lagging behind the conversation.

'Travelling on foot will make her tracks trickier to follow, slowing any pursuers. She can weave through thickets, backtrack, disturb the ground less so than hooves. Shows a shrewd mind, that. And shrewd minds survive.'

'Ah,' said Olle. 'Well that's alright then, isn't it?'

'Nothing we can do tonight, my friends,' said Birger. 'I say we rest and rally for tomorrow's search. Come, eat. The dawn will bring fresh luck for the Beastly Boys.'

'The Beastly Boys!' chorused all but Scion, who smiled weakly.

'Aye, alright then.' He sat cross-legged and spoke no more, though his fidgeting fingers said enough.

Tyr sparked a flint over the kindling. 'And speaking of luck, Olle's going to need a lot of it if he hopes to ward off any raiders with that sorry excuse for a bow.'

'Oi! What's wrong with my bow!' said Olle, with a look of false indignity.

'Well, for one, it's as short as a shrimp. And secondly, it's made of oak. Far too rigid for a decent draw.'

'Oh?' said Olle with a wry smile, 'I've been told it's not how long, it's how stiff!'

Again, all except Scion laughed.

The tinder caught and the twigs flared into flame.

'Speaking of stiff and long,' said Birger the Bear, climbing to his feet and tramping over to his horse, 'feast your eyes.'

He lifted the saddle blanket to reveal a long-handled sledgehammer strapped to the flank of his exhausted-looking steed.

Tyr groaned. '*That's* your weapon of choice?' He shook his head. 'Where did I go wrong with you fellows? I myself have a yew longbow with iron-tipped arrows, a hand-forged knife, an Ulfberht broadsword of crucible steel, and these two beauties.' He indicated the two criss-crossed axes shoved into his belt.

Olle whistled. 'Not bad.'

'And you, Scion? What's in your arsenal?' asked Tyr.

Scion stoked the fire absently. His voice was soft, his eyes down. 'Everything my father left me. Axe. Sword. Longbow.'

'Don't forget the seax in your boot,' said Birger. 'Forged it myself. Folded steel, that knife. Very tough. Very sharp.'

'Show me!' insisted Tyr.

Scion blinked into the fire and handed over the blade.

'Hmm. I'm jealous,' said Tyr, inspecting it carefully. 'What will it take to have one crafted for me, 'ey?'

'Ha! Bring me an elk as Scion did, and I'd be happy to,' said Birger, secretly dreading the idea of returning to the smoky forge.

'An elk it is, then.'

Scion stood swiftly and took the blade, sliding it back into his boot. He clasped his hands behind his back. 'I'll fetch us some proper firewood. I think we passed a fallen hazel back there.'

'I'll join you,' said Tyr, rolling sideways to rise, but Scion held out a palm.

'That's alright, Tyr. Sit. Eat. I won't be long.' He drummed his fingers on his thigh, nodded curtly, then turned on his heel to march off into the woods.

Olle raised his eyebrows and took another sip.

Birger bit off a strip of the dried bacon and chewed quietly.

An owl hooted.

'I've never seen him so worked up over a girl before.' said Tyr.

'Not surprised he's grumpy. It's been a long and vexing day,' said Olle.

'He's not vexed, Olle. He's afraid,' said Birger.

'Afraid of what?'

'Of losing those he cares for, of course. Losing *her*.'

'Ah,' said Olle.

As boys, it had been unbearable to witness Scion's struggle with the tragic loss of his parents. He had lashed out, run away, starved himself. Until Vali had stepped in and brought him back to the village, back to life.

Love can break a man's heart.

It can also break his fall.

'Well,' said Tyr, 'we won't let that happen then, will we?'

'No,' said Birger, taking a sip of mead. 'No, we will not.'

HALF-BLOOD

Dry blood stained the bandage.

'Not too much damage,' said Gudrun, admiring her own stitch-work, as she carefully replaced the dressing on her granddaughter's palm. 'I'm sure you'll be back to your old self in a few weeks.'

Astrid flinched as the fresh linen tightened over the tender flesh. She felt refreshed after such a deep sleep, back in her blue dress, washed and bone-dry, with her yellow hair clean and bundled at the nape.

'Thank you, Grandmother,' she said, growing more accustomed to using the moniker.

'You are most welcome, Granddaughter,' smiled Gudrun.

The open doorway framed a flaming pink sky. Even as Astrid breathed in the sweet scent of pine, the sun peeked over the mountains and spilled its gold along the snowline. She sighed, straightening her silver brooch.

Gudrun set a bowl of hard-boiled eggs on the table.

'Eat,' she urged. 'We must return to the village as soon as possible. I'm sure your father will be happy to see you safe.'

Astrid caught the omission. 'And my *mother*,' she added.

Gudrun pursed her lips. 'Of course.'

'Do you think they made it?'

Gudrun held her breath. Erik may well be dead, if her dream was to be believed, and Freya, the ultimate cause. The girl had a right to be told. Needed to be told.

'You know what your mother is, don't you?'

Astrid frowned. 'I do.'

'The Great Wolf.'

'The Alpha, yes. What of it?'

Gudrun failed to hide her distaste. 'Well, then I'm sure she's perfectly alright. Knows how to survive that one, whatever it takes.'

Astrid shifted in her seat. She saw a new side to her grandmother and did not much care for it. 'And just what is that supposed to mean?'

'Freya is not who you think she is, Astrid. Not who anyone thinks she is. She has a plan. One that will destroy us all.'

'Oh, really? And what would *you* know of my mother?'

Because I saw her in a vision twenty years ago, thought Gudrun. *Because she is Fenrir, the world-devouring Wolf of Ragnarök, and you are her half-blood instrument of destruction.*

'Well?' insisted Astrid.

A long silence.

Gudrun averted her gaze.

No, the truth would be too much for the poor dear. She folded the soiled bandage and placed it beside the kettle, rubbing her eyes. 'Never mind, girl. Leave it be.'

'No, Grandmother. I will *not* leave it be. Tell me what you mean.'

The old woman shook now. 'I—I cannot. Not yet.' She needed to smooth the ruffled feathers, and was about to speak when a shadow stretched into the room.

Astrid gasped.

Gorm loomed in the doorway, silhouetted by the burning dawn light. His tunic and trousers were tattered, blood-stained, musty, and there was a scabbing graze across his shaven scalp. He ducked below the lintel to enter, the wooden floorboards creaking under the heavy clomp of his boots. He walked right up to Gudrun before she had the wide-eyed sense to move.

'Get back, you!' she shouted, reaching for an axe on the table. But Gorm swatted her hand away and shook his head, those icy eyes boring into her.

'Sit,' he ordered, and she did.

Astrid trembled, frozen in place by sheer terror. This was the man who had led the attack, the one responsible for Thora's death. Snatching the axe, Gorm tossed it to the floor, and slid his gaze over to the young woman.

'The Witch's apprentice,' he stated flatly. 'And if I overheard correctly, the Alpha's daughter. That is what one might call *useful information.*'

The two women exchanged a troubled look.

With a grimace, Gorm sat on the bed, dividing his gaze between them. '*Astrid*, is it? Lovely name. I believe it means *beloved of the gods.*' He winced, and Astrid—feeling entirely *abandoned* by the gods—caught a glimpse of a darkly blotched rag around his forearm. Gorm tilted his head to the side and stroked his tapering beard. Menace radiated off him like heat.

'Food. Now. Ale, if you have.'

Gudrun slid the bowl of eggs his way. 'No ale.'

Shrugging, Gorm returned his attention to Astrid. 'Your father didn't make it, by the way,' he said, peeling away an eggshell. 'He was a brave fool, and died a brave fool's death.'

A cold statement of fact, devoid of gloating or mockery.

Astrid went white.

Gudrun's shoulders slumped. 'By your hand?'

Gorm popped the egg into his mouth. 'Yes,' he said, wiping his beard on the back of his hand.

Astrid's stomach twisted and she found it difficult to breathe. How could there be a world without her father? It could not be. She forced back tears, as though weeping would only make it true.

Gorm leaned forward, stiffly, and slipped off his tunic. Chiselled muscles bulged and rippled under a mesh of old scars and fresh cuts.

'These wounds will need cleaning,' he rumbled.

Shakily, Gudrun rose to fetch a pitcher.

Astrid swallowed. There was an iron poker by the firepit, only a few paces away. Gorm unwrapped his forearm, releasing a foul odour from the oozing black bite. He swore under his breath.

'Hurry now,' he growled.

Mother's handiwork, thought Astrid. *She's alive!*

A bowl of honey-water and strips of linen were laid out. Gudrun sat once more, her teeth clenched. The blackness of Gorm's wound conjured the image of the wounded lily from her dream...

A paralysing fear fixed Astrid to her chair.

The poker was so close.

Gorm reached for the fresh cloth and dipped it in the bowl.

Grunting, he wiped at his wrist. Fresh blood trickled through the black scabs.

Astrid took a deep breath, her father's face clear in her mind. She lunged for the poker.

A fraction too slow.

Gorm buffeted her aside with a quick boot and she sprawled to the floor, the stitches on her palm splitting open as she skidded on her hands and knees. Desperate and furious, she spun around and sprang again. But Gorm was quick on his step, catching her mid-air by the throat, holding her aloft with one solid arm.

'Oh!' cried Gudrun, rushing to her granddaughter's aid, but she was swept aside with a casual backhand that sent her clattering into the table and crashing to the floor.

She lay in a heap and moaned.

A vein stood out on Astrid's reddening forehead, eyes bulging, fighting for breath, clawing vainly at Gorm's vice-like grip.

'Do not fret, young Astrid. I will allow you to live. You will make a fine hostage to draw out the She-Wolf.' He batted away her kicks with his free hand. 'And later, perhaps you'll make a fine slave.'

Never, thought Astrid. The sense of cage bars closing in caused something to rise up within her. She clapped her hands around Gorm's wrist and tugged with all her failing strength, and her bloody palm rubbed into his open bites wounds.

Blood of a Wolf.

Blood of a Half-Moon.

Blending together.

'Now, promise that you'll behave when—'

Pain exploded up Gorm's arm like a rush of poison. Astrid felt the hairs on his forearm thicken and elongate as his fingers sprang open, dropping her to the floor. He doubled over in agony, coarse hair spreading over his mushrooming back and shoulders. Astrid scrambled away, staring in horror as Gorm's arms virtually doubled in length, fingernails flaring out into sharp yellow claws.

Blood trickled from a cut into Gudrun's terrified eyes. A Wolf-man in the daylight? This had to be a dream.

Gorm roared, deafeningly loud, his monstrous form blocking the doorway.

There was no way out.

REQUIEM

The entire village attended Erik's funeral.

Drawn and pale, Freya rubbed her eyes with the heel of her hand, seemingly weighed down by her stringed jewels and formal finery. She leant on a gnarled crutch with her right arm dangling in a sling. Weak as she was, and numb from the many soothing tonics, she was determined to pay homage to her husband.

She gazed down at him.

Brushed his cheek with the back of her fingers.

Erik had been dressed in soft furs and elaborately moulded leathers. A silk band lay draped over his hollowed eyes. His cold hands folded over a burnished broadsword that rested on his chest.

His body was laid out on the deck of a burial ship, its heavy hull resting on the cold earth and wreathed with autumn leaves. The ship sat perched on the edge of a high precipice overlooking a deep gorge far below. *Heimdall's Balcony*, they called this place, for the site commanded a sweeping view of the Northern woods and the endless blue-grey mountains beyond.

The ship had languished here for decades.

Erik's predecessor, Chief Lennärt, had ordered it brought to the overhang—a cumbersome endeavour involving rolling logs and a dozen oxen—in the hopes that he might someday be buried in stately Viking style. But rumour had it that he had died abroad and so the ship had been left to accumulate moss instead.

Freya stared absently at the bouquet of marigolds in her hands, the petals bright yellow and citrus-scented.

Right before their first kiss, Erik had slid marigolds through her hair. Had presented her with a garland of marigolds on their wedding day. Had picked her wild marigolds on the day of Astrid's birth. And yet, in this moment, the bouquet seemed all she had left of him, so she tucked them away. Instead, she placed the first stone on Erik's chest. Then, taking one last look at his handsome face, kissed his forehead.

The grief was a chokehold.

It pressed the breath from her.

Jutting her jaw, she turned stiffly, painfully, on her crutch.

The procession began to file past, each silent mourner awaiting the chance to pay tribute, each toting as large a stone as possible, the line stretching away from the cliffside and back down the dusty bank. By day's end the entire ship's deck would be covered with one enormous cairn to honour their beloved Chief.

Freya beheld the many grieving faces of Runolodda.

Tove the Songbird.

Torsten the Logger.

Knud the Blacksmith.

Fiske and Selby, the ever-duelling neighbours.

Hedda, the Nurse, and her five stout daughters.

Families and loners.

Children and widows.

Old warriors, silver-bearded and grim.

With Erik gone, the responsibility for these people fell squarely on her shoulders. They would need comfort. They would need leadership and protection. All she had was doubt, and it gnawed at the edges of her confidence.

In the past, she had dealt with the mundane affairs of the village with ease, her keen mind and quick wit guiding her decisions. But when it came to the bigger picture, it was Erik who had been the guiding force. He had possessed a gift for eloquence, using words to paint the future in ways that inspired people to press on through hardship. Freya felt the urge to throw up. The raiders would almost certainly return. How could she lead Runolodda without Erik by her side?

She limped down the ramp and past the sombre procession where four volunteer porters helped her climb back up onto a crude litter. Before they could lift it up onto their shoulders, Vali approached, hunched, his fingertips in a low steeple.

'Lady Freya, may I speak with you?'

She flitted her gaze to the old huntsman, then back to the straps on her leg. 'Of course, Vali,' she said, adjusting the buckles that pinched her throbbing thigh.

'Erik was a fine man, my Lady. Honourable and fearless in all his ways. Odin has welcomed him into his Hall, of that I am certain.' A shuffling of feet. 'He was also, I am proud to say, a trusted friend.'

Freya smiled weakly. 'He trusted you, too, Vali.' Then, seeing the man's corked sorrow, she added, 'He once told me that you had two listening ears and two helping hands.' It wasn't much, but was all she could manage.

Vali cleared his throat. 'He was always such fine company.'

'And what of Astrid? Has there been any word?'

'Not as yet, my Lady. The Boys hasten, though the road is long. I suggest we allow a few days before sending scouts.'

Freya clamped her eyes shut, but the reservoir of pain erupted. Grief can be that way sometimes, slapping like a wave, sudden and suffocating. She let them come now—the shaking, racking sobs, along with the loneliness and the fear.

Vali dipped his gaze and took a step closer, his voice low. 'Peace, Freya.'

'I cannot lose her too, Vali.'

'I am with you, my Lady. Do not walk this dark time alone. Lean on my shoulder. I will provide what wisdom I can, and what strength I have.'

Freya laced her fingers and pressed both palms to her chest, eyes closed, slowly releasing her breath through pursed lips. There was relief in her whisper when at last she spoke. 'Thank you.'

Vali gave a thin-lipped smile, bowed, and turned on his heel, when Freya spoke again. 'Vali?'

'Yes, Lady Freya?'

'I hear you hold a prisoner.'

'We do, my Lady.'

'What is his name?'

THE DAYWALKER

The shallow water babbled over Scion's boots.

He rolled the dead horseman face up. Sure enough, the wretch wore a Klo ring, the Valknut etched into the gold.

'Two of 'em. Mucking up the river with their stink.'

He crouched to pluck the dart from the rider's neck and held it up for the others to see.

'Poison,' muttered Tyr, astride his horse. 'An unnamed shooter, then.'

'Someone mad enough to wander through bear territory,' added Olle.

'Or live here,' said Tyr.

They rode on, following the river south until eventually coming upon a cottage tucked into a thicket near the banks.

The door hung askew on a buckled hinge.

Tyr pointed to the riverbank. 'Astrid's footprints there, leading up to the house.'

Scion was first inside.

The place stood unoccupied. There were clear signs of a struggle. Broken shelves against the walls, clay and glass shattered across the floor, toppled pots beside an overturned table.

'The handiwork of our unnamed shooter?' asked Olle.

'Unlikely.' said Birger. 'Why would Astrid's saviour suddenly attack her?'

'A third horseman, perhaps?' offered Scion.

'Or something worse,' called Tyr from outside. 'Take a look at this.'

Scion was first outside.

They had seen such a paw print before. Wide like a bear's but longer, evidence of a Wolf-man in the torn earth.

Tyr scratched his snowy beard. 'But how? These tracks are no more than half a day old.'

'Impossible,' frowned Scion. 'Only the full moon can turn the Wolf-kind. Not so?'

'And no other tracks,' noted Olle. 'So strange.'

'Eaten?'

'Nay. I see no blood. No remains.'

'Carried, then? By this . . . *Daywalker*? Why?'

'Best we find out,' said Birger the Bear, mounting his horse.

'Agreed,' said Scion, following the big man's lead.

The tracks led downriver.

Further from home.

Closer to Gorm and the Klo army.

*

The world blazed.

Seen through Wolfsight, the pale sky burned an electric blue over the woods that shimmered in a million dazzling hues. Fiery emerald leaves. Beetles of psychedelic violet. Fungi glinted like rubies on a carpet of bronze pine needles. Smells hung sharp as spice, inescapable as incense. All sound, too, seemed amplified. A sparrow flapped its wings, yet to Gorm it was like the snap of heavy sails. Even the squirrels, squeaking faintly in the treetops, sounded clear and bright in his ears.

It was like coming fully awake for the first time.

Every tether to the mundane had been severed.

He stared in fascination at his dripping claws, luminescent red to his eyes, then down at his kill. The reindeer had been at least thirty strides away, but in the space of a few heartbeats Gorm had closed the distance, caught the frantic creature in his claws, raked thick lines through its flesh and crushed its skull into the stony earth. He bit into the animal's throat and tore out a thick string of meat, his wide maw drooling blood.

Thinking back, he could picture King Ødger's father—Ari the Wolf-King—losing his sanity beneath the full moon. Losing control. Losing himself.

Yet this was different.

Gorm's thoughts were clear and altogether . . . human.

His mind remained his own.

But how?

It had to have been the girl, Astrid, half-blood daughter of the Alpha. She had touched her wound to his.

Her blood!

Her blood flowed with Moonlight that unleashed the Wolf in his veins and triggered the transformation. It was though the Alpha's bite had turned his blood from water to oil and Astrid was the fire to ignite it. Though with far superior results. Gorm threw his monstrous head back with elation. He possessed the best of both worlds. The form of a Predator. The mind of a Conqueror. Imagine what could be accomplished with an *army* of such creatures! The idea was intoxicating.

Dragging the deer by the horns, he trudged back into the thicket.

The women sat as he had left them, gagged and bound to a great oak. The elder held his gaze, incredulous, fearful. The younger simply stared at her feet. Gorm hooked the gags free with a thorny fingertip. Then, patiently, awkwardly, forced his broad muzzle to form the words, though they rolled off his canine tongue in a guttural slur.

'What is your name, crone?' The voice was thunder in a well.

Gudrun found herself unable to look away. 'How is it that you speak?'

'Your *name*.'

'And how are you Wolf by day?'

Gorm leaned close. 'I shall not ask again.'

'She is Gudrun,' blurted Astrid, loath to antagonise the monster.

'Gudrun,' repeated Gorm, speech forming easier now.

The truth of Astrid's power dawned on Gudrun. Of course! Astrid, the half-moon shining like a goddess in the dark. And here she was. The foretelling made flesh.

Gorm advanced on Astrid, staring quizzically down. 'Silver, is it?'

'What?'

Without deigning to answer, Gorm unclasped the silver brooch at Astrid's breast and turned it over in his claws. The pin was the length of a child's hand.

It would do.

Bracing himself, he pressed the sharp point deep into the soft tissue under his tongue. The rush of nausea was immediate. Gorm crashed to the ground, writhing, frothing, howling like a wounded hound, his whipping claws missing the women by a hair, their screams desperate, their squirming futile.

It was over as quickly as it began.

Gorm, returned to human form, staggered miserably to his feet.

'That was . . . unpleasant,' he muttered, looking himself over. Apart from the old battle scars, his pale skin was whole once more. Every ache and pain had ebbed away. Every cut and sting. Even the bites had healed shut, leaving a curve of faint pink dots.

So, silver is their weakness, thought Gudrun. *Gorm seems to know an awful lot about the Wolf-kind.*

Then the truth landed like a hammer.

There were more of them out there.

A ripple washed through her mind, rolling the pebbles into a new pattern. *Fenrir, breaking his shackles. Rising from the depths. The wave of blood crashing through Runolodda.* These images, seen all those years ago in a dream, were crystallising before her now. Gudrun cursed her stupidity. Freya had never been the Great Wolf. As Gorm dressed himself in her husband's old clothes, Gudrun saw the true meaning of her vision.

'You,' he said, casting those ice-blue eyes on Astrid. 'From where does your mother hail?'

Freya had spoken little of her past. All Astrid knew was that her mother had grown in Caledonia, a rain-soaked land to the south and west. But how she came to live in the North, Astrid could not say. In any event, she had no intention of feeding this barbarian with anything close to the truth.

'From Kievan Rus,' she lied, keeping her voice steady. 'A land to the east.'

'I have travelled through Rus. From which city?'

Astrid had heard something once. What was the name of the place? 'Rostov.'

Gorm grunted, pulled a fur over his shoulders, and stooped close. 'You're lying.'

'I'm not!'

'You're lying and you're—'

'She speaks the truth!' Gudrun weathered his glare. 'Leave

her be. She's only a girl.'

'Only a girl, is she? You've not been paying attention, crone. With her power as my tool, I will vanquish any and all who stand before me. The Klo shall be as gods among men!'

'The Klo?' asked Gudrun. 'Your people?'

Gorm tossed the brooch at Astrid's feet. 'Enough talk. We must keep moving.' With a swift stroke, he chopped the ropes binding them to the tree and slipped the axe back into his belt.

'Where are you taking us?' asked Astrid.

'I will say no more. On your feet.'

The women rose. With her wrists bound, Astrid struggled to repin the brooch.

'If silence is your wish, I will only ask one more thing. Will you release my grandmother? I will do as you say. Only, please let her go.'

'That is precisely *why* I am keeping her near. So that you *will* do as I say. Any disobedience, any attempt at escape, any more *questions*, will result in her execution. Are we clear, Moonwitch?'

'We are,' she whispered.

'Good. Now, march.'

They hurried on until noon, the pace quick but not quick enough for Gorm since the overgrown path ran unclear and untrodden. It seemed there was a thicket or a boulder every few paces, making for painfully slow travel. Perhaps he should transform once again? Carrying the hostages had certainly been quicker, though rough on the old woman's bones. No, he needed silence, not bleating in his ear.

Eventually, they stumbled upon an abandoned runestone that loomed two men tall. A granite totem from a time past. Faded runes showed on the flat side, now covered with lichen and protruding mushrooms with gilled underbellies. The stone stood in the centre of a small clearing, thick with ferns and edged by a flowering tangle, though a sickly decay wafted in the air.

'We rest,' said Gorm, apparently untroubled by the stink. He had smelled far worse on the battlefield and the women could put up with it for a short while to catch their breath. Gudrun seemed most ill at ease. She knew this place. Knew what might happen if they lingered.

'Don't stop on my account,' she quavered, swatting a fly. 'I'm stronger than I look. I can keep going.'

'Your insufferable wheezing tells me otherwise. We rest.' But even as Gorm sat against the stone a strange feeling stole over him.

They were being followed.

Perhaps it was some sixth sense smouldering in his now-dormant Wolf-blood, warning him, trying to protect him. It was time to leave the forest and head for the river, however exposed that might make them.

'There are cranberries a little way ahead,' piped Gudrun, breaking his train of thought. 'Come, we can—'

'Are you hard of hearing or just plain insolent? I told you to—' There it was again. The impression of eyes upon him. He raised a finger for silence and squinted into the bushes.

Astrid felt it too. Had Freya sent a search party? Was Scion nearby, keen blade at the ready?

The silence stretched on.

Gorm stood slowly and gestured that they follow.

He took Astrid by the arm and turned to leave when a colossal brown bear lumbered into the open. Its great bulk shuddered with each deliberate step, its mouth drooling. In place of its left eye, there was the deep groove of an old axe wound. Something unnaturally sinister burned in the remaining orb. Something evil.

Gudrun knew this bear. Knew it as the Laughing Troll, for this one killed for sport. And this was its domain. Its arena of death. She had tried to steer them wide of this place but Gorm was about as approachable as a snakepit.

Gorm drew his axe and sliced a shallow gash across Astrid's arm. She winced, seeing that he was about to lick the blood, though he stopped short when the bear turned its unholy gaze on Gudrun. It took one heavy step toward her.

Gorm drew Astrid away. Perhaps the old woman was more trouble than she was worth. And without time to strip down, another transformation would only rip his fresh clothes. The girl would be made to obey, with or without the crone's company.

Contingencies upon contingencies.

Astrid tried to wrench free. 'What are you doing? She needs our help!'

'Hush.' Pitiless, Gorm dragged her back, fixed on the bear as they steadily withdrew into the trees.

'Grandmother!'

But Gudrun did not look back. She knew this place. Knew it well. Knew of the crevice in the ground a few paces to the left, where, if she had not picked up too much weight over the years, she could slip through into an underground passage too narrow for the bear to follow.

If she could reach it in time.

She stood abandoned. As forsaken as the runestone. Alone as she'd been for all those wasted years. The Laughing Troll advanced, savouring the fragrance of fear. Gudrun steadied her breath, took a careful step to the left, her boot squelching on a rotting carcass. The foetid smell smothered like a pall, bidding her to die.

No. Not today.

She bolted.

Surprised, the bear hesitated for a single heartbeat, then came at her.

She dived, landing hard on her belly, felt a rib crack as she slid for the crevice, the ferns whipping her cheeks, blood surging in her ears. The bear swiped, raking her calf even as she scraped through the opening.

Gudrun slammed into the back wall and crumpled to the cold, moss-soaked floor. Huffing and moaning, the bear tore at the narrow entrance, thrusting its slavering jaws through, its hot breath streaming in.

Racked with pain, Gudrun urgently scanned her surroundings. The narrow passage to her right ran for a mile underground, back towards her cottage—one of the many ways she travelled safely through bear country. But to reach it would mean coming in range of the beast. Left was a dead end. But at least the rockface was jagged enough to saw the ropes from her wrists. The bear grew more and more agitated. And little by little, its thrashing head inched nearer, nearer, strings of drool licking into the dark.

Gudrun sawed furiously, and gasped as the rope finally split. Reaching painfully behind her, she drew out the hidden blowpipe, mercifully still intact, fumbled with a dart, loaded the pipe, and slowed her breath.

The bear strained forward.

One eye wild.

One eye missing.

Gudrun rammed the blowpipe into the empty socket and blew.

TRAITOR

Ulrick curled up on the damp floor.

The night was cold, and colder still down this wretched pit. Soft moonlight broke through the overhead grate kept locked and guarded by the yammering fools high above. Ulrick had quickly given up on the notion of escape. To scale the smooth walls would be like climbing a glass well. Better to bide his time. His moment would come, of that he was sure.

The one they called Vali had interrogated him, failed to crack him, set his ruffians on him. But torture was a fine art for which they lacked imagination—an artform in which Ulrick, to put it mildly, excelled.

They had also tried mind games, showing him the pile of rotting raiders, heaped high in the first of the seven pits. The one, Vali had told him, where Manning had burnt alive. Whoever that was. Ulrick had stared impassively down at his dead crewmates. Besides the growing stench, nothing about the display bothered him. Their heads had been removed for extra effect, but dead was dead. And since these men had fallen in battle their spirits now revelled in the Halls of Valhalla, fighting by day, feasting by night, in Odin's glorious company. What could be better?

Ulrick heard the sound of hoofbeats above, and a woman's voice. 'Good evening, fellows. Lady Freya sends a jug of mead to stay the cold.'

'Hmph. Call this cold?' bragged a wheezy voice.

'Shut up, you old goat. She's offering us free drink!'

'Thank you kindly, Tove.'

'Not at all, Torsten. Drink up.'

'You two should find a room!'

'Selby!'

'It's true! In my day, we'd pocket the dowry and get down to business.'

'In your day they didn't *have* pockets!'

Laughter.

More drinking.

More chatter.

Annoyed, Ulrick rolled over and tried to fall asleep when the blathering stopped all at once. After a prolonged silence his eyes fluttered open. Then, a smash, a thud, and a clang as the guards collapsed, one keeling over onto the iron grate, lying quite still.

'Who's there?' called Ulrick, peering up.

The body was dragged away and before too long a face slid into view.

'It's Tove, sir. I nursed your wounds, remember?'

Ah, the blonde Songbird in the tangerine dress.

'I'm here to set you free,' she called.

Ulrick staggered to his feet. Every muscle ached and a few of his ribs had certainly cracked. Imaginative torturers or not, they could pack a punch. 'Why?' he asked.

'You're a man in the wrong place at the wrong time.' Tove fed down a rope. 'Runolodda is blinded by grief, hellbent on retribution. And you, sir, are the luckless scapegoat.'

Ulrick stared up into her innocent, gullible eyes. *The fool. She doesn't know who I am.* 'Thank the gods! You are most perceptive for someone so young.'

'It is vengeance the people seek, not justice. To be blamed for the deeds of your foul allies . . . why, that is a sore thing.'

'I am but a humble pedlar, I assure you. Their jeweller. Nothing more.'

'I know.' Tove shrugged, planted her feet, and readied the rope about her waist. 'You swore on the gods.'

Ulrick smirked in the dark. Aye, he had sworn on the gods. What of it? Ever had the gods failed to heed his words so why would they start now? When he had spied on the village and heard this vixen sing—so passionately of the old ways, so earnestly of Odin and the gods—he knew right away that she was a true believer. And belief is such an easy thing to exploit.

He took the rope in his fist and shinnied up, every bruised muscle screaming to stop. When at last he reached the top, the girl stood waiting beside her horse, alive with nervous energy. Ulrick lay on his back and breathed deeply.

'My thanks, young lady,' he rasped at length.

'Come, sir. We must hurry.'

Ulrick stood, carefully, painfully. The guards—two old men and a larger, younger third—lay still beside the grate, the shattered remains of a clay jug on the grass nearby. He prodded Fiske with his foot but the old man did not flinch. 'What happened?'

'I slipped them a sleeping tonic. It should last an hour or so.'

'So, what now?'

'Take me with you. They will do worse to me for this betrayal.'

'Take you with me, 'ey? Where would you like to go, girl?' There was an unsettling edge to his voice.

Tove swallowed. 'To Hvalvik, of course. I can hide out with you for a time. It's the least you can do, sir. I'm saving your life.'

Ulrick turned his back, stooping to take Torsten's cloak. He scarcely hid his wicked grin. 'Now why would I want to go to Hvalvik? For the harlots, perhaps?'

Tove took a step back, for the first time seeing the bold Valknut tattooed across Ulrick's shoulder blades. 'No . . . Y-You swore—'

He whirled the cloak around his shoulders and mounted the steed. 'My thanks for the horse. You shall see him again when the Klo return.' He winked. 'Trust me.'

'Return? Ha! There will be no return, oathbreaker! Your crew is *dead!*'

Ulrick smiled at that. His tongue clicked and the horse plodded forward. 'I say again, little lass. We are the Klo. Trained warriors under King Ødger of Klo Island. Our ranks are three hundred strong, with a ship for every score.'

Tove backed up, yet still Ulrick advanced. 'We have horses,' she stammered. 'We can—'

'We have more. Eight for every ship. Your pitiful band of farmers are in for a—'

His eyes widened as a pitiful band of farmers emerged from the shadows, arrows drawn back and aimed at his bare chest.

'—surprise?' finished Tove. The corners of her mouth quirked up.

'Well, that was bloody easy!' beamed Fiske, creaking to his feet.

'He just blurted it all out!' laughed Selby, brushing grass from his sleeves. 'What an idiot!'

Gnashing his teeth, Ulrick tried to wheel the horse. But Torsten was too quick. He gripped the reins in one hand and Ulrick's wiry bicep in the other, yanking him from the saddle. Ulrick landed clumsily, rolled to his feet, face twisted in a scowl.

Surrounded.

The sound of hoofbeats came from the woods across the meadow, and Ulrick spun in a low crouch to see Freya emerge, torchlight glinting off her steed's caramel mane. Vali rode alongside her. He seemed rather pleased.

Cursing, Ulrick glared at Tove. 'Is this your idea of justice, then?'

'No,' smiled Tove. 'This is Freya's idea of eavesdropping.'

Ulrick spat, glaring as Freya neared. 'Freeze in Hel, She-Wolf! You think you can hide behind a few pitchforks? The Klo will be back with a fury you can only imagine!'

'My oh my,' quipped Selby. 'Ever seen a dog barking at a wolf?'

'Never,' said Fiske. 'Seems a foolish thing to do.'

Freya winced in the saddle. Her leg burned hot with pain. 'It warms my heart to hear you speak so freely, Ulrick. My thanks for such useful information.' Laughter rippled through the huddle. 'Well done, Tove. An excellent performance. I shall have another cask sent for you and your *acting troupe*.'

'Much obliged, Lady Freya,' chorused the delighted Fiske and Selby.

'And much to ponder,' said Vali, leaning closer to Freya. 'We have work to do.'

Freya's heart sank. Where would they even begin? Runolodda would be overrun by such a force as Ulrick had described. Nevertheless, as Chieftain she had to maintain a firm facade.

'That we do, Vali. That we do.' She turned to Ulrick once more, sizing up the man. 'Toss him back in, Torsten. We have what we need.'

'Of course, my Lady.'

Turning their horses toward Two-Mile-Hill, Freya and Vali made off for the village. Tove caught Torsten's eye and smiled, making him blush like a bride as he hurled Ulrick into the pit.

STRANGE NEW WORLD

'By the gods!'

Hvalvik was immense. Each year its borders crept ever outward, the once nondescript trading port growing into a handsome Viking city. Astrid stumbled down the hillside ahead of Gorm, unable to tear her eyes away. She could see the river Hreim snaking through the sprawl of buildings, its long journey ending in the Silver Sea that lay sparkling in the sun.

Gorm untied her wrists and lifted her chin. 'If anyone asks, you are my niece on your way to a funeral. That will explain your glum expression.'

My glum expression? Thought Astrid. *And why do you suppose that is?*

'Keep your head down until we reach the harbourside. Understood?'

'We're to sail?'

'The Klo fortress is out to sea, yes.'

'An island fortress? How impressive.'

Gorm raised an eyebrow. Little by little the girl grew more impudent. It would not stand. And yet, he needed her now.

Needed what she could help him achieve.

And she knew it.

'May we at least eat?' She dabbed at the scab where Gorm had nicked her arm beside the runestone. 'It's been hard travel on an empty belly.'

Impudent, but not impractical. 'If it will shut you up,' he growled and shoved her forward. 'Now, no more questions.'

Hvalvik had no fence, no gates, not even a hedge. When the dusty road became cobbled street, and the rumble of voices grew louder, Astrid knew she had crossed into a strange new world. The first houses were squat, straw-topped, familiar. But the stone buildings soon rose two or three levels tall, their timber frames pressed together, their steepled roofs horned with twin rafters, each more decoratively carved than the Great Hall back home.

Before long, steps spilled down into a bustling market square, alive with the din of people haggling amid makeshift stalls and trundling carts. Astrid blinked, trying to decide whether all this colour and clamour was paradise or Hel.

'Silks from Serkland!'

'How much?'

'Beeswax for your leather!'

'Three coins, not two.'

'That's walrus ivory, my Lady.'

Everything was on offer. From silver and spice, to swords and slaves. Most folk wore northern garb, though there were more than a few unfamiliar travellers come to trade their curious wares.

'Stay close,' said Gorm, his meaty fist around her arm. 'We'll find a quiet tavern.'

They approached a spindling vendor, whose bright satin robe and conical hat bore the emblem of a red dragon that made him stand out even in this culturally mixed bag. Beside him stood a large gilded cage overcrowded with birds—an exotic rainbow of feathers, screeching behind those ornate bars.

He stroked the long tendrils of his moustache and smiled, eager to make a sale.

'We seek a tavern,' said Gorm, quaffing an invisible drink. 'Food? Ale?'

The man's face dropped and he waved vaguely to the south, turning his attention to another potential customer.

Astrid squinted into the birdcage.

It held a truly dazzling display of colour.

But all she could see was red.

*

Scion held out Thora's beaded necklace.

'Jade-and-turquoise, see? She wears one just like it.'

The cheesemonger rubbed his chin. 'A pretty blonde, you say? Look around you, young man. There's one on every corner!'

Scion sighed.

Hvalvik was a big place indeed, folk teeming like fish in a net. How could they stand it? And how in Odin's name would he ever find Astrid here? He thanked the man and set off once more into the maze and was soon swallowed up by the crowd.

*

Astrid hissed as her toe caught on a cobblestone.

'Keep moving,' urged Gorm. 'It can't be far.'

They threaded their way through alley after narrow alley before reaching a seedy establishment, entered, and sat in a dark corner away from the fire.

Gorm smoothed his tapered beard. 'There are a few hours before the cargo ship sets off. We'll wait here.'

There were shadows in the windowless gloom. Rough folk at rough tables, already drunk or well on their way. A busty serving maid sauntered over and leant on the sticky tabletop, one hand resting on her wide hip.

'A coin apiece for bread and ale. Another for a plate of mutton. Anything else . . . is negotiable.' She leered at Gorm, ignoring Astrid.

He produced two coins from his drawstring purse, all that remained of his Klo wardrobe. Gudrun's husband's old clothes were warm but tight-fitting. And the chafing was beginning to wear on Gorm's patience.

'Be quick about it,' he murmured. 'We have a pressing engagement.'

Astrid cocked her head at that. Gorm had a tendency to bark orders even when they weren't necessary. The maid straightened stiffly, sweeping the coins away with a huff.

'Right you are, sir.'

She stomped off and Astrid unintentionally caught Gorm's eye. She held his gaze for the first time since he had stormed into her life, regarding him now with unveiled contempt, aware that she was about to dine with the man who had murdered her father, her Witch, and her people. The man who had left her grandmother to die.

No more questions be damned!

'What is it that you *really* want, Gorm?' She felt like a cornered fox under his gaze, though the strength of her own voice surprised her.

Gorm picked a piece of lint from his sleeve and stared straight back. In times past, he had owned slaves who starved or harmed themselves, rather than *subject* themselves to the Klo. This girl had the same look about her. And although her cooperation was not integral to his needs, it was preferred. Perhaps she might prove more willing if she could be persuaded to share his view of the world.

'Dominion,' he stated flatly.

'Governance is not to be coveted, believe me. It's all duty and responsibility.'

'Governance will be left to the bureaucrats and politicians. But it is I who shall cut their path clear.' Gorm leaned back in his chair, indicating the dimly lit room. 'Look around you. The North is full of petty men squabbling over trinkets, competing over crumbs. You are too young to remember, but once we were Vikings. *True* Vikings with an appetite for conquest. But alas, we have melted into the soup, content to be diluted versions of our former selves.'

'An appetite for peace does not lessen a man.'

'Peace, you say? Living in the backwoods, you would not have heard the tides bring endless news of our defeat. Of expulsion from distant shores. Of loss, of shame. We Northerners have put down roots in wastelands, bargained for foreign thrones, instead of stretching wide our jaws as once we did.'

An interesting choice of words.

'The Klo will change all that. We will take back all that the North has lost. Remind our people of who we are.'

'By attacking us in the dead of night? By leaving us to the bears?'

'The weak will not survive what is to come. History grows frail with age, girl. Sometimes, only war can revive it.'

'Oh, I see,' she leaned forward and slid her fingertips across the table, her lips a sneer. 'Your army is here to *help*.'

Gorm shot forward, clutched her hand, and squeezed. The shock of pain made Astrid gasp and squirm to pull free as her stitches split open once again. 'Blood cleanses, Astrid of Runolodda. We shall saturate the world once more, by the tooth and by the claw.'

Her face turned red as the pain intensified. 'This tale sounds familiar,' she whimpered. '—All things swallowed up by the Great Wolf.'

Gorm's cruel eyes shone in the sputtering firelight. The sheer impudence! He tightened his grip. Her knuckles might crack soon, but what did he care? He needed her blood, not her bones.

'The End of Days?' he sneered. 'With *you* the heroine and *me* the vile Fenrir?'

'Please,' she gasped, her head jerking back. 'No more.'

Gorm scoffed, releasing her, the girl sucking in air, cradling her hand.

'Surely you know the story does not *end* in devastation?' he probed. 'After Ragnarök there will come a new beginning, a new cycle in which true order is possible.'

Astrid stared down at the table, catching her breath.

The maid arrived with the victuals, set them down without a word, and shuffled away.

'Ah, ale. Finally,' said Gorm, putting a prompt stop to the conversation. He reached for the mutton even as he drained the first cup.

Astrid flexed her bruised fingers. *True order? That's the key, isn't it?* Gorm was good at hiding his thoughts, guarding everything behind those hooded eyes. And yet, time after time he had given himself away. He cared not for the North. He cared for no-one at all.

Gorm craved conflict.

And Gorm craved control.

Be silent. Hush. March. Come. Go.

True order.

A man who needs that degree of obedience must go through life gathering frustrations like a dog gathers fleas. And sooner or later the dog must stop to scratch.

That's when the fox leaps free.

She looked around the tavern.

It crawled with just the right sort of pests.

*

'I still don't get it.'

Tyr rolled his eyes. It wasn't that Olle was stupid, per se, but he did tend to glaze over at anything vaguely complicated.

'The unnamed shooter. The one with the blowpipe.' Tyr shoved through the press, narrowly avoiding a cart weighed down with carrots. 'That's who killed the bear.'

Olle scratched his belly. 'But no tracks?'

'No tracks. The shooter slipped underground and through the caverns. Probably passed right beneath our feet, heading the other way.'

'Why?'

'No idea, my friend. But it's not our concern right now. We're looking for Astrid, so—Hey! Put that back!'

Olle chomped happily on a carrot as the cart rattled away behind him. 'They won't miss *one*. Besides, a man can search and snack at the same time. I wonder if Birger's had better luck?'

'You heard Scion. We meet at noon by the docks. Let's hope she turns up before—'

'You mean *those* docks?'

Tyr followed Olle's chubby finger. Sure enough, Hvalvik's harbourside could be seen through an alleyway to the right. And as if to confirm the sighting, a seagull landed at Olle's feet and squawked.

'Shoo!' He hugged the carrot to his chest. 'I'm hungrier than I look.'

Tyr blew a strand of silky white hair from his eyes. 'Alright, now we have our bearings. Come. I'd say we have another hour before midday.'

Olle half-heartedly kicked at the gull, missed, and followed Tyr back into the bustle.

And stole another carrot.

*

'Time to go,' said Gorm.

Astrid rose, scratching the itchy scab on her arm and peering through the smoky haze. The group she had singled out sat clustered around the fire, gulping down mead between peals of laughter. They bristled with strange weapons. Some wore turbans and baggy trousers. Others, the distinctive fur hats of the Eastern Rus. There was even a dark-skinned warrior from the far South, lithe and austere, a lion's mane about his shoulders.

Their leader, too, was hard to miss.

Morcant was a Celt from the West—a towering beast of a man with wild red hair and blue tattoos, both of which covered his back, his bare chest, and ruddy face. A pair of enormous hounds sat at his feet. They growled loudly, gnawing on the same juicy bone. Morcant snapped his fingers and they sat bolt upright, silent as shadows.

'Och, enough 'o that,' he scolded, pausing for a dog's eternity to take a sip. Eventually the nod came, and once more the hounds fell upon the bone like vultures.

Astrid held her breath and took a step in their direction. These men were likely a pirate crew. Or mercenaries. Regardless, they looked dangerous. And dangerous was good.

'I said to keep close,' muttered Gorm, but she rushed ahead, and before he could say more she pretended to stumble, falling into the arms of the red-haired Celt.

'Down, boys!' boomed Morcant, as the hounds tensed. He held Astrid in hands of iron, rather pleased by this beautiful intrusion. 'And what have we here?'

'I . . . I can't do it.' She whispered. 'Please. Tell him I can't.'

'Eh?'

Gorm swept to her side, grasping her arm once more. 'Come, niece. You've had too much to drink.'

The hounds growled deeply and Morcant stepped close, the room crackling with thunder. The two huge men locked eyes. 'And just who might ye be?' At his back, blades sung from their scabbards. 'Her owner, is it?'

'Her uncle,' growled Gorm, sweeping his gaze over the crew as they swaggered into a circle around him. Cocksure men from all corners of the map.

The world against the North.

'And what would yer *uncle* have you do, lass?'

'Rob you, sir,' gulped Astrid. 'He'd make a thief of me for his . . . habits.'

Gorm had to smile. Clever fox.

'Something funny, *Uncle*?' Morcant's sour breath stung Gorm's nostrils. 'Where I'm from, the penalty for theft is death. That sound funny to ya?'

'You talk too much,' said Gorm, touching Gudrun's axe to Morcant's bare stomach.

'Eh?' The steel felt cold and sharp, and no one had seen this shaven-headed Northman slip it from his belt. He was quick indeed, but a fool all the same.

'You've thought this through, have ya, Uncle?' Morcant backed away and the hounds filled the space between them. They snarled now, long teeth drooling. 'A few more bones fer the pups.'

The Turks grinned. The Rus gave a brittle laugh. The dark-skinned Serk simply glared.

Then Astrid saw Gorm lift the axe to his lips.

Saw her dried blood on the sharp edge.

Saw Gorm lick it.

She fled the tavern and did not look back.

*

'You've not seen *vellum* before?'

Birger had not. The object resembled a rolling pin and seemed about as interesting as one, too. He passed it back to the trader, a hunched man who kept licking his lips.

'What is it?'

'Snatched these on a raid many years back,' boasted the Liplicker, theatrically opening the scroll. A grin cracked his leathered face. 'An entire monastery full of 'em. Ha! They never saw us coming. Took their gold. Took their stories.'

Birger's mouth fell open.

Stories!

Though made of sheepskin, the parchment was almost thin enough to see through, and graced with . . . marvels. Of course, he had seen writing before—angular runes etched into talismans to give them magical potency. The initials of swordsmiths stamped into blades. The names of dead men on runestones. But this *vellum* was covered in line upon line of elegant red text, with the larger first character elaborately painted in coloured inks and gold leaf. Strange, curled lettering stood in neat rows like soldiers at attention. More words than could be uttered in an hour.

'What does it say?' whispered Birger.

'Only one way to find out,' winked Liplicker, closing the scroll and holding out his palm.

'I . . . I can't read.'

Liplicker tossed the scroll back among the stolen merchandise cluttered across his trestle. 'Hmph. And can't pay neither, I imagine.'

'Well, I—'

And that's when Astrid dashed by, Scion hurtling after and calling her name.

Though all anyone could hear was the screaming crowd.

BLOOD IN THE STREETS

There was a terrible shriek when the Turk's gut split open.

The spray of blood followed Gorm's claw in a great circle through the air.

Spatter seemed to hang there, scarlet droplets drifting lazily across Morcant's vision.

He reached for the hilt of his sword.

Felt the warm flecks patter his cheeks and settle like ash in his wild red hair.

Heard the slow echo of a dog's bark, the sound dull and distant.

Saw the Turk doubling over, unable to stop slippery entrails from tumbling through his fingers, his body floating down to the floor.

Morcant's sword scraped from its sheath.

The Creature dragged its gaze over to him.

Saliva stretched thin between its widening jaws.

It stepped over the Rus lying crumpled at its feet.

Stepped into the dark blood that pooled from his burst skull.

Morcant knew tales of the Northern *berserkers*—frothing, crazed warriors who ran naked into battle, possessed by the spirits of wild beasts, reputedly impervious to flame or steel.

But this . . . what was *this?*

Morcant's lips pulled back into a snarl.

Firelight danced along his shining blade.

He roared.

And time rushed up to meet him.

He lunged forward, feinted a thrust, and spun low to hack at the Creature's ankle. Which wasn't there. Instead, a fist of stone caught him in the chest, blasting the wind from his lungs and smashing him across the tavern. He hit the ground, slid through hound-blood into the doorframe, hearing bones crack, no breath left to cry out.

The crew moved as one.

Lion's mane flapping like a cape, the Serk leapt from a table to skewer Gorm from behind even as a second Turk came head on. But Gorm had the Wolfsight. Could hear heartbeats. Smell fear. Taste victory. He waited until the last moment, then pivoted low, shot both claws out to their full reach, sharp points punching both men through the chest.

In that instant, the remaining hound went for his throat but snapped at empty air when Gorm flung his head back and drove a knee into the animal's ribs.

Morcant heard the crunch from where he lay, heard the whine of pain, saw the hound drop from view behind an overturned table. He tried to breathe, tried to move, but his legs would not respond. The room began to spin, to blur, so he rolled over onto his belly and dragged himself toward the sunlight, the noise at his back dampening to echoes once more as terror seized his heart.

The street looked emptier than ever. Morcant scraped his shattered ribs over the cobbles and a scream came out at last.

There were footsteps, some mad fools heading for the tavern, curious as cats and eager for a fight. Morcant tried to warn them but coughed blood instead. He took a ragged breath and the fight left him. There was no escaping.

Death drew near.

He listened as one by one his crew fell silent, the fools fell silent, and Gorm emerged from the shadows like smoke, a great Wolf-man dripping thick gore.

Morcant lay still, unable to lift his gaze.

'What . . . are you?' he gurgled.

'I am the End of Days,' growled Gorm, and ground the Celt's head under his heel.

He snuffled the air, caught Astrid's scent, and swept away.

*

'Astrid! Wait!'

Now that they had reached a reasonably safe distance from the Creature, the frantic crowd came to a halt, and folk craned to see back down the street.

Scion shoved through, elbows swinging. 'Move!' And received more than a few resentful elbows to the ribs in return. 'Astrid! Stop! It's me!'

Eventually, he reached the open square and spun about, eyes wild.

'Oh, for pity's sake!' No sign of her. She must have slipped down one of the numerous alleyways that spoked off into the labyrinth.

Curse this city with its ridiculously tall—

There was a ladder against a ridiculously tall building. Only three levels high, but to Scion it seemed a watchtower. It would certainly provide a better vantage point than down here in the sprawl.

He clambered up the rickety rungs and onto the steeply pitched roof, the pale thatch prickly to the touch. Carefully, he crawled up to the peak, then jogged along the spine with arms out wide for balance, taking in the city that spread out to the sea. It looked a lot higher from up here, by Thor. And the straw slopes to either side of him wouldn't offer much grip if he slipped. Scion reached the far gable, palms sweating. Shielding his eyes, he squinted down at the winding streets.

There!

She was careening down a lane, blonde hair swishing, blue dress hiked up.

'Astrid!'

But she was out of earshot.

Scion stood poised to holler once more when the memories came. Unexpected and unwelcome, as always. His parents, drowning beneath the ice, sinking from his reach. His desperate, futile reach. That old fear loomed before him once more and whispered in his ear.

Give up. You could not save them. You cannot save her.

He knew this voice well. Had heard it all his life, a plague in his heart that sought at every turn to erode his courage. A worm, nibbling at his confidence from the inside out.

You're just a boy. A failure. Weak and useless and foolish.

Vali had raised him to recognize the voice. To imagine it a ghost, separate from his own mind, seeking control. All talk, no truth. And the only way to silence it was to prove it wrong.

He peered down and sized up the distance to the building across the street. He could jump that. He could.

He thought of Astrid's catchword again.

Ascertain. Aye, I'm sure I've correctly ascertained the gap.

Scion backed up for a run up and took a deep breath.

That was when the square erupted with screams.

*

Birger the Bear stood his ground like a rock in a raging river.

The mob rushed past, a woman crying out as she was knocked down, others trampling her in their desperation to escape the Creature barrelling on all fours toward them.

Birger hefted his sledgehammer and set his teeth. The Wolfman was almost upon him. Gods, it was huge! A rampaging boulder of muscle and fur with overlong arms and overlong teeth. And eyes of astonishing rage.

The Daywalker.

It slammed a cart aside, took two bounding strides and leapt into the swarm, claws flashing. Birger could see blood and worse in those fangs now. Smelt the sharp musk of its breath. He cried out, more a knee-jerk screech than a battle cry, and swung a savage arc.

Crack!

For all his wrath and power, Gorm was still only flesh and bone. And as he soared overhead the hammer smashed up into his hip bone, flipping him mid-air like a coin. He crashed clumsily on his back and skidded through tumbling legs into a stall that exploded in a shower of grain.

Birger stared open-mouthed at the hammerhead. Up until now he had only ever used it for driving in fence posts or breaking rocks in the barley fields. It had almost been a joke— the blacksmith taking a *hammer* into battle. Yet here he was, clubbing monsters like some sort of Thor impersonator.

Gorm spat a curse. 'Fool,' he growled, rearing up to his full height and loping forward. 'You will pay for that.'

The words rolled clumsily off that canine tongue, and Birger noticed how the Daywalker favoured its bruised hip.

He hoisted the hammer and held his breath.

Gorm tasted bile, felt the fractured bone already start to heal itself, and spread his claws wide, when—out of the blue—an arrow whistled through the air. Now more attuned to his surroundings, Gorm heard it, dodged it, and caught it by the shaft.

From his throat came a rumble like an approaching storm. The girl was slipping away and he had no time to swat at every pesky fly.

He glowered up at the rooftops.

'Blast!' Scion hunkered behind the forked rafters and sighted a second arrow through the gap. 'Back away, ya bastard!'

Birger saw an opening and darted forward with another wild swipe. But Gorm danced aside and smacked a ball of knuckles into the blacksmith's shoulder that sent him reeling with a cry into a wall.

Scion's second arrow overshot by a hair.

Unexpectedly, a third arrow hissed from elsewhere and struck Gorm above the back of his knee.

'Yes!' Tyr emerged from an alley with his fine longbow bent again, his boots thundering toward the Daywalker as though it were no great threat. Birger the Bear was back on his feet, blood weeping from a swollen eyebrow, and Scion yowled like an ape as he loosed yet another shaft.

Gorm moved like a flickering shadow and the arrows skittered harmlessly across the cobbles. *Enough!* It was time to go. He dashed from the square, back on Astrid's trail, swiping people from his path as he barreled through the alleyways.

'Baldur's balls! He's quick!' gasped Tyr, running to Birger's side.

'And tough as oak.' Birger wiped blood from his eyes. 'Where's Olle?'

'Left in my dust, as always. We heard the commotion and came running, one of us quicker than the other. As always.'

Scion yelled from the rooftop. 'I'm taking the scenic route! You boys catch up!' And with that he sprinted back across the roof with more abandon than was wise. He sped to the far end and leapt for all he was worth, sailed like a hawk over the stream of people far below, and landed ribs-first on the opposite roof.

'Oof!' His lungs screamed for breath. He scrambled up, urgency driving him up and on, and he ran like the wind.

*

Astrid could hear the screams grow closer.

Her chest burned, her feet ached, and she'd cracked a toe on these wretched cobbles. But nothing was about to hold her back. She thought of *freckled* Hermod, her fleet and faithful steed, and felt a touch of homesickness. A strange sensation to experience while running for one's life.

She glanced back before rounding a corner, hysteria at her heels, and ran headlong into the tendril-moustached vendor.

'Hey!' he barked. 'What is this?' And his birds twittered in the cage.

'Pardon me, sir.'

He seized her roughly by the arms, sharp nails digging into her skin. 'Need to look! You stupid girl!'

Astrid thrashed against the unexpectedly crushing grip. 'Let me go, you fool!'

Pandemonium spilled into the street and smeared by, startling the man. 'What is this? What you do?'

The next thing he felt was a sharp knee to the groin, and he folded with a high wail.

Astrid wasted no time.

She flung the cage door open to let the screeching rainbow bustle out, an iridescent flurry of wings taking to the sky.

Free.

She followed their flight up into the blue and caught sight of a figure on a rooftop. She could just make him out through the feathery blur. He was waving at her. Calling for her.

Scion!

A part of her needed to run, needed to flee the Wolf-man. And another part could live forever in this glorious moment in which a young man from her village had come to take her home. A man who had searched for her. And found her.

Time reined in, and Astrid wondered what Scion saw in her.

The Chief's daughter? A half-breed? The Witch?

Or something more?

He waved at her. Frantically.

'Run!' he yelled, and she woke from her trance with a start.

Run! And she barged into the stampede without looking back.

*

Wolfsight made colours of smells.

It took focus, intense focus, but Gorm could literally *see* Astrid's route as a blue streak weaving among hundreds more that trailed like ribbons of smoke through the streets. The scent was stronger now. His pace quickened, as did his heart. And as he turned into a wider road—and passed an overturned birdcage— he saw her.

I have you now, Astrid of Runolodda.

That was when Scion's arrow struck.

'Up here, ya sack of fleas!' He took aim once more and let fly.

Him again! Gorm tore the arrow from his shoulder, slapped

the second aside, and snapped his gaze back up the road. There seemed to be a fine line between intense focus and fixation, the latter leaving him vulnerable to distraction. He would need to develop stronger control over his Wolfsight. But that could wait since his prize was plainly in view.

Don't stray too far, young Astrid.

Gorm wrenched a heavy wheel from a nearby cart and hurled it like a spinning plate. Scion yelped and ducked to his haunches as the disc whooshed close enough to graze his hair. And before he could say '*close shave*', he'd lost his footing, tumbled down the rooftop, and plunged over the edge with a screech.

Gorm was off, yet could not resist glancing back.

An awning caught Scion in a tangle, stretched like a slingshot before tearing at last, and spat him to the cobbles. Scion lay in a breathless heap. Then, cursing, he struggled free of the tarpaulin in time to hear the clop of approaching hooves.

'So much for the scenic route.' Tyr scooched forward on his mount. 'Hop on.'

'Gladly.'

Birger the Bear slowed briefly as he rode by. 'Victory or Valhalla!' he roared, his mighty hammer raised high, and the Boys echoed his cry in return.

'Victory or Valhalla!' Chief Erik's famous battle cry, taken up by three untested warriors chasing a Wolf-man through a terrorised city.

*

Astrid panted so hard she could taste blood.

Close behind, torn bodies flew left and right, screaming, flailing, slapping into walls. She ran. She jostled. She yelled. And still the reaper came, closer, closer, harvesting blood and bone and the souls of men.

And then he was upon her.

A great claw clutched her waist and yanked her from her feet. She reeled in that crushing grip, tried to pry free, but Gorm swung her bodily over his shoulder and drove on through the crowd, roaring and tearing as he went.

*

'Hyah!'

Tyr's steed overtook Birger's despite carrying two, which said something about the big man's weight on the unfortunate animal. It also said something about Tyr's insatiably competitive spirit.

'A little closer!' yelled Scion, lifting his bow, though it occurred to him that shooting from horseback was a terrible idea.

*

Gorm could smell the sea.

People slipped off into every available doorway, nook, and alley, allowing him a clearer view down the long street to the harbour. Masts swayed there like distant trees, and Gorm put on a burst of speed at the sight.

'Oof!' Astrid's ribs bruised with every jolt.

But her hands were free to feel for the silver pin of her brooch.

*

The street seemed clearer now, although narrow and uneven as it neared the harbour.

Scion had to relent. 'There's no smooth shot!' he yelled, lowering his bow.

Birger's horse caught up, hooves pounding alongside.

'Look out!' shouted Scion.

They reined in hard, the horses skidding on the cobbles and rearing to a halt as a colossal white stallion sprang from a side street to bar their path, its nostrils snorting steam. The rider was a barrel-chested Northman, beardless and bald, his face twisted in a murderous snarl. He carried a painted shield, round and wide, and the spear in his coiled throwing arm looked heavy and sharp as winter.

'Thieves!' he shrieked, twisting the stallion this way and that. 'I'll have your heads and your hands and your balls for this!'

Scion groaned as the fog cleared. 'Stolen horses . . . Of course.'

'Borrowed,' murmured Tyr, looking uncharacteristically sheepish.

'Move aside, sir,' barked Birger the Bear. 'A young woman is in danger!'

'She's not the only one!' shouted Barrel-chest. Sunlight glinted off the spear tip.

'We'll return the horses!' cried Scion. 'You have my word! Just let us—'

Barrel-chest spat. 'Curse your tongue and get yer asses down! All o' ya! Right now!' Clearly, he itched for a reason to hurl that harpoon.

'Alright,' conceded Tyr. He floated his hands to his head, cool as steel. His expression remained blank, lips barely moving as he whispered. 'Shoot him, Scion. On my count.'

'No!' came the hushed reply through gritted teeth. 'We can't kill an innocent man!'

'Who said *kill*? Stick him in the shoulder. The arm, maybe.'

Tyr slid down from the saddle. 'One . . .'

'Wait. *Tyr.*'

'What's happening?' whispered Birger, a glassy smile fixed to his face.

'Two . . .'

Scion found that an arrow still rested in his bow. 'I don't like this, Tyr. *Tyr!*'

Veins throbbed in Barrel-chest's thick neck. 'What are you lot gabbing about? I told ya ta *get down from me horses*!'

Tyr took a breath. 'Thr—'

Frothy ale exploded from the barrel as it struck Barrel-chest's bald head. The stallion spooked, thrashed its pale neck, and its rider rocked forward, slumped, and flopped to the street like a rag doll.

Scion's mouth fell open, then broke into a smile. 'Olle! Well done, brother!'

Olle waddled over and frowned at the malty spillage. 'Such a shameful waste.' But there was a wink in his worry.

'Thanks, Olle,' grinned Tyr, mounting up. The stallion's silky white mane and his silky white hair swished in time. 'Let's go get—'

But Scion was already riding.

*

Shaded alleyways abruptly gave way to dazzling light.

Astrid screwed her eyes shut, tasting a light spray of salt on the air. Then her waist twisted painfully as Gorm rounded the corner and barrelled down the length of the dockside, barging through the screaming blur.

Nauseous and slung like a sack of oats, she could only catch dizzying glimpses of the place. More cobbles. Bobbing ships, great and small. Folk stowing cargo. Fishermen hauling nets. Wharves of barnacled timber reaching into the icy tide. Her hands jerked, her elbows jarred, and it took a great deal of effort to keep hold of the brooch, let alone open it.

At last she did.

And the pin shone like hope.

At the same time, Gorm spotted the Klo cargo ship and made a quick turn onto the wharf, whipping Astrid's neck so hard she felt it might snap. The brooch slipped free and flew away, glittering as it caught the sunlight, her fingers willing it back. Her father had given it to her. Had told her to keep it close to her heart—the only place he now lived. It had meant something to her, as all things that hold fond memories do. It clattered to the dock now, out of her grasp and out of her story, and became a commonplace bauble once more.

The ship had cast off, its crew already rowing out to sea. Still, Gorm thundered down the dock and made a leap for it, Astrid's golden hair trailing behind as they soared over the cold water. The craft was small but sturdy and weighed down with supplies. So, when a massive claw bit into the rail and rocked it portside, the crew cried out in fear and confusion. Gorm vaulted onto the deck and slapped Astrid down like the day's catch.

'Heave!' he commanded.

The crew were a ragged band of Benedictine monks in grey cowls, their hoods drawn back to reveal shaven crowns and shaven chins. Each face wore the same question: had a ten foot Wolf-man just ordered them to heave?

Gorm grabbed the nearest oarsman by the scruff and leaned in. 'It is I, Gorm of the Klo. And I say again—heave!'

The monks heaved.

Staggering to her feet, Astrid watched the harbour recede swiftly into the distance, the ship skimming over the swell under full sail. And there on the docks rode Scion, out of time, out of luck, and out of reach. She called his name, knowing that the cruel wind would steal her words away.

And there was still so much to say.

*

'Astrid!'

Scion sprang from his horse and called for help. 'A ship! We need a ship, brothers!'

Folk poured onto the dock, terrified, flashing suspicious looks his way, asking questions he had no time to answer.

'What was that?'

'You know the Creature, do ya?'

'Where did it come from? Tell us!'

Scion opened his mouth to speak when a hand came to rest on his shoulder, giving him a start. 'Peace, my son. You won't want to sail this day.'

The voice, like the man it belonged to, was frail and reedy. He too wore a grey cowl, tied at the waist by a frayed rope, his feet wrapped in fur against the cold.

'Oh, aye? And why is that?' Scion waved for Tyr's attention, the white stallion pacing behind the gathering crowd.

The monk lowered his hood and Scion saw deep wrinkles on the face of a man long thought dead. A face from his childhood. A man who had once ruled Runolodda.

He tossed Scion a silver coin, the Klo insignia stamped on its surface.

The Valknut.

'They call me *Father* Lennärt now. And you had best come with me, Scion.'

HALF A WARNING

Were they memories or dreams?

Gudrun could remember the Laughing Troll—that one-eyed, black-hearted bear—breathing his last pungent breath. Remembered the searing pain in her torn leg, her cracked rib, that came when her heart had stopped racing. She remembered the cold underground passageways that snaked and banked all the way back to her cottage. Remembered finding Astrid's bandage beside the kettle. Passing out on her bed. Waking later, perhaps much later. Remembered setting off for Runolodda, each step a struggle against a fever that boiled hotter and hotter as the miles wore on. Causing her to shake. To retch, dizzy and faint.

And then—

And then she must have found a horse. Or a horse had found her. For she sat straddled on one now. A cream-coloured colt covered in brown spots like freckles. Hermod snorted over a steep knoll and galloped through the trees, rattling Gudrun's teeth, her ribs screaming. Everything ached. Her neck, her back, her head. The forest blurred again.

Went black.

And when she jerked awake the sky was a deepening grey and they were in a glade, the horse kicking up mushrooms as it ran. Pain had woken her. Pain that pinched her leg where the dressing had come loose to hang laced around her ankle. Gently, she pressed the swollen lacerations. Gods, it hurt! Pus wept out onto her fingertips, and she lifted them to better see. The foul stuff was a pale green and stank like the grave.

Gudrun threw up and slumped forward to hug Hermod's neck weakly.

She would die as she had lived . . . alone.

All because she had clung to a certain point of view.

Erik had been right about Freya. She should have trusted his judgement. Should have welcomed Freya into the family. Been there to celebrate their wedding, to witness the birth of her granddaughter, to share in their life.

Instead, she had slept all these years, believing a lie.

Tears streaked her wrinkled cheeks and all light left the world.

*

Candles flickered.

Voices barked and murmured.

The smell of thatch.

Prickles of a feather pillow against her head.

A glimpse, impossibly, of Freya's face.

Gudrun lurched awake, knocking a pitcher to the floor with a crash that startled the huddled nurses, one shrieking instinctively. The nurse quickly recovered her composure, cheeks flushed.

'Easy now,' soothed Hedda, easing Gudrun back down. 'Girls, fetch more water. And more poppies for the pain. Hurry, girls!' Her daughters set to work, ever eager to please their hard-to-please mother.

Gudrun felt queasy. Smoke choked the already stuffy room and she blinked, eyes stinging. When they cleared, Freya stood beside her with the orange glow of a fire at her back. She appeared taller, sterner, more regal than Gudrun remembered. But also more . . . world-weary. Freya was older now, of course, though the years had been kind. And Gudrun caught a glimpse of how Erik had seen her.

Beautiful and brave.

'Where is she? Where is Astrid?' A mother's desperation.

Gudrun tried to speak but her throat caught, dry as chalk. 'Gorm . . .' she managed. 'G-Gorm has her.' Reaching into her cloak, she fished out Astrid's blood-stained bandage.

Freya snatched it, holding the grubby strip up to the firelight.

'What happened? Is she *alright*?'

'Better than her pursuers,' grinned Gudrun feebly.

But Freya was in no mood for jests. 'So, Gorm lives . . .' she whispered, then glared at her mother-in-law. 'Where are they?'

Gudrun coughed and the room swirled like paint. 'There is much to say, Freya. Much that you must—'

'Where *is* she, Gudrun?' Half a demand, half a plea.

Hedda lifted a cup of water to Gudrun's cracked lips. This conversation required more strength than a broken old woman had to spare. 'They call themselves the Klo. But you—'

Freya sprang to her feet. 'We must leave at once. Ready my horse!'

Gudrun hacked again, and shadows formed around her vision. She caught Freya by the sleeve. 'No! If you go to her, Gorm will be waiting. You will both die. This—' she sputtered, 'This I have *seen*.'

Freya's mouth formed a hard line. Ah, yes. Gudrun the Oracle—she who foresaw doom where there was none. The cryptic crone who sowed discord and panic. Her dreams may have fooled others, but not the Alpha. Not today.

She jutted her jaw. 'You see much, Gudrun of the woods. But you do not always see well.' There was steel in her tone. And hurt.

'I . . . I saw Erik fall. My son is dead. I have seen well enough.' Gudrun slumped and felt herself slipping away. Freya clutched her hand, the young woman's fingers so warm, her own shrivelled palm so cold. 'G-Gorm will bring Astrid to you, Freya. I know this. Her blood is—'

Sleep took the old woman.

'Gudrun? Gudrun!'

'She lives,' assured Hedda, feeling for a pulse. 'But she'll need rest and plenty of it.'

The nurses clustered, each with a pitcher or a cloth or a blanket, when Gudrun jerked awake again, eliciting a second shriek from the shrieker.

Eyes locked with Freya, Gudrun cried out in a strong, steady voice.

'The mountains will reveal the Wolf Victorious!'

Then her lashes fluttered closed and she sank into dreaming.

THE BROTHERHOOD

'Aren't you meant to be dead?' asked Tyr.

The question took Father Lennärt by surprise, and he drained his mead before speaking. The Beastly Boys chewed a little slower, not wanting to miss his response. All but Olle, of course, who took another drumstick to his greasy lips, lost in his own personal Paradise.

Their table took up most of the room—a modest scullery-come-dining area in the centre of the equally modest monastery—with half a dozen monks sitting squeezed in between them on rough benches, leaving little space to spare. They were a quiet lot, all smooth-chinned, speaking the Northern tongue slowly and with thick Saxon accents.

'Are we not all dead in some ways, but alive in others?' Father Lennärt had an annoying habit of answering a question with a question. 'Those rumours also reached my ears, and in the days following my leaving Runolodda, I wished they were true.'

'Why?' asked Olle, lips smacking as he ate.

Lennärt pushed an onion around his plate. 'Shame, my son. The Alpha had stirred up turmoil in our village, and what did I do?

I passed the problem off to Erik and left.'

'Oh, aye,' said Olle, with the tact of a jester at a funeral. 'I remember that.'

Tyr shot Olle a reproachful frown. 'Forgive him, Chief—I mean, *Father* Lennärt. We were children at the time, and some of us, it seems, still are. Olle meant no offence.'

Lennärt shrugged. 'It was wrong of me. I should have been there for my people in their hour of need. But fear overcame me, and that is why, upon arriving in Hvalvik, I spent weeks drinking myself into a stupor. To numb the shame, you see.' With a warm smile, he gestured to the monks. 'The Brotherhood took me in. They gave me—'

'We're wasting time,' interrupted Scion. 'Maybe it slipped your notice but the Daywalker has Astrid.'

'Daywalker?' asked Lennärt.

Another bloody question.

'Daywalker, yes. Though how he transformed without the full moon is a mystery we have yet to riddle out.'

'Intriguing,' said Lennärt, noting the worried expressions all around.

'You have their coin,' said Scion, flicking it onto the table where it landed with the Valknut facing up. 'How? What do you know of these men?'

Scion remembered Lennärt, of course. As Chief, he'd known much about farming and livestock, yet never seemed equipped to handle a crisis. *Coward* was perhaps too harsh a word for the man, though Scion could not help but think it.

In the awkward silence, Lennärt stabbed the onion and took a bite.

'Are you certain you wish to know?'

Scion held his gaze. 'I wish to know.'

Lennärt sighed, and exchanged a nod with the monk beside him, who slipped into an adjacent chamber and returned with a bundle of scrolls. Birger's face lit up as plates were cleared for the scrolls to be laid out. His face fell when he saw their contents. Every scrap of parchment was filled with hasty scrawls and messy sketches, a hodgepodge of diagrams, instructions, names, and numbers. After the beautifully decorated vellum he'd seen in the marketplace, this was a monumental disappointment. Where was the elegant calligraphy? Where was the *artistry*?

Still, there was a story here, and Lennärt needed to tell it.

He stretched out a map that followed the winding River Hreim from its source in the Northern mountains, past Runolodda, through miles of woodland, and down through Hvalvik where it spilled into the Silver Sea. An island, some distance from the port's shoreline, bore the ominous mark of the Valknut in vivid red ink.

'A long time ago,' began Lennärt, 'Hvalvik became the official meeting place for the annual assembly. Tribes would journey for miles to hear the Lawspeaker pass judgement. And while most charges brought forth were trivial, some involved the most heinous of criminals. The worst of the worst. Their crimes were so despicable that the verdict led to their banishment. And where do you suppose they were sent?'

Scion nodded. 'The island.'

'Precisely. So, naturally, when the Brotherhood caught wind of these stranded souls, we took pity. Out of compassion, we decided to take supplies. However, we were astonished to discover that the outcasts had not only survived, but thrived. They bore the name of their own choosing: the Klo, which translates as the Claw, and had forged a kingdom unto themselves, complete with a formidable raiding fleet.'

'And they simply set you free?' asked Tyr.

The monk to Lennärt's right spoke. He was a large man with a rasping voice, and hands like gnarled bark. 'Not at first. We were taken to their slave barracks, little more than a poorly kept pen. A woman was brought before us. They . . .' Lennärt gave an encouraging nod. '. . . they cut off her hands and feet. We were made to carry them back to our boat, told to keep them as a reminder.'

'A reminder of what?' asked Tyr.

'To serve the Klo in secret. Should the Brotherhood fail in our duties, more women would suffer.'

Birger the Bear swallowed. 'Duties?'

'To be their ferrymen, transporting cargo to Klo Island. In the beginning, we were not good seamen, though we learned quickly. The waters are dangerous. Many rocks.'

'Father Frank is putting it mildly. Every crossing to that cursed place is a brush with death.'

'So, take reinforcements,' suggested Scion. 'Fight back. Surely there are locals who might help?'

'No-one in Hvalvik knows the truth. Every year, more outlaws are banished to the island. The Lawspeaker is oblivious to the fact that he is inadvertently swelling the Klo ranks in the process.'

'No-one knows?' asked Tyr. 'I find that hard to believe. The Klo trade slaves here in Hvalvik, for pity's sake!'

'They do,' agreed Father Frank, 'but through a third party. They are careful to keep all movements secret, only sailing at night, raiding distant shores, paying off the prisoner escorts. Klo Island is barely visible from Hvalvik, and what goes on there has remained hidden.'

Lennärt traced his finger from Runolodda down to Hvalvik. 'By the time I arrived, the Klo had found further use for the Brotherhood, forcing us to melt down stolen silver to mint their coins. Hammer, hammer, hammer . . . that's all we ever seem to do. To this day we are paid a single coin for that weekly *service*,' he sneered.

'I say keep it,' mumbled Olle, between mouthfuls of bread. 'Take their loot and run.'

Father Frank lowered his gaze. 'Once, we withheld a few extra coins to help Hvalvik's poor through a particularly bad winter. The Klo found out and sent us the head of a slave woman in response—a warning to never short-change them again.'

Lennärt spat. 'And a reminder to keep our mouths shut.'

Scion shook his head. 'You could have left the Brotherhood, Lennärt. Isn't that what you do? Leave?'

Lennärt made no attempt to defend his reputation. 'And miss the opportunity to learn more of the Wolf-kind?' He swept the map aside to tap his fingertips on the scattered parchments. 'I found these on the island. They describe one of their own—King Ari—who transformed at the full moon.'

The Beastly Boys leaned closer, understanding the drawings if not the words.

'And Astrid is heading his way,' gasped Scion.

'King Ari died years ago,' said Frank, 'though we have kept a close eye on the Klo ever since. And his son, King Ødger.'

'There's more,' said Lennärt, shuffling the parchments. 'We found a few accounts given by Klo slaves of the Wolf-kind in far off lands. How their bite transmits the disease, their Wolfsight, their healing abilities, hunting patterns, and so on. The Klo have learned much of the Wolf-kind.'

'Fascinating,' grumbled Scion. 'But how does this help us now?'

'See here?' Lennärt slid an architectural diagram to the centre of the table. It offered a bird's-eye view of the enemy's stronghold. 'This is everything you need to know about Klo Island.'

Scion immediately perked up, committing every detail to memory.

The main hall had a roughly rectangular shape, although its perimeter ran unevenly, appearing more like the handiwork of nature than of man. A crudely hewn cavern, perhaps? There were adjacent structures, too: slave quarters to the left and a larder to the right. A second diagram, showing the side view, revealed its towering height, reaching almost one hundred and fifty feet. From this angle, one could see dense bramble atop the hall. Behind this thicket, a small, level plateau extended back before rising up sharply into a sheer rock face. And if the artist was to be believed, it seemed that houses were scattered all the way up the cliff, somehow secured to the vertical rock face.

It reminded Scion of Mount Varda back home.

'Looks like a huge stiff one!' chuckled Olle. 'See? There's the mountain sticking up and this cave-hall covered in bushes looks like a pair of hairy b—'

'This is their fortress,' continued Lennärt hastily. 'My guess is that your Astrid has been taken to the slave barracks. But there would be hundreds of Klo warriors gathered in the hall between you and her, I'm afraid. And if this Daywalker, as you call him, can transmit his power . . .'

Scion glanced around, taking in his friends' sober expressions. Chasing Gorm across the sea might have led them to a swift demise. It was a fortunate thing that Lennärt had stopped them when he did.

'Excuse us, gentlemen,' said Father Frank, rising to his feet. 'But I'm afraid it is time for afternoon prayers.'

'Ah, yes. Thank you, Father,' nodded Lennärt.

The monks rose, making space on the benches at last, and donned their hoods as they murmured their apologies, sweeping away like grey ghosts. Lennärt, however, remained seated.

'Will you not be joining us, Father?'

'Shortly, Father Frank. I wish to attend to our guests' accommodation first.'

'Of course. I'm sure we can squeeze a few more pallets into the dormitory.'

With a dignified bow, Father Frank withdrew.

'We won't be staying,' said Scion. 'Our thanks for the meal, but we must be on our way.'

Lennärt gestured for them to remain seated, discreetly leaning forward to ensure that Frank was out of earshot.

'One more thing, gentlemen.'

He reached into his robe and produced a hidden scroll, more ancient and beautifully embellished than the others. Birger drank in the sight. The vellum was snow-white and fine, and adorned with a blue Mediterranean script, a unique blend of angular precision and flowing elegance.

'This document reveals the Wolf-kind's one weakness—' Lennärt tossed the Klo coin back to Scion. '—Silver.'

Scion rubbed the insignia with his thumb. 'Are you offering us what I think you're offering us?'

Lennärt reached back and drew a curtain aside. There, balanced on rows of rickety shelves, was enough silver to feed all the poor in Hvalvik until next winter.

'There'd be a poetic irony in using the Klo's ill-gotten gain against them. Take their plunder. There's a forge at the end of the alley. Melt it down to plate your blades.'

'And tip our arrows?' asked Tyr. The thought of enhancing his weapons sent a quiver of joy up his spine. But before Lennärt could agree, Father Frank returned with a bundle of blankets.

'I found these in the—Father Lennärt? What are you doing?'

Lennärt sighed. 'Giving them a fighting chance.'

Father Frank gently lowered the blankets to the table. 'A fighting chance, is it? And when the Klo learn of our involvement? How many heads will they lop off this time?'

This conversation had been a long time coming. Lennärt took a deep breath and braced for the response. 'Not if we make it look like a robbery. A slaughter. We'll turn the monastery upside down, splash goat's blood around. Their silver will be gone, and so will we.'

'We leave?' Father Frank locked his gaze on Lennärt in disbelief.

'We leave, yes. Have we not spent enough time under their thumb, Father? We can rebuild elsewhere. No-one need die.'

'*They* will!' Frank swept a hand over the foursome, almost slapping Tyr. 'Klo Island is crawling with seasoned warriors, more vicious than any I've had the prior misfortune to meet. I doubt these gentlemen will make it past the watchmen!'

Lennärt pointed at Scion. 'This one survived the Alpha's attack when he was but a sapling. Have faith, Father.'

'I cannot allow it. There is too much at stake.'

Scion had been brooding over the map. He would face the fury of the gods and all the horrors of Hel to save Astrid.

His father's wisdom sprang to mind.

Better to catch a bear snoring than roaring.

He rose to his feet. 'I have *ascertained* an idea.'

FREYA'S TALE

Knud the Blacksmith had been busy.

Every man and woman of Runolodda was issued a crude helmet and iron reinforcing for their shields, including a domed boss in the centre. Most folk already owned their own swords and axes. Knud had carefully inspected these, forge welding any cracks together for greater resilience. Some watched eagerly as he ground their scythes and sickles to a razor edge, sparks flying in the forge.

Today, however, the people trained.

On the open gravel just beyond the village gates, the motley group of farmers, housewives, and swineherds sparred in pairs, sweat dripping from their brows. Vali wove between them, correcting their form, offering encouragement.

'Anticipate! Angle your shields to deflect incoming strikes! I want to see wide, steady stances and a keen eye for openings! Keep at it! Push through the fatigue!'

Some folk were as old as he, or older, having seen battle in their youth, though now more accustomed to wielding a hoe than a sword. Yet, they did not grumble, knowing that their lives and the lives of others depended on their readiness. The younger generation duelled amongst them. Trained from childhood in the rudiments of combat, they had honed their skills in the quiet periods between planting and harvest. But for all their swordplay, they had never tasted the bitter sting of battle, their blades untested, their courage yet to be measured.

Even gentle Tove the Songbird was present, her soft hands uncomfortable and clumsy on the thick hilt. She was paired with sausage-fingered Torsten, whose hands appeared to swallow his own hilt whole.

'You're doing well, Tove. You can go harder.' Torsten blushed, wondering if Tove might take his comment as a suggestive innuendo. Fortunately, Tove was far too innocent for such things. Taking up a sword had brought home the gravity of what was to come and she seemed distracted by the dread of it.

'Are you alright?' asked Torsten. 'You look quite pale.'

Tove gazed up into his eyes. 'This is no performance, Torsten. This is real. I fear my hands won't obey when the time comes. What if I falter? Will the gods mark me unworthy?'

Torsten blew out a long breath. What did a simple logger know of divine opinion? Tove lived her life close to the gods, ever eager to honour and please them. The thought of falling short in their eyes troubled her greatly.

After a long moment of reflection, Torsten finally spoke.

'I have seen you hold the village rapt with song, Tove. That takes courage of a sort. Perhaps you doubt needlessly.' He said it like a question, not wishing to offend. 'If it helps at all, there are many here who hide their fear beneath their fervour. That is the plain truth.'

Tove glanced around the training ground. 'They seem so self-assured. So resolute.'

'We train not for the love of conflict, but for the love of what we hold dear. Bear that in mind, and your courage will hold.'

Tove tilted her head, sensing deep waters in this quiet man. Torsten watched people. Listened more than he spoke. Yet when he did, his words proved measured and meaningful.

'Thank you, Torsten. I shall.' She smiled, and saw him blush.

'Shields up,' he said. 'Let's go again.'

Vali had overheard the exchange. He appreciated men like Torsten. In little ways, they helped carry the burden of leadership. Vali rubbed the bridge of his nose. There was still so much to be done. If the battlements could be constructed in time, people like Tove might hold their courage a little longer against the might of the Klo.

'That is all for today!' he called, cupping hands around his mouth. 'Remember to keep your blades oiled and sharp. Rest well. And don't drink too much!' The crowd laughed, dispersing as the smell of woodsmoke wafted through the late afternoon air.

Vali yawned, stretching his aching back. Freya had been scarce of late, spending much time at Erik's gravesite. Grieving and healing as she was, he would not press her to join the training. Though a part of him wished she would. The people looked to her, and he would not want her absence to be mistaken for despair.

No, let Freya be.

He would prepare the village for war in her stead.

Violence was simply not in her nature.

*

'To what do I owe the pleasure, Little Sparrow?'

Blood dribbled through the gaps in Ulrick's goblin grin. Ropes held him fast to a tall post that poked splinters into his neck and back. Still, he grinned. And if the icy sea breeze troubled him, he hid it well. Freya sat three paces away on a rock, digging her bare toes into the sand.

Marigolds in her hair.

She appeared not to have noticed his question, choosing instead to gaze out at the setting sunlight dancing on the ocean. Her injuries still throbbed, though she no longer needed a splint or buckles on her leg and she could roll her shoulder with relative ease. Wolf-blood healed, clearly. Yet besides that one blessing, what had it brought but suffering?

Ulrick held his smile. 'Do I get to see what's in the basket? Are we having a picnic, Little Sparrow?'

Freya smiled too. The basket rested in her lap, its contents concealed by a simple homespun cloth. She placed it at her feet, hugged her cloak tighter, and let her gaze crawl up her prisoner's naked legs, bruised ribs, and battered face.

Until their eyes met.

'I grew up on a farm in Caledonia with my father and sister.'

'Ah,' nodded Ulrick. 'Storytime.'

'Seems an age ago but I still remember the stubble on Father's cheek where I'd kiss him goodnight. The smell of our cabin. The sound of Maisie's laughter, so high and free, as we'd skip stones over the loch. Sometimes I wonder if it was nothing but a dream.'

Freya shifted her weight.

'It was a spring morning when one of your Klo raiding ships arrived. Father died fighting. Gorm was there. A captain then, I think. And he treated us . . . roughly.'

Ulrick's grin began to melt.

'Maisie died on the voyage to Klo Island. My sweet, silly, gentle sister. Left to rot on the deck without so much as a prayer or a poem. The other women, likewise torn from their homes, tried to console me. But I crawled inside myself. Cowered in the shadows of my mind.

'When at last we made it to Klo Island they stripped us bare. Lined us up like lambs to be inspected. Klo Island was a hard place, naturally. I was allowed a linen tunic, a ratty woollen blanket, and—oddly—a glass vial of white powder. Of course, you'd know what that powder was, wouldn't you?'

Ulrick's smile was gone, replaced by a scowl.

'My sister's bones, yes. Ground down and presented as a souvenir from your mad King Ari.'

Freya closed her eyes, remembering King Ødger's late father.

Ari the Butcher. Ari the Tyrant. Ari the Insane.

A man possessed of a macabre sentimentality.

And a frightening strength.

'At first, I thought I'd be sold at market. But, no. I was to suffer a fate far worse.'

Freya placed the basket at Ulrick's feet and lifted the cloth away.

He turned pale as frost.

'Ari took a liking to me. I spent many nights in his bed, enduring his cruelty and the stench of his hot breath on my neck. Shame was my constant companion. Shame and Fear.

'Imagine my relief when he left one morning for a raid to the South, though Gorm and his men kept me *occupied* for weeks. There were only a handful of survivors upon Ari's return. For it was whispered that a great Creature had come in the night and laid waste to the men, biting Ari before skulking back to the hills.

'A full moon shone on the night of the King's return, and the sounds of battle echoed from Klo Hall until morning. Ari the Wolf-man survived, though many did not. His mind was gone. His condition, a threat. So, at Ødger's orders, Ari was locked away in his chambers for the remainder of his days. A madman too dangerous for this world. A madman with a taste for *human flesh*.

'Once a month, out of sorrow for his father's fate, Ødger would send a slave into his chambers. Their bones never left the room, where Ari would grind them down to powder, singing sea shanties as he worked.

'I would gaze fearfully at the swelling moon, silent and cold in the sky, knowing my turn would eventually come. And sure enough, it did. I thought to smuggle in a weapon but knew I'd be stripped before entering. So, I broke the vial containing Maisie's remains and slipped a shard beneath my tongue. She would have her revenge, even in death.

'They locked me in with mad King Ari and he wasted no time in pressing me down. The moon mocked me through the open window. Fear choked me. However, anger roused me.

'Midnight was fast approaching, so when Ari moved in close I took my chance. Biting the shard as tightly as I could, I lashed it across his throat. It opened like a ripe plum. I watched him reel back, spluttering blood, and I sprang for the window even as Fear pawed at me to stay.

'Midnight struck. I should never have looked back. I should have ignored the howling, the thrashing. But before I knew it, The Change was complete, and the Wolf-man bit! Through the door, I could hear the guards talking, yet they never entered. I was, after all, that night's dinner. Screams were to be expected.

'I tore my leg free and time seemed to stop.

'I might have stayed there, frozen in terror, had it not been for the look in those bestial eyes. King Ari, Lord of the Klo, Tyrant, Monster . . . was more afraid than I. Afraid of death and the cold Hel that awaited him.

'What came next was a blur. Leaping through the window. Falling through the night. The freezing wind. The black ocean. I took a skiff across the water and scrambled ashore. Somehow, I survived out in the wild for a full month—for when the next full moon appeared, I underwent my transformation. I must have strayed through the bowels of the mountains, for when I came to my senses, I found myself at the mouth of a bear cave with Runolodda's hunters bleeding in the snow around me. I looked up to find Erik cradling me in his arms.'

For some reason, the memory brought Gudrun's prophecy to mind—*The mountains will reveal the Wolf Victorious.*

A smile, the first since Erik's death, played on her lips. Freya rose and gazed at her prisoner.

'You've been a most receptive audience, Ulrick. Thank you for listening.'

Head to toe, Ulrick bristled with knives, each one thrust into him so deeply that only their hilts protruded. Blood pooled at his feet and soaked into the white sand. Freya took a moment to find somewhere to drive in the final dagger and decided on his left eye.

'I hope Gorm gets a good look at you before I meet him again.'

She turned on her heel, swinging the empty basket as she crossed the beach, warmed by a comforting thought.

Ulrick would never grin again.

ALL HAIL THE KING

'Oh, how the mighty have fallen!'

King Ødger wrung his hands with delight, his red cape trailing like a serpent as he descended the throne to meet Gorm. You could hear a pin drop in the great cavern of Klo Hall. Scores of warriors gathered around, gawking at the sorry state of the General, stripped of his signature black battledress, clad instead in a grey monk's cowl. The crisp taper of his beard had flared into a wiry mess and his ever-shaven head now sprouted dark stubble.

Long had Ødger waited to see the General brought down a notch. Long had he felt threatened by the man's stature and status, of his esteem among the Klo. Esteem rightfully owed to their ruler, by Thor!

'My King,' said Gorm, bending the knee.

'And it would seem——' sneered Ødger, peering down the length of the Hall and through the gigantic open doors to the beach beyond where the monks offloaded cargo, '——that your ship has shrunk.'

Gorm gritted his teeth. His raiding party was dead, his grand warship wrecked, and Ødger dared to jest? Gorm's mood had already soured during the treacherous crossing from Hvalvik. Navigating the jagged reef that pierced the ocean's surface was challenging even on a clear day. So, when a gale had blown in, the crew had fought furiously to avoid the razor-sharp crags and stay the course to the island.

The monks had managed surprisingly well in the end. Astrid was still alive, thank the gods, though the effects of her blood had worn off, shrinking Gorm back down to his naked human form. The youngest monk, a chinless rake of a lad whose head bobbed like a barn owl, had kindly *volunteered* his cowl.

'I have come to report,' said Gorm. 'And to lay a plan before you, my King.'

Ødger made a point to appear bored. He sipped his wine absently and watched the monks work, distant insects in the moonlight, then motioned for the monolithic doors to be closed. They sealed shut, casting the vast cavern into darkness where only the flickering torchlight defied the gloom.

'A plan? How generous of you, General.' Ødger leered down at Astrid, drenched through at Gorm's side. 'And would this soggy sprite have something to do with it?'

Astrid, weak as a whisper after that stomach-turning voyage, lifted her gaze to Ødger, intending to fix him with a murderous glare but only managing a miserable look. Blood in her wet hair, where she had hit her head on an oar, betrayed her poor rowing skill.

'She is the key, my King.'

Ødger looked Astrid up and down, a thinly veiled amusement dancing in his eyes.

'Is she? Is she indeed?'

Engaging with Ødger was like trudging through a swamp.

Gorm took a shortcut.

'The plan relates to your father's . . . *curse*.' The word tasted sour in Gorm's mouth now that he himself was bitten, but he knew this was how Ødger regarded the Wolf-kind.

Cursed.

The word was a slap in Ødger's face. He stepped back from Astrid, immediately alert.

'I seem to recall sending you off to quell their kind, Gorm. Have you now brought the sickness into my Hall?'

'Their kind is no more, my King. All but one. Their Alpha lives—a woman named Freya, mother to this half-blood girl who possesses a power employable to our advantage.'

'What are you on about, Gorm?' sputtered the King. 'What power?'

'Simply put, she can actuate the Cursed into their Wolf form. Day or night, regardless of the phase of the moon.'

A murmur burbled through the Hall.

Ødger's walrus moustache twitched. 'And how, pray tell, is that to our advantage?'

'Only the body is impacted by her power, my King. Not the mind. Would a Wolf-man still be deemed cursed if he could maintain his rationality?'

Ødger took another step back. 'Where is this leading, Gorm?'

The King's Guard perceived their master's nervousness and crowded closer, hands on hilts. Their Captain, Björn, was larger than the General and quick as a viper. Gorm would need to tread carefully.

'Envision an army of lucid Wolf-men,' said Gorm. 'Such a force would be unstoppable.' Gorm glanced about the Hall. Warriors had pieced his intentions together—nodding, smiling, exchanging eager looks. Their conquests would be spun into songs sung across the world *forever*. Such glory would be theirs! Such as never before.

Gorm stood to his feet. 'We could take back the North.'

'*We?*' Ødger's bellow reverberated through the cavern. '*That* is your plan, General? To fetch the *Alpha* to poison our veins? To align us with Fenrir the Wolf, enemy of the gods?'

'My King, your father—'

'My father was an abomination! He brought a plague to our shores and I charged you to end it once and for all. Now, abandon this madness and return to Runolodda. And this time, bring me the Alpha's head or I shall stick yours on a pike!'

There rose a susurration of voices like the rustling of dead leaves. King or not, it was unwise to threaten Gorm.

'You are right about one thing, King Ødger. I shall return to Runolodda and slay the Alpha. However, her bite is not *poison*. It is a gift.' He pulled up the sleeve of his robe to reveal the teeth marks. 'Nor do I need her anymore to transmit the gift.'

Ødger recoiled as though scalded by steam. 'Guards!'

Gorm shut his eyes. He had expected as much from Ødger. The man was a complacent fool, a superstitious hedonist who had worn his father's crown for far too long.

It was time for new blood.

Men closed in, though Gorm could see their conflict. Each warrior had sworn loyalty to Ødger, and oaths were a sacred thing. Yet each man felt as Gorm did—that the Klo could be so much more than bandits in service of a drunk glutton.

They could be legends of war.

Björn drew a great axe, speaking softly. 'I am sorry for this, General.'

For the second time today, Gorm found himself encircled by armed warriors. However, these were no Celts. No Turks or Serks or Rus. No, these were men of the North. Men who had bled the same soil as he, been swept off their feet by the same bitter wave of history as he. These were *his* men. And his war was not with them.

'I challenge *you*, King Ødger, to *Holmgang*—a duel to the death—for the Klo throne!' The words echoed throughout the vaulted cave, finding every cowering shadow and every wavering heart.

Ødger spluttered. 'You have no claim and no right to challenge me, General!'

'Have I not, my *King*?' He spat the word, lifting off the robe to let it fall at his bare feet. 'You have insulted my honour and threatened my life without provocation. I have killed greater men for far less.'

Ødger's complexion went bright red and he flapped his cape aside with the petulance of a child. Golden torchlight danced on his polished armour, every steel plate and rivet a defensive wall against the naked General.

'How dare—'

But Gorm was not finished. 'I have issued my challenge, Ødger! Will you fight or stand there drowning in your father's garments, baying like a mule?'

Laughter—some stifled, some not—began to ripple through the Hall, and Ødger found that his tongue had stuck to the roof of his mouth. Instinctively, he lifted his drinking horn, only to find it empty. Astrid flinched once more as Ødger, with a thunderous bellow, hurled it aside, narrowly missing her head.

'So be it, Gorm!'

Ødger wasted no time. His challenger stood unarmed and stark naked, low-hanging fruit, so to speak. With unexpected speed, he seized a round shield and a thrusting spear—tall as a man—and lunged. Gorm had anticipated an underhanded manoeuvre and turned effortlessly aside, tripping Ødger as he rushed past. The King fell on his belly, his armour clattering and scraping on the stone floor.

Björn offered Gorm his axe but he waved it away. 'On your feet, Ødger son of Ari. Your reckoning draws near.'

Ødger rose slowly, his breath short, his temper shorter. 'You're an *obvious* man, Gorm. Did you suppose your ambition went unnoticed? Am I so blind in your view?' He peered over his raised shield, the spear poised above the iron rim, and began to circle. 'I name you Traitor! Poison-tooth! Throne-thief!' cried the King, his face a sickly pallor.

Gorm's eyes smouldered. 'Traitor? It was not *I* who locked your father away. You could have shared Ari's power with the Klo. Instead, you chose to isolate him from us. That was *your* great betrayal. That was *your* great theft!'

The Klo came closer, tightening the circle, their murmurs rising like steam. Gorm had finally given voice to their long-held misgivings. Had lifted the lid on their simmering unrest. Yes, raiding was a comfortable life—the wealth, the wine, the women. Even so, comfort breeds restlessness. And restlessness breeds wrath.

War would scratch that itch.

Ødger's eyes flicked around the Hall in fear. 'Enough, you insolent bastard!'

He feinted a thrust, then threw the spear with all his strength. Gorm ducked, and the point dug into a warrior's shield behind him. Ødger gasped, struggling to draw his sword as Gorm closed in. He swung wildly, but in one fluid motion, Gorm caught his forearm, pivoted, and sent him tumbling once more to the floor.

This time, Gorm moved swiftly and mercilessly. He pounced, ramming a knee into the King's chest and pinning his wrists to the floor with such force that the sword sprang free of his grasp.

'Bring the girl!' roared Gorm.

Astrid had to look away as Gorm smashed his knuckles into the King's face. Once, twice, three times—sick, wet, thuds. Two rough men hauled her closer to the General, and she saw beads of sweat on his naked back as he panted over the mess he'd made.

Ødger groaned, consciousness slipping, though his eyes were wild with fear.

'Come,' said Gorm, beckoning her nearer, and she flinched as he reached for her. 'Now, warriors of the Klo, I shall demonstrate how your glory will be won.'

He ran a finger through Astrid's blood-soaked hair and licked it clean.

The Hall erupted with cries of astonishment as Gorm twisted, writhed, unfolded, swelled—a nightmare creature come to life. Some remembered the night of Ari's transformation, seizing weapons and shields, ready to kill or be killed. Gorm roared loud as thunder, his colossal Wolf-head thrown back.

Then he settled, wild eyes sharpening, and turned his attention back to Ødger, still pinned to the floor under his great weight. 'Your reign—' he growled, and the Klo shivered at the sound of that startling voice, '—is no more.'

The Wolf-man's knee pressed down into Ødger's breastplate. Ribs crunched. Pulverised lips released a shriek of agony. The King could do nothing but stare as Gorm took him by the head and began to twist.

There was a piercing cry.

Then a snapping of bone.

Astrid dropped to her knees and threw up. And still Gorm twisted, around and around, until the spine separated. A tearing noise, and the King's head came away. In all the excitement the man with the shield had not removed Ødger's spear, and he tensed now as the Wolf-man approached.

'Fear not, comrade,' said Gorm, dislodging it to inspect the sharp point. 'We are on the same side.'

It remained deathly silent while Gorm worked the spear tip up through Ødger's severed head; quiet enough to hear the faint crunch when it poked through the crown. Then he raised it high, blood and brain dripping down the haft in thick globules.

'It's no pike, though it will have to do.'

For a moment, the jest echoed in the silence. Then the Klo began to grin, to chuckle, as a weight lifted from their shoulders. Before long, they erupted into a jubilant uproar. Axes were thrust into the air, voices boomed and bellowed, fists pounded chests like war drums, and hearty cheers echoed through the Hall.

'All hail King Gorm!' thundered Björn.

The Klo took up the chant as Ødger's blood pooled at the Wolf-man's feet.

'All hail King Gorm!'

Björn was first to roll up his sleeve and present his bare forearm to Gorm.

'All hail King Gorm!'

Drooling jaws inched closer, teeth gleaming—

'All hail King Gorm!'

—and bit.

THE WORLD TREE

They called her the Oracle.

Gudrun slept.

Gudrun dreamt.

She found herself atop a giant ash tree on a sea of leaves so thick she could walk across them. Lush and sparkling like emeralds, they seemed to stretch for miles in every direction. It was wise to tread cautiously, for the branches below swayed gently. There was a noticeable springiness to the surface which was both pleasant and slightly unnerving.

She recognized this tree at once. Yggdrasil, the mythical World Tree, whose roots hold the Nine Realms of the cosmos together.

The sky shone clear and ocean blue, the sun hot, as she set off in no particular direction.

After some time, she noticed a point of light glowing in the distance. When Gudrun neared, she saw it was a contained ring of flame—only flame, no smoke or ash—with two obscured figures in its midst.

A gateway appeared, wide as a cottage door, and Gudrun was startled to feel the leaves beneath her feet come to life and carry her forward through the gap, each branch passing her like a torch in a relay until the ring sealed closed behind her. Only then did she see who the figures were.

Her mother and father.

This was her oldest vision, the one that had set her on the path to becoming a Seer. Mother stood stunned, her shoulders sagging, while Father sat weeping in the dust.

'What's the matter, Father?' And Gudrun was surprised to find her voice sweet and high. She was twelve summers old again, her hair in a plait and her nightdress covered in soot.

'The crop is burning, child. The winter will be cruel and we will starve.'

'No Father, the villagers will help us through. Please don't cry.'

Father's gaze briefly lifted, a fleeting glimmer of recognition in his red eyes as they met his daughter's, before dulling once more as he turned his attention back to the mesmerising flame.

'The crop is burning, child. The winter will be cruel and we will starve.'

'Did you not hear me, Father? We will survive. Everything will be alright.'

'Why didn't you warn us, Gudi?' It was Mother who spoke, eyes distant and sad. 'You saw this coming.'

'The crop is burning, child,' repeated Father. 'The winter will be cruel and we will starve.'

'It —It was just another dream to me. How could I have guessed its significance?'

'Why didn't you warn us, Gudi? You saw this coming.'

'The crop is burning, child . . .'

Then Gudrun felt the years rush through her bones like poison, and she was old again.

'Aye, I was a *child*. A confused child, and you stirred such guilt in me for my silence. I am grown, now, see? I've changed.'

Instantly, the air shifted. Gudrun spun about as the ring of flame closed in, shadows burning away, the heat intensifying.

Wait, this is not what happened.

Mother remained hunched, staring.

Father sat weeping.

'Mother! Father! Hurry!'

'. . . We will starve . . .'

'Why didn't you warn us . . ?'

Gudrun dropped to her knees and started tearing at the leaves. 'I became what you wanted!'

'. . . You saw this coming . . .'

The blaze roared, more noise than heat.

She ripped a hole in the canopy, thick boughs visible through the opening.

'I became the warning drum!'

'The crop is burning, child . . .'

Gudrun squirmed through the hole, even as the branches pushed to close over, and the roar rose to a fever pitch.

'I am the warning drum!'

Then she was through and all was silent.

Gudrun felt her ears pop, and worked her jaw to ease the sudden pressure. Above, the gap had snapped shut. The leaves were solid crystal now, beautiful but impenetrable, cutting off the path upwards. She steeled herself to look down, summoning all her courage. Below, thousands upon thousands of branches descended the trunk of the mighty Yggdrasil. The ground below resembled a map, with mountains reduced to wrinkles and great rivers like silver strings. Gudrun clung white-knuckled to the uppermost branch, overcome by a paralysing sense of vertigo, her breath coming in short, terrified gasps. Everything swam before her. She squeezed her eyes shut until the dizziness subsided.

There was only one thing for it.

She would need to climb down.

*

Days seem to pass, though the sun had not moved.

And although the branches were thick and easy enough to clamber down, there seemed no end to their number. Ancient bark, rough as stone, scratched her palms, scratched her legs. Dream or not, this was sweaty work.

Yggdrasil hummed with life and it seemed to Gudrun that the great tree was aware of her presence, whispering her name through the leaves. If it had a heartbeat, it was a sound too deep for mortal ears. Too deep and too slow.

Every so often she would pass a small hollow in the trunk, like a portal into a mind older than time. An inner voice told her not to look in, though she could not help herself. She was a Seer, and Seers *see*, by Thor!

She crouched beside the next hollow down, and peered in.

At first there were only shadows, yet the shadows swirled like mist, and a scene swiftly took shape. There, impossibly, were four young men in a forge, slathering molten silver over their weapons—swords, axes, even a large sledgehammer. The tallest of the four was big as a bear and wore a blacksmith's apron. One had hair as white as snow, and he worked the bellows with a stouter, jolly-looking fellow. The fourth was the brooding sort, who melted silver artefacts—jewellery, plates, chalices—over the searing fire.

Gudrun watched, and waited. But their movements simply repeated. Over and over. This was the here and now, the frozen present, never fading into the past, never advancing into the future.

She dropped to a lower branch, finding another hollow.

Again, figures materialised from the shadows.

This time she saw Astrid bound in a gloomy room. Men held her down, drawing her blood into tiny glass vials as she writhed and cursed their black hearts.

'Unhand her, you beasts!' screamed Gudrun, but what she was seeing was an echo of reality, not reality itself, and her cries went unheard. The scene repeated, and she had to look away, the shadows filling the hollow once more.

Down she climbed. Down, down, and hollows continued to appear. One showed Freya visiting Erik's grave, over and over. Another showed Vali, overseeing Runolodda's fortifications. Another, the villagers training for war. Then Gorm the Wolfman, infecting soldiers one by one. Monks at prayer. A dead man on a beach, riddled with knives.

She risked a look down. Then a look up.

Damn! She had descended less than halfway.

Gudrun reached down for the next branch when the blast of a Great Horn took her by surprise. A powerful surge of wind shook Yggdrasil as if an earthquake had taken hold. Branches thrashed. Air roared. Leaves whipped Gudrun's eyes and she cried out as her hand slipped. Then, the branch she stood on twisted, pitching her forward past the tipping point, and she plummeted with a shriek.

Every other branch swung aside, each refusing to break her fall, and the ground rushed up to meet her with terrifying speed. She plunged like a falling star, limbs flailing, throat screaming, and buried her face in her arms as she struck the green grass.

And passed through.

It was as if she had slipped through a cloud.

And what lay below left her breathless.

The roots of Yggdrasil sprawled like colossal serpents, their sinuous tendrils reaching across black and empty infinity. They pulsed with an otherworldly glow, alive with colour, alive with light, though hard as dead stone. Gnarled and knotted, they resembled the intertwining limbs of great giants, burrowing through the very fabric of existence itself.

Such beauty. Such magnificence. The spectacle brought tears to Gudrun's eyes, and it took her a moment to realise she was floating. Alive, and gliding through the abyss as though swimming the ocean depths.

Instinctively, she gave a kick and felt herself drift forward, closer to the nearest root. Faded runes adorned its surface. She ran her fingers over the patterns. These had been carved so long ago that it was difficult to make out their meaning. Old scars that had forgotten the shapes of their original wounds.

She *swam* on.

The closer she came to the central root, the clearer the runes appeared. Fresher wounds. Nearer futures. Gudrun swallowed, a sinking realisation setting in as she understood her destination.

These were the Runes of Reality, the irrefutable predestiny of all things.

Carved by the Sisters Three.

The Norns of Fate.

KLO ISLAND

Scion had never believed in Fate.

Scion believed in Possibility. Accepting Fate would erase the significance of his choices and his actions, like surrendering to an ocean current. So, as the very real, very powerful current towed their boat inexorably closer to Klo Island, he felt Fate mock his disbelief.

None of the Beastly Boys had ever sailed on open sea. The vessel was larger than their riverboats back home, and nowhere near as robust as a longship. They strained against the oars, their muscles taut and trembling. Each of them conjured their own image of nightmarish creatures rising from the depths of the churning murk.

Tyr had his eyes closed, exhaling slowly. A spray of saltwater splashed the deck, causing Birger the Bear to grit his teeth, sweat dripping into his eyes, while Olle gripped the boat's edge, white-knuckled and green-faced, and threw up everything he'd eaten since leaving Runolodda. Scion appeared calm, if only on the surface, as he scanned the darkness for a glimpse of the island.

'It shan't be much longer, my son.' Father Lennärt sat on a barrel beside him, his breath wisps of mist in the cold. 'Do you feel adequately prepared?'

Scion drew his seax from his boot. Moonlight shone brilliantly off the polished silver plating and cast a gleam along the razor-sharp edge.

'More than we would have been. Thanks to the Brotherhood.' Scion hated to be indebted to another, but he could not allow their sacrifice to pass without expressing his gratitude.

'Why did you do it?' asked Scion.

'Do what?'

'Give up the silver. Risk your lives on a mere . . . possibility.'

Perched on a barrel, Lennärt drummed his fingers against it.

He cast his mind back. Once, he had been Chief to these young men. And when starvation threatened their village he had called for a hunt. But rather than personally joining in, he had sent good men out into the cold. Good men and young boys. And they had faced the Alpha without him. None who returned were ever the same again.

'Upon my arrival in Hvalvik,' began Lennärt, picking his words with care. 'I was a man burdened with the need for forgiveness. Father Frank convinced me that divine absolution would relieve that burden. However, it appears that prayer was but the first step toward redemption.' His gaze darted briefly to the silver seax. 'Perhaps I take my second step today.'

'You've carried this guilt for twenty years?'

'Do we not carry the same burden, my son?'

A memory flashed before Scion—his parents thrashing and drowning beneath the ice, his young hands powerless to reach them.

He slid the blade into his boot. 'Do not presume to know my mind, old man.'

'That is not my intention, Scion of Runolodda. But ask yourself why you pursue Astrid.'

Scion shrugged. 'Well, we can't very well abandon a kinswoman in peril, can we?'

'Do not speak for the others. Speak for yourself. Why do *you* pursue her?'

'She is—' Scion searched for the most neutral descriptor. '— worth pursuing.'

'You care for her?'

'I—' Scion gazed out across the surging water. 'I do.'

'Good. That is good, Scion. Your parents would be proud of the man you've grown into.'

The unexpected compliment caught Scion completely off guard, leaving a lump in his throat, an equally unexpected reaction.

'Oh?' he managed, though his voice cracked.

'For whatever merit it holds, so am I.' Lennärt interlaced his fingers and turned his gaze away to grant Scion his privacy. 'I have fond memories of them, you know? Your parents, that is. Your father, if I recall correctly, was a champion keg roller.'

Tears stung Scion's eyes, but he laughed at that. 'A what?'

'You've not partaken in the sport? Ah, it was a delightful pastime, rolling those hefty kegs loaded with stones across the festival grounds, with the young lasses cheering us on toward the finish line. Your father took on all contenders. Took them on and won.'

Lennärt rested a hand on Scion's shoulder.

'He was a strong man, son. But the cold was stronger that day.'

'I know,' whispered Scion.

'Do you?'

Scion remained silent, his jaw clenched, willing back the tears.

'Guilt is a heavy burden. And often a fruitless one. My intent is not to add to that burden, but to help you to lay it down. You long to save Astrid. Good. Yet perhaps you also seek to absolve yourself by succeeding where you once failed?'

Scion was about to speak, to deny it. In the end, he simply nodded.

'You love this Astrid. That much is clear,' said Father Lennärt, holding his gaze, 'But I think it's time for you and I to take the third step toward redemption.'

'The third step?'

Lennärt leaned in close and whispered.

'We need to forgive ourselves.'

*

Astrid fluttered open her eyes.

How long had she lain here? A fresh incision on her forearm stung like a cattle brand. The Klo had not been gentle, drawing her blood with a hollow reed to fill glass vial after glass vial, only to casually stow them away in a small wooden chest. Mercifully, they had stopped when she passed out, no doubt loth to kill their sole donor.

Slowly, she sat up.

Scion's voice, as he called out her name from the harbourside, still echoed inside her. There was such pain in that voice, a mingling of strength and fragility that drew her toward him, stirring the first soft whispers of love. Did Scion feel it too? He had walked through fire to set her free. Astrid felt a yearning to soothe his wounds in return, to offer him solace and understanding. To embrace him and to have him embrace her.

Hope gave way to a creeping dread as she glanced around the room.

Her bed was large, a heavy timber base draped in soft pelts and dyed wool.

Fit for a queen.

Apart from this one luxury, the chamber had recently been stripped bare. A table bore dusty outlines; imprints of goblets, candleholders, drinking vessels. Perhaps the Klo feared she might use them for self-harm. Or try to inflict harm on them.

Astrid's chest tightened. Thick stone walls hemmed her in, with an iron door and iron bars on the window, through which an icy breeze blew. The floor was bare but for a bucket and a pitcher of water.

And the metal trapdoor.

Two great chains extended up from the hatch to a wall where they passed through openings in the masonry. Astrid guessed they were part of a pulley system, though she could not say whether they led up or down.

The chains weighed a ton and could not be budged, not by a dozen men. She ran fingers up the chain and checked the openings in the wall. Unfortunately, they were too snug to squeeze a hand through. She tried the trapdoor. Locked? Or simply too heavy? Lastly, she felt around the iron bars in the window, feeling for any cracks or weaknesses.

Rust.

She could cut through rust.

What to use, what to use? The pitcher was copper, a metal too soft to saw through iron. Ah! Astrid smashed the bucket against the wall, lifting the solid band from the debris.

Steel. That could work.

As she started scraping away at the first bar, she heard the whoosh of a passing flock of birds. Exotic birds. An iridescent blur of wings.

Beautiful and free.

The watchman's tone was as biting as the sea breeze.

'About time you showed up!' he sputtered, nearly stumbling over the small pile of firewood in the sand. He hurried across the narrow beach to his fellow guard. 'I've stood half the shift on me own, ya scurvy layabout!'

'Don't get yer tits in a twist, Holger,' grumbled the *Layabout* as he stepped out from Klo Hall, his furs casting a bristly silhouette against the warm, beckoning light within. By the time he had shut the huge doors behind him, his breath had turned to white fog. 'I was snagging meself one o' these.'

With dramatic flair, *Layabout* produced a glass vial and hurried over to the fire where he swirled its gloppy red contents in the flickering light.

'Where's mine?' complained Holger, trying to snatch it away.

'First come, first served,' grinned Layabout, swiping the vial out of reach and taking a seat closer to the fire.

Keeping watch at Klo Island was often this chilly, even in the summer months, owing to the cruel onshore wind. Not that anyone would think to attack the mountain stronghold. As far as Hvalvik was concerned, this was where lowlifes and criminals were taken to rot in exile—the last place anyone would care to visit, let alone break into. Still, shivering watchmen patrolled the thin strip of beach between Klo Hall and the pitch-dark sea. Just in case.

'How's the bite?' asked Holger. 'Mine's gettin' there, I reckon.'

They rolled up their sleeves to compare wounds. Holger's was swollen and tender, the holes shallow and even, while Layabout's looked a ragged gash.

'By the gods,' winced Holger. 'Seems King Gorm got a bit careless towards the back of the line.'

He prodded his own bite gently, hissing at the pain. It was hours old now, already a darkening brown, though not yet black.

'Won't be too much longer for me,' he gloated.

'Well, won't do you any good without one o' these,' smirked Layabout, tucking the vial back into his cloak and rubbing his hands over the flames. 'But you'll have to wait. They'll let the lass recover before bleeding her again. Sweet-looking honeypot though, ain't she?'

Holger grinned a gap-toothed grin. 'Ay, I'll bet she—'

'Good evening, gentlemen,' came a nearby voice.

Spears snapped up, menacingly fixed on Father Lennärt, who stood like a spectre from the sea. Behind him, moonlight revealed four monks, their faces concealed by grey hoods, as they hauled the boat ashore.

'It's only us, sir. The ferrymen.'

Holger blew out hard and lowered his spear. 'Almost jumped out of me skin, ya halfwits!' he bellowed. If his tits were in a twist before, they were now a pair of double-tied knots. 'What're ya doing here at this hour?'

Father Lennärt lifted his cowl. 'Apologies, sirs. Our rudder broke and we were blown off course. We had to wait for the wind to turn.' He moved to join the monks, already in the process of unloading the barrels. 'Very good, brothers. Hurry these indoors, if you please.'

'Hold yer horses a moment,' growled Layabout, keeping his spear level. 'No-one enters Klo Hall tonight.'

Lennärt was momentarily taken aback, but kept his composure all the same. 'As you wish, sir. No need for concern. We'll stock the larder and be on our way.'

Holger stepped closer. 'Not the larder, neither. Understood?'

'But gentlemen, we have always—'

'Not tonight!' shouted Holger, shoving Lennärt back.

The four monks shuffled uneasily. One even took a step forward, though pulled up short at Lennärt's gesture.

'Would the King find it agreeable that his cargo failed to arrive?' asked Lennärt.

'The King has other things on his mind than cheese and ale, priest. Now clear off before I cut yer flapping tongue out.'

At that moment, the larder door swung open. After all these years, it still unsettled Lennärt how Klo Hall's imposing doors dwarfed the adjacent larder's entrance, making it seem as small as a mousehole. A man burst out in a hurry, untying his trousers to relieve himself in the sea.

'Oi! Don't piss into the wind!' yelled Layabout.

'Use the Hall's chamber pots, ya dolt!' added Holger.

'Pots are full,' cried the man. 'Too much excitement tonight to be bothered with cleaning duties, by the looks of it.'

Lennärt tensed as the largest monk edged closer to Holger.

'So you'd rather spray us out here than empty the pot yerself?' cried Holger.

'Desperate times,' laughed the man, still draining his bladder.

The larder door remained ajar, and Lennärt could glimpse Klo warriors milling about inside, drawing mead from a cask, now and then brushing a curious glance their way. And with a speartip at his throat, there was nothing to do but retreat.

Hoods low, the monks seemed to agree, and, exchanging reluctant nods, headed back to the boat. The large monk paused to peer over his shoulder, seeing the watchmen push the barrels across the sandy shore and into the larder, where the warriors let out a cheer.

He clambered into the vessel and lifted his hood. 'Well it's up to them now,' rasped Father Frank.

The remaining monks removed their hoods too, and took to the oars, conversing in their Saxon tongue.

'Let's hope they make it past the storeroom,' murmured Father Lennärt. 'Didn't expect such a crowd at the outset of Scion's plan.'

'One more part for us to play,' said Frank, opening a chest at his feet. 'We'll row out and wait for the signal.'

The Brotherhood nodded, keeping their voices low.

The night, however, was about to get loud.

*

The larder was spacious and torchlit, though chill as a crypt, the scent of dank mould clinging to every corner. Odours tangled and fought—onion and offal, barley and blood, leather, sweat, and smoke. The shelves, unevenly hewn from the rock, held provisions and supplies in disarray, the clamminess warping wooden crates and dampening sacks of grain.

Two Klo warriors loitered around the large table in the centre of the room, cracking jokes and sloshing mead while the watchmen rolled the barrels to a corner alongside a row of stout iron pots.

'We gettin' more armour?' asked Holger.

'No. Not for another week or so,' replied a warrior, crumbs spraying as he spoke.

'New skillets, maybe?'

'No, nothing like that. What's the fuss?'

Holger scratched his chin and tapped a barrel with his spear. 'Something's rattling like a bag o' bells in this one. What ya reckon's in there?'

'Well, open it and find out,' said the warrior, going over to see for himself.

Holger pried open the lid and reached in to discover a collection of silvered weapons. Axes, swords, arrows. Even a sledgehammer bristling with spikes.

'What in Odin's name . . ?' exclaimed the warrior. He tested the sharp edge of an axe against his thumb and whistled in awe. 'Could be a special requisition for the new King.'

The other warrior joined the huddle, marvelling at a sword, turning it over in the torchlight. 'Can't be. Gorm's only held the crown since nightfall.'

'Must be a mix up with them monks, then,' suggested Holger.

'I'd wager it's—' began Layabout, when a silver seax sliced the words from his throat. And before the others could react, hands clapped over their mouths, knives slit their windpipes, and they slumped wide-eyed and gurgling to the stone floor.

'A little help?' whispered Birger the Bear, still stuck halfway out of his barrel.

Olle, not one for tight spaces, had been first to poke out from his own barrel. Now he flapped his arms around, trying to get the blood flowing again.

'My neck,' he moaned. 'My back. My knees. This must be what hard work feels like.'

'Let's slip into something more appropriate, shall we, brothers?' said Scion, peeling the fur cloak from Holger's body, careful not to drag it through the puddles of blood. 'Best to look the part if we're to fool a horde of parboiled Wolf-men.'

'And collect your weapons,' said Tyr, cradling his silvered broadsword as if it were a cherished family heirloom. He swished it into its sheath, then slid his prized pair of axes into his belt and slung the bow and quiver over his shoulder. To finish off, he pulled on one of the Klo cloaks, donned the dead man's helmet, and hoisted Layabout's roundshield onto his back.

'Not bad,' grinned Scion, noting the painted Valknut

emblazoned across the oak surface. There was a gratifying touch of irony in using the Klo's shields against them.

Birger and Tyr grabbed anything and everything flammable, scattering woven baskets and kindling across the floor, smearing fish oil and lard across every surface.

Olle set the flaming torch in place.

'Right, boys,' said Scion as they huddled together. 'For Astrid.'

'For Astrid,' repeated the others.

Scion strode over to the larder door, still ajar. The Brotherhood would be somewhere out there in the dark waves, waiting for his signal. He gave the Beastly Boys a nod, and off they went, slipping through the side tunnel that led to Klo Hall.

Scion took a deep breath.

'Victory or Valhalla,' he whispered under his breath.

*

'By the hammer of Thor!' hissed Tyr.

Klo Hall crackled like a gathering storm. More than three hundred Klo warriors swarmed, hornets in a nest, comparing bite wounds, laughing, shouting, chanting. Some stood on tabletops, stomping their boots to tunes of their own invention, imagining what the skalds would sing of their conquests. Others gambled for the rare blood-vials, eager to be among the first to undergo the transformation.

Tyr stole a glance at Gorm, who now sat the throne, returned to human form and wrapped in nothing but a fur cloak. Tailors undoubtedly stitched together a fresh set of battle attire for him. He had shaved his head, but there was still blood in his beard. And he had the look of a proud father. The Klo were his now, and he had altered their fundamental nature. A god, shaping men into his own image.

Tyr shivered and weaved carefully through the throng toward the great doors.

Birger came next through the tunnel, staring wide-eyed up at the cavern's high vault. Olle, surprisingly, put on a better performance, swaggering in like this was his local tavern. Their disguises seemed to be working, so, with a nod, they separated, positioning themselves on opposite sides of the Hall, eyes down, helmets low.

Tyr reached the enormous doors, nervous as a cat. He exhaled slowly. Scion would soon give the signal, angling his sword to reflect moonlight out to sea. With any luck, the Brotherhood would see it and—

There!

Mighty War Drums boomed in the distance.

The Klo came to a standstill.

A great Battle Horn sounded across the water.

Gorm sprang to his feet. 'What's happening?' he bellowed.

Tyr was ready, sliding open the peep-hatch. 'We're under attack, my King! The watchmen have been shot dead!' He'd added a growl to his voice which seemed to go unchallenged.

Gorm stormed across the Hall, warriors pouring in behind him. Could it be? Had the Alpha come for him? Would Freya dare? Oh, he hoped so.

'Björn! How's that bite progressing?'

Gorm's Captain of the Guard fell into step beside him. 'Not quite ready, my King.' The seventh hour approached but his wound had yet to ooze black.

'No matter,' said Gorm, motioning for the doors to be opened. 'If these are the dogs of Runolodda, we will grind their skulls either way—whether we be men or wolves.'

Tyr leapt into action, lifting the bolt and heaving the doors open.

'It seems our prey has come knocking,' roared Gorm. 'Forward, comrades! Show no mercy!'

The drums continued to sound from across the water, the horn continued to blare. Olle and Birger added to the fervour. 'To battle!' they cried, slapping nearby warriors on the back. The Klo stampeded through the Hall and spilled out into the night air, spirits raised, voices raised, axes raised. Gorm led the throng to the shore and squinted out across the dark waves.

In an instant, the drums stopped.

The horn cut short.

Everything fell into silence.

Gorm swiftly took a blood-vial to his lips. The transformation into Wolf form was quick, but still gruesome enough to turn a few stomachs. He crouched, fur cloak still clinging to his back, though now stretched and torn to tatters. His Wolfsight quested out, penetrating the mist and darkness almost supernaturally. There, bobbing on the distant waves were a handful of monks rowing off into the night.

There was a drum propped up against the rail.

Björn was at his side. 'I see no watchmen, my King. Dead or alive.'

As one, they peered slowly back to the Hall in time to see Tyr throw them the middle finger and shut the heavy doors. And before anyone could react, he pulled the inner lever. A mechanism came alive, springing a cascade of iron bolts across the doors from top to bottom.

Clangs rang out. Echoed. Echoed. Then, faded on the breeze.

To a man, the Klo stood stunned. They were locked out of their own fortress.

Gorm snarled. He whirled angrily back to the sea and, for an instant, contemplated swimming after those grey *snakes!* Yet, their scent was already blowing away, even to his heightened senses. And he would much rather fight the tricksters in his Hall than the powerful ocean currents, Wolf-man or not.

He would have to deal with the Brotherhood at another time.

Eager, a handful of warriors raced to the larder door ahead of the rest. And at the same moment, Gorm caught the whiff of an odd smell.

'Wait!' he cried. 'It's a trap—'

The warriors barged through. The torch dropped. The oil erupted.

Whoomph!

The blast threw men back, flames curling out like a Dragon's tongue, licking their furs, feasting on their flesh, their screams shattering the short-lived silence. Men staggered back from the heat. One ran shrieking, his entire body wreathed in fire, and collapsed only a few strides short of the shore.

Gorm scowled against the glare. Curse it! *Gorm the Great Strategist*—outsmarted on his own soil! Not to mention the weeks, maybe *months* worth of supplies gone up in smoke. Whoever these troublemakers were, he'd see their balls in a bucket by sunrise.

Men shouted, and Gorm turned to see axes being swung into the heavy oak of the enormous locked doors.

'Leave them!' he roared. 'Concentrate all efforts on dousing the flames!'

It was the wisest plan of action. Chopping through into Klo Hall would be like mining through granite. At once, the Klo stowed their axes and set to work, scooping sand and seawater in their helmets to throw into the blazing larder.

Björn moved to pitch in, but Gorm stopped him with a massive claw.

'Not you, Captain. If we can't go through, we shall have to go over.' For Gorm, there was always another way. Contingencies upon contingencies.

Björn hesitated, his gaze crawling up the exterior of Klo Hall—sheer rock, worn smooth by the elements, and crowned by a tangle of thorny vines and loose stones. It would have made an ideal lookout were it not so treacherous. Did Gorm really expect them to slither over the top?

He opened and closed his mouth a few times before speaking.

'Surely, no man can scale *that*, my King.'

'Indeed, no man could,' said Gorm, sniffing the air. 'But we are more than men now. Is that not so, Captain?'

Björn looked puzzled, then took Gorm's meaning, lifting his own sleeve.

The King was correct.

The seventh hour had come and his bite oozed black.

SISTER SLAVES

'Step back! We're coming in!' yelled Birger the Bear, hoisting his sledgehammer.

With a single blow, the door crashed open, and he stepped into the slave quarters with Scion shoving in after him.

'Astrid! Astrid!'

The barracks were squat, little more than a hollow opposite the larder tunnel, which billowed thick smoke into the Hall. There was no ventilation in the slave's chamber, if one could call it that, and Birger almost gagged on the combined stench of mildew and human waste. More than a dozen women in ratty tunics huddled against the barrack's far wall, away from their straw beds that lay strewn on the cold floor as if for cattle. They looked terrified. Feeble. And no-one moved a muscle.

'It's alright,' soothed Scion, hands spread wide. 'We're not Klo. We're here for the new girl.' He took a small step closer, casting about the room. 'Is she here?'

A dark-skinned woman spoke up. 'She go. They take her to the . . .' she searched for the word, and a pale woman on her arm filled in the rest.

'She eez in ze King's Chamber, my lords.' She spoke with a Frankish accent, her voice a whisper.

Tyr rubbed his eyes. 'Did she just say the King's Chamber?'

'I think she said the King's Chamber,' nodded Birger.

'Not the pissing *King's Chamber*,' groaned Olle.

Scion had seen Lennärt's diagrams, and knew precisely where to find the King's Chamber. He grimaced. The plan had been to release Astrid from the barracks, then quickly escape through a rear exit tucked behind the King's throne. From there they could follow the tunnel that led to the Klo ships. Slogging up to the King's Chamber would be suicide.

'Are you certain?' he asked, stepping back towards the ruined doorway.

'Yes. Up, up,' said the first woman. 'But we come. We come, too.'

She motioned for the slaves to move out, a mother hen with her chicks.

Tyr hesitated. 'You'd be safer taking a ship. Go while you can. The Klo will be focussed on us.'

'Long path up to King's Chamber. Many houses. Our sisters there. Trapped. Cannot leave them.' She wasn't asking, she was insisting. And the others nodded, a loyal Sisterhood of the Chain. Birger smiled at the poetry of such a gesture.

Scion glanced around. 'You all wish to follow us? Gorm will want us dead, and anyone else who dares cross him tonight.'

'Sisters be dead if they stay. We come.'

'Of course . . .' said Scion, a raised eyebrow inviting her introduction.

'Nala,' supplied the woman, and rushed out into the Hall without wasting any more time on pleasantries.

The Beastly Boys exchanged a shrug.

'For Astrid,' repeated Scion.

'And everyone else, it seems,' replied Tyr, breaking into a smile.

Carved into the solid rock, the staircase led them upward, boots and bare feet careful not to slip on the unevenly hewn steps. Scion looked back down at the empty Hall, grateful to be leaving the thickening smoke behind.

Before long, they came to the narrow exit at the top of the stairs and stepped out into the bracing night air. Nala was already hurrying toward the sheer rock face that loomed before them. Gods, it must be as tall as Mount Varda back home!

'Still looks like a cock to me,' said Olle, rushing to keep up with the women.

Father Lennärt's diagrams had been fairly accurate. Indeed, thatched cabins dotted the vertical face, anchored to the rock by angled supports. Each cabin had its own deck, a precarious wooden platform lit by its own burning brazier. A web of rope bridges and ladders joined the cabins, a zig zag reaching all the way up to a single peak with a larger dwelling perched on top.

The King's Chamber.

From this distance, the overall effect was beautiful. Magical. Like a festive maypole lighting up the night. Then again, what went on in those pretty points of light was far from merry.

'What do we do when we reach the peak?' asked Birger.

Scion blew out, his breath icy. 'Not sure yet. Any suggestions?'

There was a not-too-distant growl.

They whirled to face the rocky flat that covered Klo Hall, overgrown by a dense thicket of thorny vines. The foliage shook. The growler growled louder, closer, soon joined by others, until a chorus of wolf howls rippled through the air.

'Run!' yelled Scion.

Wolf-men came tearing through the bramble, quicker now, keener, hungrier. They were about twenty strides away and gaining, though slowed somewhat by the wildwood. Some laughed, calling out human words through inhuman teeth. Others roared and whooped while still others cursed as the thick thorns dug into their limbs.

Tyr was crouched low, arrow poised, when the first Wolf-man broke through. He had not expected it to be wielding an axe and shield—an almost comical image if it weren't so terrifying. The beast snarled, lips curled back. Cuts in its fur were already healing, and it hacked through the final vine as Tyr took aim.

The silver point flew, punching into its chest, and the creature shrieked as if burned. It crumpled, imploding like a burst lung, claws retracting, body hair receding, muscles shrinking back to pale human form. Tyr gasped. The silver had worked swiftly indeed. But there was no time to lose and he had already turned to run before the man hit the ground.

Olle caught up with the women and began helping them up the first rope ladder.

'Hurry! It's about to get very hairy out here!'

'Follow me!' cried Nala, reaching the top rung. The first deck felt solid enough. It supported a small cabin and, near the doorway, a heavy-looking iron brazier that glowed with red embers.

Cautiously, she peeked inside the cabin.

No sister-slaves here.

She raced along the first suspended bridge. It rose in a gentle incline, and Nala kept one hand against the rockface to maintain her balance, before leaping onto the next deck.

Scion and Tyr were last to catch up, glancing back to see if any more Wolf-men had breached the thicket. So far, there was no sign of them other than the incessant howling. With any luck, some had slid on the loose rock and fallen back down to the beach. Crushing those below, hopefully.

No-one lingered to find out.

Up a ladder they went, across a bridge, up the next, across again—a rising switchback pathway—poking their heads into each cabin they passed, until at last they found a woman chained to a heavy storage chest at the foot of a large bed. She barely moved, curled up on the floor like a dog.

Birger recoiled in disgust at the sight. What sort of men could do this? 'Step aside,' he said, smashing the shackle cleanly from her ankle.

'Come, young one,' soothed Nala. 'We be free of this place.'

Then a roar boomed from the thorny thicket far below and a pair of Wolf-men came tearing across the open space for the first ladder.

Scion loosed an arrow but the Wolf-man was quick, lifting its shield in time as he ascended. Tyr, strategically positioned, saw the gap appear in its defences and exploited it, aiming through its raised armpit with a precise shot. A howl became a wail as the silver withered the creature back to human form, and his corpse dropped away.

The second Wolf-man ignored the ladders entirely, digging powerful claws directly into the rockface to climb with surprising speed. Tyr let fly, missed. Scion too. The creature climbed on, weaving, rising closer and closer. Another volley. Another miss!

Scion darted a glance upward. Birger and Olle were doing all they could to press the group on.

'Come on, Tyr!' he yelled, stringing another arrow. 'These bastards can't get past us!'

The creature was now only one level down. Yet before they could shoot, it slipped beneath the bridge and clung to its underside, using it as a shield as it scuttled along like an upside-down spider.

Curse it! Scion took aim for a gap in the planking, guessed the timing, and fired. He heard a yowl as the arrow found its mark. The beast fell, hit a bridge that rattled and writhed with the impact, then a second, and had reverted to pale naked flesh before it hit the ground with an audible crunch.

'Thor's nuts! Here they come!' yelled Tyr.

Far below, half a dozen more Wolf-men strained through the thicket. Only two held shields, the others trusting in their thick hides. Their claws. Their slavering teeth.

'Push forward!' yelled Scion, though he knew the group climbed as fast as humanly possible. Not yet halfway up, the Wolf-men would soon be on them.

And who knew how many more were on the way?

THE VIKING WAY

Vali could not sleep.

The fire had dwindled to embers, so he tossed another log in. Looking across to Scion's empty bed, Vali worried. He knew he shouldn't. The Beastly Boys were a cunning pack and had survived many a tight spot before. After all, he had trained them to fight and hunt since they were knee high. And yet, no matter how many cuffs to the back of the head he had doled out, they could still be immature and foolhardy at times.

He hoped they'd not run into any trouble.

Vali tossed his woollen blanket aside and climbed out of bed.

Dawn was a few hours away. The village lay sound asleep, holding its breath for the coming wave. He strode through the empty streets, inspecting door bolts at random. To withstand a siege, the womenfolk had stockpiled provisions in the stables. Others had helped set up stockades between the houses, designed to impede the Klo and make it easier for the villagers to control chokepoints.

He made his way up the stairs to their new parapets. Torsten had done well, fitting battlements every five paces for the archers to hide behind. Vali was impressed. Many of the archers slept at their post beside a bucketful of arrows, their bows reinforced and freshly strung. All seemed quiet. Preparations had been carried out as thoroughly as possible. Gazing over the palisades, he chuckled at the deep encircling trench. If nothing else, farmers knew how to dig.

'Something amusing?'

'Lady Freya! You really shouldn't sneak up on an old man like that.'

Freya smiled, leaning on the palisade to stare up at the stars. 'I thought that Vali the Huntsman could hear a grasshopper fart in a forest.'

'Ha! Perhaps my ears have aged, after all,' he grinned. 'Having trouble sleeping?'

'Aye, though this time I cannot blame the pain, given that it has all but vanished.' She stretched her leg, rolled her shoulder.

'Thank the gods for the healing power of Wolf-blood, 'ey?'

Vali's grin faded as Freya offered no smile in return. Instead, she lifted Astrid's blood-stained bandage in one pale hand.

'Speaking of blood—you sent the Boys to find my daughter. Where are they, Vali?'

There was no use giving assurances. Nothing but the bare truth would satisfy Lady Freya. 'In truth, I don't know.'

She nodded. 'Gudrun claimed Gorm would bring her to me. That I must wait rather than act.'

'What does your heart tell you?'

Freya tucked the bandage away. 'Only that she yet lives.'

'Well that is hope enough for tonight,' smiled Vali. He straightened, stretched his back. 'I saw what you did to the prisoner. *Ulrick*, was it? That will send Gorm quite the message.'

'Good.' She said no more. Simply stared into the darkness.

'If I'm being honest, I never imagined you had it in you. You've always exuded a sense of gentleness. Of restraint.'

Freya dipped her head. 'And why do you suppose I gave off that impression?'

'Ah,' said Vali, revelation dawning. The roars and the screams echoed down the years, and he smelled the blood and the pine and the snow once more. 'The Battle of the Bear Cave. You frightened the village back then . . .'

'. . . So I needed to tame myself in their eyes. Give them no cause for concern. Would the people have forgiven me so readily if I showed any sign of aggression? Of rage?'

'Though the rage simmers within you.'

'How could it not?' whispered Freya. 'After all I have endured.'

Vali looked away, wringing his hands. Over the years, he had been close enough with Erik to learn much of Freya's past. There was great strength in her, he realised, to rebuild her life from such sorrow. He picked his words with care.

'And yet, you are gentle too, Freya. Runolodda is blessed to know that side of you. Perhaps, when the time comes, you will speak your heart to the people. They may find courage in your story.'

Freya straightened, breathing out slowly as she turned to face the rooftops of Runolodda. For a long moment, she gazed at the moonlight resting on the sleepy village below.

'Despite my given name, I am not Viking-born, Vali. I was taken by Vikings, torn from my home by Vikings. To serve and to suffer. That is all I know of the Viking Way. You, on the other hand, were among those to see battle before settling in the valley. You were raised on the sagas and the legends that shaped your thinking, your speech, your very being.'

Vali frowned. 'What are you saying, Freya?'

'I cannot lead Runolodda,' she admitted at last. 'The task must fall to you.'

Vali blinked in astonishment.

If ever there was a daughter of the Viking North, she stood before him in that moment. The settlers of Runolodda had given up the raiding life for a reason. There was far more to the Viking Way than blooding one's hands. Surely, Freya had gleaned as much from her years in Runolodda.

'Draw your sword,' ordered Vali, a sudden gravity in his voice.

'What?'

With a practised hand, he whisked his own sword from its scabbard. 'You heard me.'

'Vali, this is foolish What if—' She winced as the flat of Vali's blade slapped against her arm.

'Show us who you are,' demanded Vali.

He took the hilt in both hands, settling into a fighting stance. Freya's eyes widened, disbelief spread across her face. Some of the sleeping archers woke, murmuring and confused as they rose to their feet. Were their minds playing tricks on them, or did Vali threaten Lady Freya?

At length, she drew her sword and widened her stance.

Vali stood still, waiting.

She lunged, the thrust easily swatted away.

'Show us who you are,' repeated Vali.

She renewed her attack, this time with more aggression. But Vali parried, rapping her knuckles with his pommel. 'I said . . . show us who you are!'

She roared, came at him with a feint, then barged her shoulder into his chest. Absorbing the impact, he swivelled, shoving her off balance, tripping her to the ground.

'Are you Tame Freya, meek and mild?' he asked, sword tip

hovering dangerously close to her wide eyes. 'Or are you something more?'

'Yah!' She struck the blade away and rolled to her feet. The archers stood transfixed, aware at least that there was no deadly intent in the air. Though what had sparked such a confrontation remained a mystery.

Vali unleashed a flurry of strikes, each deflected in rapid succession. He shouted, and curious folk began to trickle from their homes.

'Show us who you are!'

Freya felt the rage rise, and her sword work moved steadily from a defensive footing to a more assertive one. She forced Vali back, back. Steel rang and sweat began to run, despite the cold. Freya found the fire inside her and channelled it from the depths of her soul to the tip of her sword arm. Vali's eyes bulged, struggling to block each explosive strike as they landed with dizzying speed.

'Aye! Show us!'

He surged forward, but Freya ducked, dropping her sword to seize his arm in both hands, and executed a swift toss that sent him crashing to the ground. The breath was driven from his lungs, and a bolt of pain shot through his back.

Wincing, he sat up.

Freya came to loom over him. 'Is that what you wanted?' she screamed. 'Are you satisfied?' She caught movement from the streets below. People milled about, murmuring amongst themselves, the hour too dark to read their features. The archers looked away, intent on inspecting their bows once again.

'There you are.' Vali grinned, standing. Freya glared at him, shaking as he turned to face the village. 'Get some rest, people! Tomorrow will demand much from us all.'

Then, he turned on his heel as though nothing significant had happened, and headed back the way he had come.

Freya blew out a jet of cold air.

And exhaustion hit her all at once.

THE BATTLE OF KLO MOUNTAIN

Astrid listened intently to the distant commotion.

Either her blood had driven the Klo mad, or they were facing challenges with a few rowdy trespassers. She smiled, guessing the latter. If Scion was to reach the King's Chamber, he would need a way out. Or they'd all be trapped for good.

She lifted her steel to the rusty iron bars.

And sawed with a rabid fury.

*

They came like the rising tide.

The Boys were able to pick off a few with their bows, but most of the climbing Wolf-men were too cunning, too quick. Some slipped into the cabins, out of their line of sight. Some dodged, climbing nimbly, or leaped between thatched rooftops. Others deflected arrows with shields, or swatted them away.

Scion had almost crossed a particularly shaky bridge when he caught movement from the corner of his eye. Some of the creatures were scrambling wide, hoping to sneak past.

He reached into his quiver. *Empty!*

'Tyr! Do you see them?' yelled Scion.

'I see them!'

Tyr swung his bow and shot the beast furthest up through the ribs. It tumbled, sweeping another comrade off the cliff with a cry of pain.

Scion whooped.

He had not seen the third Wolf-man.

'Scion! Behind you!' cried Tyr, as it bounded along the bridge.

Sharp claws reached, and Scion spun his sword in a wild arc to sever the talons with the silver edge. Carried by its own momentum, the Wolf-man collided with Scion, and together they crashed onto the nearest deck with a force that knocked the blade from his grasp. Scion's vision swam for a moment while the silver worked to reduce the creature to its naked human shape. The man cursed, maimed but not dead, and Scion scrambled to his feet to reach for the seax in his boot.

The man rushed in, tackling him to the ground once more. They wrestled, punched, yelled, blood squirting from severed fingers into Scion's eyes, blinding him. He bucked madly, and the brute was thrown clear. Scion's hands shook, wiping desperately at his eyes while fumbling once more for his seax. Through the muck, he saw the man reach for the silver sword, sweeping it up for a kill stroke.

Fortunately, the man was instantly crushed by a falling brazier, a downpour of fire and iron smashing him into the deck.

'You're welcome!' yelled Olle from above, his boot still extended out over the platform.

'Fine thinking, Olle! Burn the lower levels!'

What followed can only be described as a rain of fire.

The slaves dropped burning braziers onto the underlying cabins, the thatch roofs erupting into flame. Birger and Olle shot fiery arrows down at the wooden structures, the bridges, the ladders—anything flammable. Including their pursuers. Wolf-men shrieked in the roiling inferno, fur catching, flaring, blazing. Soon the lower cliffside was engulfed in flame, a tower of black ash rising, structures collapsing and crashing down on all that lay below.

Still, the Wolf-men came.

Scion climbed, glancing back as often as he dared. Wolf eyes flashed, pinpricks through the smoke, boiling with hatred and dogged determination. Scion watched Birger shoot his final arrow. Tyr and Olle were empty too.

Scion drew his axe.

Felt the heft of the blade.

He had sincerely hoped to avoid close quarter combat.

*

The far smaller fire in the larder had finally abated.

Gorm entered the thick smoke, particularly bothersome to his heightened Wolf senses, and coughed, growling with irritation. He crept through the charred debris. It radiated heat, and the Wolf-men who followed were careful to avoid the scalding cookware strewn across the floor.

Gorm slipped through the tunnel and into the Hall.

The stone floor lay paved with ash, though most of the smoke had risen to hang like thunderclouds against the high ceiling. Wisps had floated up the twin stairways to find open air where the tricksters had fled with the slaves. However, Gorm had another route in mind.

'To the Ascentor. We shall cut them off at the top.'

The Klo grinned and hurried across the Hall to the tunnel behind the throne. They entered, Wolfsight penetrating the gloom. The passage twisted this way and that, and the scent of the sea at the mountain's rear grew sharper the further they went.

About halfway through, they reached a locked door on the left wall. Gorm didn't bother with a key. With a giant fist, he splintered the oak from its hinges and stepped inside.

He allowed himself a rare smile.

The Ascentor was a clever apparatus indeed.

And it would be the intruders' doom.

*

'Nearly there! Keep climbing!'

Scion peered down.

Felt a pit in his stomach.

The only thing more terrifying than the drop was what you'd pass on the way down. The group had grown by four, the freed slaves expressing a mix of gratitude, confusion, and fear as they stepped out into the rising smoke. Nala had taken the lead, Olle and Birger in the middle, hauling up the slower climbers, while Scion and Tyr brought up the rear.

Tyr lay prone on a deck, gazing down at the Wolf-men who, like ice climbers with their hatchets, dug claws into the rock below.

He was not pleased.

He had hurled one of his prized axes, only to see his target catch it by the grip, laughing as he tossed it away.

Wolf-men were arseholes.

'I count at least a dozen!' shouted Tyr. 'What do we do?'

Across the bridge, Scion crouched on a second deck, squinting down through the plume. 'Well, we didn't dip these in silver just to pretty them up,' he called, raising his sword.

Tyr groaned. He revelled in weaponry, but the thrill of battle was quickly losing its charm.

'I shouldn't have asked.' And he drew his broadsword, grasping the hilt with both hands. The pair almost jumped out of their skin as Birger the Bear dropped to the bridge between them with a startling thump.

'Careful there, you dolt! It's a long way down, by Odin!'

'Relax, Tyr,' grinned Birger. 'They may wobble a bit, but these things are as sturdy as steel.' He shook the bridge by its corded handrail. 'Unless a flaming cabin lands on us, we'll be fine.'

The big man hefted his spiked hammer and peered down. *More* than a dozen, by his count, crawling like lizards up the sheer cliff.

He spat. 'Looks like the smoke is giving them some trouble.'

'We don't need to kill them in one,' called Scion. 'Just pierce their hides, and the silver will level the field enough for you to finish the job.'

'Good to know!' hollered Tyr.

'Hold onto your helmets,' said Birger. 'Here they come.'

The first Wolf-man sprang up for Scion's platform, claws wide, jaws wide. As it seemed to hang suspended in the air, Scion swung his blade, but missed when the creature twisted before landing on its haunches. It stood not three paces away. Quick talons swept low to reach beneath Scion's shield, but he jumped in time, landed, and whipped the point at the beast's face. The Wolf-man moved with unnatural speed, leaning out of reach and kicking a clawed foot into his shield. Scion felt his arm go numb on impact and almost staggered over the edge of the deck.

He found his balance and lunged again, sword point extended as far as possible. The Wolf-man took the bait, swatting the flat aside, and Scion spun with the momentum to slice his seax across its thigh. The creature howled, morphing back to human. Scion bore him to the ground, roaring as he smashed the pommel of his sword into the man's forehead, again and again, until his skull was a bloody pulp. Grunting, he hurled the body over the edge. And with the smoke momentarily obscuring their vision, it knocked one Wolf-man back into a second, sending both flailing and shrieking to their deaths.

Another Wolf-man came, stretching from below to grab for the bridge. It had to raise a shield to block Birger's blow, but the hammerhead smashed through and the spikes sliced into the monster's forearm. As the brute plummeted away, yet another scrambled over the bridge handrail and charged along the planks, teeth like polished daggers. Birger did not hesitate, rushing forward to meet it head on. And when they were about to collide, he slid through the beast's legs, hammer raised, and felt the sharp spikes rip through its groin.

Tyr saw it happen and winced.

There were worse ways to die, he supposed, though none sprang to mind.

From the corner of his eye, Tyr glimpsed claws reaching upward, their tips digging into the platform a mere hair's breadth from his foot. He was quick on his step, grinding them under his heel, though the Wolf-man simply grunted and scrambled up onto the landing. Tyr darted forward, but the beast's sidestep caused him to swing wide and be thrown off balance. The creature struck from behind with frightening strength, splintering the shield affixed to Tyr's back and knocking him headlong into the cabin. Tyr tripped over a wooden chest and scrambled to his feet in time to see the Wolf-man loom in the doorway with eyes wild and drool dripping from its open maw.

Tyr held his breath and waited for it to enter. In the confined space, the colossus would struggle to dodge a throw of his remaining axe.

Discreetly, Tyr slid it from his belt.

The creature paused at the threshold, sensing a trap.

Tyr ground his teeth. 'Come at me, ya ratbag! Or are you only brave enough to take on defenceless women?'

The Wolf-man growled, standing its ground.

Then it broke into a hideous grin.

'Hmm, now there's an idea.' A feral voice, wicked and wry. 'Why waste time with the likes of you when I could keep them ladies company?'

It backed away, eyes on Tyr's axe.

'I'll leave you to play *Viking Werewolf* with my comrades,' it jeered, bounding out of view.

Tyr rushed from the cabin, glimpsing the Wolf-man ascending once more. Climbing steadily, it was already ten feet above where Birger fought on the bridge.

Tyr breathed out.

Took aim.

And flung the axe with all his strength.

Like its comrade before, the beast anticipated the move, swivelling swiftly to catch the axe by the handle. What it had *not* anticipated was Tyr throwing a knife as well. The blade spun like a spindle, flashing moonlight, and sank into the creature's throat with a wet thud.

Its blood splashed over Birger below, and the corpse crashed onto the bridge beside him, startling him out of his wits. '*Now* who's the dolt!? I could have been squashed flat!' he yelled, shaking a fist at Tyr.

However, Tyr's attention was elsewhere. He watched wearily as the axe—the second of his treasured pair—slipped from the Klo's lifeless fingers and plunged into the billowing smoke below.

Hearing the cry as another Wolf-man took it in the eye was *some* consolation. Though not nearly enough. Rage took him, and he swiped his sword at the next hairy bastard to rear its head. And the next. And the next. Severing talons, limbs, and—with one lucky swing—a head.

Scion raced across the bridge toward Birger, stopping briefly to retrieve Tyr's knife from the dead man, whose face remained frozen in a surprised grimace.

'How long can we keep this up?' asked Birger.

'Not very. Best we get a move on,' said Scion.

Scion reached the platform first and hastily followed Tyr up the ladder. Birger followed, then paused to kick the brazier over, adding to the fiery chaos below. Through the haze, he caught sight of the ground far, far below, and felt ill. Had they climbed this high already?

The women were almost to the top. Nala guided them across the last bridge to the ladder for the King's Chamber, while Olle waited on the preceding deck for the Boys to catch up. He seemed to be dragging something from the cabin.

Tyr pulled up short, midway across the bridge, Scion and Birger almost slamming into him.

'Shift to the left, fellas!' cried Olle, wheezing from above. 'I have one last surprise for our furry friends!'

'Olle, wait!' They yelled in concert.

But Olle didn't wait. He kicked a heavily loaded red oak chest, filled with plundered loot, over the landing's edge. It plummeted, dragging a sturdy wooden bed along by a chain. The only option was for the Boys to hold on tight. If the chest destroyed the bridge they'd have no way across to Olle's deck. And if it came down on them . . . well, that could pose a problem.

The running joke was that Olle consisted of one part laziness and two parts luck. *Hamingja*, they called it. A kind of living, breathing Luck passed down the generations, usually bestowing wealth and good fortune upon the bearer. His family had never been wealthy. Their hand-me-down laziness tempered any chance at financial gain, and Olle was not one to break the pattern.

Good fortune, on the other hand, he had in abundance. Yes, he was clumsy. Yet he'd never broken a bone. Yes, he carelessly ate whatever he foraged. Yet had never run a fever. And yes, he was slow at times. Yet his hare-brained ideas—when he took the trouble to form them—always worked.

The red chest dropped.

Bounced off a bulge in the cliffside.

Plunged past the bridge, narrowly missing, and yanked the bed along its trajectory.

The chest smashed into a Wolf-man, and the bed swung level. The chain between them stretched out and caught another Wolf-man in the neck, tearing the creature from the rock face. Both the bed and chest collided with the remaining beasts, wiping them away like smudges from a window.

The inferno burned on.

But other than that . . .

Silence.

'Well?' called down Olle. 'What are you waiting for?'

THE DARKNESS BELOW

Astrid pressed her ear to the door.

There were voices. Definitely close now. Women.

'Hello? Who's out there?' The door was solid iron, though if she could hear them through it, they could hear her.

The sound of stamping boots, coming closer, closer.

Had the Klo caught up?

'Astrid! Are you alright?'

Relief crashed through her like a river.

It was Scion's voice.

Her throat tightened and she fought back the tears. She had been torn from her home. Hunted. Beaten. Bled. Her father was dead, her grandmother abandoned to wild beasts. And the fate of her village hung in the balance.

And yet she smiled.

'In here! I'm in here!' She rattled the handle once more, despite knowing it was locked.

'Hold on!' yelled Scion. 'We'll get you out of there!'

The joyous moment shattered when a metallic grating noise pierced the air. Astrid whirled to see the floor hatch shudder as the two great chains began to recede into the wall. Then came the muffled sound of creaking timber and rattling iron.

The pulley system had been activated.

Something was on its way up.

*

Tyr was last to arrive on the final platform.

This one spanned wider than the others. A balcony for the King to look out across the sea, if he could stomach the terrifying elevation. No Klo stood guard here tonight. Not with the new King's insistence on biting every man without delay. The slaves huddled together, and Tyr realised how cold they must be in their threadbare tunics. He draped his cloak over the nearest shivering woman, cursing that he had not thought to do so earlier.

She turned, eyes bleary, black hair matted against her pale face.

'Thank you, Monsieur,' whispered the Frankish woman.

She turned her back. Stretched to see over the others. Curious to know how the men planned to break into the King's Chamber.

Tyr watched the floating ash settle in her hair.

Moonlight trickled through the velvet curls.

Exhaling deeply, he bent forward, hands on knees.

He had to catch his breath.

Close his eyes.

Just for a moment.

That's all he needed.

And in that moment, the Wolf-man attacked.

It must have slipped around their defences, climbing wide, melting into the shadows, choosing its moment as it clung to the concealed underside of the King's balcony. Soundlessly, it swung up, delivering a swift blow that sent the Frankish woman tumbling over the precipice. She shrieked, eyes wide as she fell, and Tyr jolted to attention.

Bristling, the beast advanced.

Fixed its hideous gaze on him.

Time

waded

through

water . . .

Tyr raised his sword.

Lunged.

The Wolf-man bared its fangs.

Pounced.

If the gods were watching, they seemed divided on which side to favour. With a calculated flourish, Tyr flicked the point up, plunging it between the creature's teeth, over its tongue and out through the base of the skull.

Reflexively, its jaws snapped shut like a spring trap.

Chomping clean through Tyr's wrist.

He screamed.

And screamed.

Blood spurted, voices cried.

A swirl of legs rushed to his aid.

A few strides away, his amputated hand still grasped the sword hilt.

Shadows pressed against the edges of his vision.

He saw the Wolf-man shrink.

Smelt the copper tang of blood.

Felt the cold blackness.

And fell asleep.

*

'I'm sorry, old friend, but this may sting a little,' whispered Olle.

He drew his sword from the brazier, hands shaking, and sealed Tyr's wound with the red-hot steel. With a start, Tyr's eyes snapped open, his body rigid, only to slip back into oblivion without a sound.

'Is he alright?' yelled Birger from the doorway.

'The bleeding's stopped!' called Olle. 'Now, get us off this cursed mountain!'

With a mighty roar, Birger swung the hammer. The clang was deafening, and he staggered back, teeth rattling. The iron door had barely dented, though the hinges in the timber frame had at least loosened.

Scion hacked around the hinge with his axe, once, twice, then stepped out of the way.

'Again!' he cried.

Clang! The bolts tore at the beams, though not enough to come away.

Scion chopped for a second time, harder, the blade biting a deep wedge into the wood.

'Again!'

Crack! At last, the frame split.

They kicked. They bellowed. Then, summoning every ounce of strength, Birger and Scion shouldered through.

When the dust settled, there she was.

Astrid.

'Boys! Over here!' She was bent, trying to drag the heavy bed over the trapdoor. 'They're heading this way!'

Scion rushed to her. This had not been the reunion he'd hoped for. In his fantasy, he envisioned Astrid flying into his arms. Smothering him with grateful kisses. Not rearranging the furniture.

'Are you hurt?' he asked.

'I'll survive. But not if they make it inside!'

'Who?' Then he saw the chains receding into the wall, the hatch in the floorboards. Maintaining a flat expression to hide the immense strain, he heaved it open and peered down.

Cold, musty air wafted up. He gazed into the mountain's hollow crater—what might have been a volcanic heart—now a chasm that stretched down from the narrow top to a wider base. From the shadowy depths there emerged a rectangular platform, resembling a river raft made of trussed beams. It rose steadily up the shaft, drawn by thick chains that coiled around well-worn pulleys.

The Ascentor.

And riding this contraption were the Klo Wolf-men. In one claw, each carried an iron-plated shield—identifying them as the King's guard—and a blazing torch in the other. Crimson flames spat and guttered, illuminating Gorm standing front and centre, glaring up at his prey.

Scion slammed the hatch shut, cursing.

They had very little time indeed.

'His breathing is shallow,' grunted Olle, as he hauled Tyr through the shattered doorway, the women pouring in after them.

Birger lugged the bed over the trapdoor. 'Not sure how much good that will do, to be honest. They're coming up fast.'

Olle frowned. 'There was a shortcut all along?!'

'It wasn't in any of the charts, if that's what you're asking,' soothed Birger. 'Here, let me take him.' But as he reached for Tyr, Nala slapped his hand away.

'Not finished. You wait.' She had a commanding presence, and Birger wondered if Nala was perhaps royalty. A Queen from a far-off land. She reminded him of Lady Freya. Regal, commanding, and compassionate.

'As you wish. But please hurry.'

Nala huffed, binding the wound as best she could and barking orders at the other women.

Scion noticed the window.

The bars had been sawn through.

'I see you've been busy.' He winked at Astrid, and immediately regretted it. Now was certainly not the time for playful banter.

Astrid blushed, frowned, shook her head. 'Everyone!' she called, and all heads turned her way. 'That window's our way out. It's a fair drop to the sea, but it's our only chance right now. Quickly, single file. Let's go!'

'Wait!' Scion rushed to the window. He poked his head through and peered down the full expanse. This was the rear of the mountain, just as steep though lacking any climbing framework. Naked, sheer, slippery cliffside. And far below, a scattering of jagged rocks reached up like spears, moonlit waves exploding against them.

He felt immediately ill. 'Have you seen what's down there?'

'Do we have any other choice?' asked Astrid.

Scion scratched his chin. 'Have you at least *ascertained* the depth?'

Astrid scrunched up her nose. 'Have I . . . what?'

'Never mind,' he mumbled.

Blast! Have I not made sense of that word after all?

Some of the women were crying, one began to wail. Nala tried to maintain calm but they jostled each other, pawing, stirring up panic.

'What's the matter?' asked Scion.

'Some no swim,' said Nala. 'They want you fight the Klo. They want you kill them.'

The Boys exchanged an anxious glance. Now that Tyr was injured, it would be three against twenty. With nowhere to run. Moreover, these Wolf-men were the best of the best, Gorm's elite. And not even Birger's hammer could damage their iron shields.

'People!' cried Astrid. 'We cannot linger!'

Nala swallowed, uncertain for the first time.

'Birger! Give me your hammer,' urged Scion, palm out.

'What? Are you mad?'

'Please! And your sword! You too, Olle!'

Reluctantly, they handed them over, and Scion rushed to where the chain slithered through the wall, and shoved every hilt and blade through a single link.

Clang!

The chain seized up, jammed. Even through the trapdoor, one could hear the great mechanism shudder and whine as it thudded to a halt. Muffled shouts came up from below. Gorm could not be pleased.

Scion beamed. At last, Astrid had witnessed one of his cunning plans come to—

The chains rattled and bobbed, rhythmically, like a pulse through an iron vein.

Birger backed away in astonishment. 'I think they're climbing the chains.'

'You must be joking!' Olle had just about had enough of this night.

Birger withdrew his hammer from the chain, and made short work of smashing the wooden bed-frame and table to pieces.

'Grab one! Timber should keep you afloat! I'll stay back until everyone is away.'

'We're out of time,' called Astrid, clambering up to the window frame. 'Come, sisters. Each of us will help who we can! We can survive this if we keep our heads!'

Then, without even taking a breath, she jumped.

'Astrid!' cried Scion.

'You heard her!' Olle thundered across the room, his belly scraping the window frame as he leaped through. It was difficult to distinguish whose shrill scream could be heard plummeting toward the sea, but it lasted for an unsettling length of time.

Scion leaped up to the window's ledge.

He gazed down the mountainside one more time.

Bile burned his throat.

And he leaped.

As the wind howled past, it drowned out all other sound. The air, sharp as a blade, cut through his clothes, stung his eyes, and the black sea rushed up to meet him. Slamming into the surface was like running headlong into a wall. The crash wrenched his shoulder from its socket, his scream strangled by a gulp of water. Instantly, the iciness clenched its fist. Inky waves surged from all directions, carrying salty foam and stinging spray. Dragged under, Scion wriggled free of his cloak with his one good arm, battling the pain and the numbing cold.

He swam. Gasping. Sputtering.

The rear of the mountain loomed in moonlit silhouette, and Scion saw the beach at its base, thinner here than at the island's forefront. It was too dark to see if Astrid or Olle had made it.

A wail crescendoed until the first woman crashed into the water, not a stroke away. Swallowed by the waves, she reached up in desperation, and Scion caught her by the wrist. More screams, more splashes—a hailstorm of women crashing all around. One poor soul took a dive into the rocks, her head splattering open like a ripe pumpkin. Then another smashed feet first into the same rock—spine, legs, and ribs crunching on impact.

Birger was next, narrowly missing the reef. Surfacing, he gasped, struggling to keep Tyr's lolling head above the churn. He could see the stronger swimmers trying to drag the weaker ones to the floating timbers, but there were too many, and some sank into the everlasting deep.

At last, Scion collapsed upon the shore.

Astrid was there with Olle, hauling women away from the slurping backwash. Scion vomited salt water, dragged himself to his feet, and peered up the mountain. It did not seem that the Klo would be taking the same way down. Why risk the drop when they had the Ascentor?

Birger passed Tyr over to a pair of women and strode towards Scion.

'Need a hand with that?' asked Birger.

'A hand with w—argh!' Without warning, the big man wrenched Scion's shoulder back into place.

'My thanks, brother,' groaned Scion, glancing around. 'How many made it?'

'Not all, but more than expected, if the truth be told.'

Olle rushed over. 'Scion! There's a shipyard here! The Klo's entire fleet!'

'Show us!'

Sure enough, a great and shadowed hollow—not quite as large as Klo Hall—housed a dozen ships, each tied to a mooring post. They bobbed in shallow water, polished and proud.

'We can't wait for the tide,' urged Birger. 'We'll need to drag one across the beach.'

'Agreed,' said Scion.

He raced back to shore, darting about wildly in search of Astrid and found her helping the last staggering woman from the sea.

'Nala didn't make it,' she declared, as he rushed to her aid.

'I'm so sorry,' said Scion, and those nearby wept, heartbroken and spent. Perhaps Nala had been a Queen after all. Perhaps, *their* Queen.

'How soon before Gorm gets here?' asked Astrid.

'Soon.'

'Then let us be free of this place.'

'Aye,' said Scion.

And they hurried to the shipyard, side by side.

A SHARED JOY

Freya's cloak fluttered in the whipping wind.

Beneath it, she wore the embroidered mint-green dress that Erik had liked best. She had come here, to the place of his burial, to feel something of his presence. But all she felt was the cold, so the dress remained hidden beneath her furs.

She sat on a fallen log beside the funeral ship.

Dead leaves at her feet.

It was a proud ship, with its carven figurehead facing the cliff's edge and staring out at the panoramic view. Stones covered the deck, piled high, tokens of the people's love for their fallen Chief. Stones that would forever hide her husband from her. The only way to see him again would be to die fighting. Perhaps the Valkyries would find her on the battlefield, and take her on golden wings to the Halls of Valhalla, where the fallen brave feast at Odin's side.

She looked down.

Erik's sword lay in her grasp.

Strange, she could not recall bringing it here . . .

Come to think of it, was this sword not buried with him?

'That blade looks familiar,' came a familiar voice.

Freya gasped. 'Erik!' The sword clattered to her feet. 'How?'

He chuckled at that, slumping down beside his wife.

'Gudrun isn't the only one who dreams, Freya.' He lifted the sword to dust off the leaves. 'Well? Stop gawking and say hello.'

Freya wanted to fling her arms around him, but, as in dreams of this kind, sensed that yielding to the impulse would shatter the delicate reality around her.

'Erik . . . They killed you.' It was all she could think to say.

Erik placed the sword between them.

'Looks like you're fixing to right that wrong,' he said.

'By Thor's hammer, you will be avenged.' A vow, strong as steel, fierce as flame.

'I would expect nothing less from the Alpha.'

A sudden weariness came over Erik, and Freya had to restrain herself from touching his arm. 'Around and around we go, Freya. Violence begetting more violence begetting even more.'

Her hand recoiled. 'What is that supposed to mean? You would have me let the matter lie?'

He flashed her one of his roguish grins. 'I would not presume to persuade you of anything, Wife. But I would have you think of the future once all this is over.'

Freya shifted in her seat. 'You assume I will *survive* this.'

'I hope it. For your sake, and for Astrid's.'

Astrid. Had Vali's Boys found her? Was she safe?

Erik eyed her tenderly.

'She loves you, you know? For all your squabbles, a mother is the sun and the stars to her daughter.'

'And she is the bright shining moon to me.'

'Then all you need do is let her shine.'

Something in the way he said it made her wonder if the dead kept secrets from the living. And for some strange reason, her mind drifted to a tale from her childhood—of the fabled Wolf, Hati, relentlessly pursuing the Moon across the sky.

'Gudrun has returned,' she said.

'I know. *Mother Dearest*. And what will you do?'

Freya sighed. 'I don't know. She could never see my true self. Perhaps she is too old to change her view of me.'

'While there is breath, there is time. Mine is spent, Wife, but Gudrun's is not.' He shuffled closer. 'Do you remember the day she left the village?'

'Aye. She left you a gift.'

'That's right. A battle horn, engraved with runic patterns, and laid at our doorstep. I think, deep down, she's been waiting all these years to hear it call her back home.'

The wind swept between them.

Leaves rustled at their feet.

At last, Erik lifted his gaze to the ship. 'I thought you might have brought me marigolds.'

Freya bit her lip, grappling with her shame. The day of Erik's funeral was a blur. She had meant to lay their favourite flower on his body but, at the last instant, withheld them—afraid to lose something in the act of giving.

She deflected with a joke.

'Well, I recalled that their pollen made you sneeze.'

'Ah,' nodded Erik, choosing not to press.

'Vali says I should speak to the people,' said Freya, steering the conversation into new territory. 'Deliver a rousing speech to prepare them for what's coming.'

'Freya, the Orator,' grinned Erik. 'Now that would be a sight to behold.'

'Don't tease! I'm being serious!'

'*Warriors of Runolodda, we stride into the fray, for glory awaits those who dare!* Thus spake Freya the Fearless!'

She rolled her eyes. 'Erik the Erudite. Cheeky charmer with a silver tongue.'

His mouth quirked into a lopsided smile. *'A well-spoken thought kindles the hearth of understanding.'*

'Ho! Now you're just showing off!'

They laughed as they always had, high and free, two souls warmed by a shared joy.

Freya stood and strode over to the ship. She ran her fingertips across the hull. Each plank overlapped the next, keeping it secure.

Keeping it safe.

'You always knew the right thing to say, Erik. And the people loved you for it. I wish I had your words right now. Things being what they are.'

'There are many ways to speak, wife. And some are far greater than words.'

She strode to the cliff's edge and gazed out at the far Northern mountains, snow on their ancient heads. 'I was ever in your shadow, Erik. Making the small decisions while you tended to the grand. I fear I may not be able to give the people what they need.'

'It's the small decisions that matter most. They stitch the cloth together and make the garment strong. The people look to you now, Freya. Not because of me, but because of every small thread you sewed. Every wound you healed. Every divide you bridged.'

The air shifted, and Freya sensed the moment begin to fade. And with it, the ghost of her dead husband, who, she realised at last, was only speaking her own thoughts back to her.

'Please. Don't leave,' she begged.

His words came as soft as an echo. 'Where you go, I will go.'

'How can I lead without you?' she asked him. Asked herself.

'You lead them already, though you cannot see it. They trust you, Freya. Trust yourself. That's all any of us can do.'

And then he was gone.

She stood in the icy wind for a moment longer.

The air was colder than before.

And yet, a warmth had spread through her.

RED DAWN

'Help! He isn't breathing!'

Astrid rushed across the deck toward the cry. After many hours under sail, the sea still tossed and hissed like a restless serpent, buffeting her as she ran.

'Step back!' she ordered, dropping to her knees where Olle tended his wounded friend. She pressed her ear to Tyr's chest. The pulse was fading, a feeble echo in his veins. All eyes settled on her now. Expectant. Imploring. She was the Witch, after all. She could perform miracles.

Yet again, Astrid wanted to weep.

The journey had been an ordeal, fraught with challenges.

In the first hour, the ship skirted the saw-toothed reef at a speed that made her hair stand on end. And when a wave hit their flank, one woman lost her footing and toppled overboard.

They spent the second hour shivering, looking over their shoulders for the Klo fleet to appear. Clouds draped across the starlit sky, limiting the crew's navigational means to the direction of the wind.

The sky began to lighten by the third hour, and they made good speed across open water, their hearts lifting with hope.

But the fourth hour dampened that hope. A fine mist rolled in, swaddling the ship in a ghost-like shroud. And with no supplies on board, thirst took hold, exacerbated by the many bouts of seasickness. Scion suffered through the nausea while he leaned out at the prow, calling warnings to Birger and Olle who manned the rear steering oar.

The fifth and sixth hours had been hardest. The mist had thickened, further impairing visibility. Astrid had heard Scion mutter to his men about the Klo, urging them to stay vigilant, even as they struggled to keep their heavy eyes open.

And now, as the seventh hour descended upon them, Tyr lay dying in her arms.

She whispered a swift prayer to Njord for aid and safe passage.

And then it struck her—she could perform *one particular* miracle.

It occurred to Astrid that she had not yet told Scion of her half-blood power. Her gift. Her curse. How would he see it? How would he see her? Was he the sort of man to be intimidated by an *unnatural* woman?

She would soon find out.

Wincing, she pricked her finger on a splinter and squeezed a drop into Tyr's mouth.

'What are you doing?' snapped Olle.

She saw Scion frown.

Take a step toward her.

Then her blood took effect.

Tyr jerked awake, his limbs stretching out rapidly, extending, thickening, growing hair, growing claws. His ribs seemed to cave in, then spring out wider than before, with his head thrust back, teeth growing into vicious points, and his chest bulging like dough in the oven.

'By the gods!' yelped Olle, scrambling away.

Healing power coursed through Tyr's new body, sealing the wound and sending blessed breath to his lungs. Tyr the Wolf-man stood, and Scion rushed forward with a roar, ready to fight. Snapping back to his senses, Birger shook off the shock and raised his hammer, unsure of his next move.

'Hold, brothers.' It was Tyr's voice, after a fashion, though he spoke as if chewing gravel in a thunderstorm. 'It's me. It's alright.'

He held up his hands, examining them with keen interest.

One was a claw. One wasn't there at all.

'What's happened to me?'

For the second time, all eyes turned to Astrid.

'It was the only way to save you,' she said, palms raised. 'You were bitten. The wound had turned.'

'Turned?'

There seemed no way to sweeten the truth. If Scion could not bear it, well, that would be beyond her control. 'Once the blood of the bitten has darkened, I can provoke The Change.'

'How?' asked Tyr.

It was Scion who answered, stepping closer. 'Because she is Moonlight. Is that not so?'

Astrid swallowed. Scion had looked beneath her skin and seen true. And the way he had said it . . . as though she were *his* moonlight. 'A living reservoir, yes. Earmarked by Gorm to bottle and store for his master plan.'

'Which is *what*, exactly?'

She was about to speak when the Klo ship struck.

Its prow sliced through the mist and rammed into their starboard side, the impact sending ripples through the juddering timbers. The jolt threw Scion into the mast. Sent women reeling across the deck. The ship pitched on its keel, dangerously close to capsizing. Miraculously, no-one fell overboard. In the time it took for the ship to right itself, the Klo vessel had swung alongside, fierce faces roaring across the narrow gap between them. Though it must be said that the sight of a one-armed Wolf-man gave them pause.

Astrid scrambled to her feet and ducked behind the colossal Tyr.

'They are but men once more,' he growled. 'It would appear that your Moonlight wears off, Astrid.'

'You only have a few hours,' she said. 'Make the most of it!'

Scion reached for his sword.

And cursed.

His sword—his *father's* old sword—was in the King's Chamber, lodged in the chain.

He took a quick inventory: one axe, one seax, and a bow with no arrows. Birger had retrieved his hammer. Olle had a stubby hatchet, and could borrow Tyr's knife. It would have to do. There were Klo shields hooked to the ship's rail, and he snatched one, rallying everyone to grab theirs. Astrid took one for herself and tested its weight in her slender arm.

She joined a group at the steering oar. Without weapons, it was all they could do to help. One stout-hearted woman—a sandy-haired Norman—replaced Scion's position at the prow, standing by to guide them clear of danger while more women raced to the rowing benches.

There came a shout from the enemy, followed by a strange whistling noise. Like a row of vipers, iron grappling hooks flew and bit into their rail, narrowly missing Birger's hand. In an instant, retractable footbridges were in place—each slung between twin chains—connecting the two vessels.

Scion bellowed, axe raised. 'Forward! There's one for each of us!'

True enough, there were precisely four bridges, soon creaking and swaying with the advance of Klo warriors.

Tyr sprang forward, tearing the first grapple free with his great claws. A section of the rail went with it, and the bridge collapsed, dropping men into the waves. Archers fired a volley in his direction. And while most found his shield, a few arrows pierced his shaggy hide. Thankfully, these tips were iron, not silver. With a primal roar, Tyr leaped the gap and landed on the Klo ship, swiping savage claws through his attackers.

Tyr, the living weapon.

Scion rushed to meet the second line, ramming his shield into the front-runner. The man staggered back into his comrades, and Scion stole a momentary glimpse of Birger wobbling on the third footbridge as he hammered the foe left and right into the drink. Olle, beyond his line of sight, bounced on the fourth bridge with all his considerable weight, causing a wave rather like the crack of a whip. The Klo were forced to hold fast to the chains or be flipped into the air.

Now on the Klo ship, Tyr tore through the enemy, splashing blood across the planking with every bite and jagged swipe. Having one arm did not seem to slow him down. The stump held his shield. It was also his hammer. And the Klo were his anvil.

However, these were no disorderly thugs.

As one, the Klo flowed from one manoeuvre to the next, questing, seeking a way through his agile defences. They darted in and out of his reach, forming shield walls in varying configurations. Here and there, a blade found purchase, and Tyr needed to work as hard on his defence as on his offence. He caught sight of their bitten forearms, and envisioned how swiftly the battle would be over if they were to reach Astrid and drink her blood.

Vaulting onto the Klo mast, he shredded the sail, and the vessel quickly lost speed. He would need to leap back to the other ship. If he could remove the remaining grapples, his company would be free to make their escape. A sudden pain blossomed when a spear skewered the back of his thigh. He roared, dropping to the deck and backhanding the culprit with his shield arm.

Tugging the spearhead free, he shot a glance toward Scion. The Klo were shoving him back, inching closer to their prey's ship. Tyr ran with a subtle limp and catapulted himself into the air. He crashed down on Scion's gangway, the sheer force sent some men tumbling into the abyss. Others clung desperately to the swaying handrails.

'Help the others!' roared Tyr. 'I'll get the grapples away!'

'Good thinking!' yelled Scion, and thundered back down the footbridge.

Tyr followed, dodging arrows until he reached the rail. Then, with both claws, he twisted and crunched the wood until the iron hooks broke free.

Failing to retreat in time, the Klo plunged into the water.

Two bridges down, two to go.

Scion nodded at Tyr, rushing towards the stern.

Birger fared well on the third gangway, though Olle's tactic had run its course on the fourth. Now, joined by some of the courageous women, Olle held back the Klo, the bridge swaying wildly over the splashing waves as their ship was forced to drag the slower Klo vessel. Blood ran down Olle's leg where a sword had poked under his shield, but still he pushed back, roaring like he'd never roared before. An arrow took one woman in the chest, another in the gut, and Scion called for them to keep their shields raised.

He shoved his way up the footbridge to reach Olle. 'You alright, brother?'

'Thriving,' groaned Olle.

Scion grinned and slammed his shield into the enemy's line.

With the first and second footbridges disabled, Tyr positioned himself at the third grapple.

'Fall back, Birger! I can unhook it!'

Birger the Bear glanced back, met Tyr's gaze, and felt an arrow pierce his side. He winced, fell to his knees, and the Klo shoved him over onto his back.

Without a moment's hesitation, Tyr pounced.

Stretching, he grasped the chain, and swung beneath the footbridge, his clawed feet skimming the water. Spray arced up as he launched high, twisting mid-air to dive down on those who would dare trample his friend. His landing sent a shockwave, barging men into the depths. It was a miracle that Birger didn't tumble in after them.

At the same moment, the Norman woman cried out from the prow, in chorus with the Klo's lookout man. Both had spotted a rock loom through the mist. Both called for their ship to veer clear. Astrid's group heaved their rudder left, while the Klo banked right, pulling the footbridges taut. The chains shuddered violently and the grapples tore at the rails.

Then, with a dreadful crack, the wood splintered.

And the remaining footbridges plunged into the sea.

Men shouted in horror, and Scion struggled with Olle to stay afloat amid the panic. He felt himself pulled down, and the last thing he saw was Tyr enveloping Birger in his arms before the waves sucked them under.

With the sudden slack, both ships lurched off-kilter, sending their crews tumbling like dice across the deck. Women flew, fell, crashed into one another. The Norman lookout was flung overboard with a shriek. Astrid clung to the steering oar, feeling her arm go numb as her elbow struck the deck.

'Scion!' She leaped to her feet and sped to the splintered rail.

The Klo ship had narrowly missed the rock, though it lagged behind now, its shredded black sail fluttering uselessly. The sea roiled. There was no sign of the Boys.

'Scion!' she cried again, but he was lost in her wake.

Beyond her reach once more.

*

'All hands to the oars! Row! Row! Row!' roared the Klo Captain.

'We'll never catch up,' muttered his second-in-command. 'They're under full sail and already the mist is clearing.'

The Captain seized him by the throat. 'Will you be the one to tell Gorm that his prize got away? He gathers the entire fleet as we speak! So, shut your mouth and join the others! We have a slippery salmon to catch!'

The crew seized the oars and heaved.

No-one noticed the claw that clung to the stern.

THE NORNS OF FATE

Gudrun swam through the Dreamspace.

She had followed Yggdrasil's roots from their tapered tips to the base stem that stretched down into endless darkness. The Runes of Reality were clear carvings now, bony letters that spoke of the future in shimmering colours: Snow-white sacrifice. Blood-red battle. Golden hope and raven-black death.

She drifted closer to the central root.

A doorway of starlight materialised on its surface, opening to reveal a much brighter light within. Gudrun had to shield her eyes. Beyond a doubt, the light was a living thing, a sentinel permitting passage only to those granted permission by those waiting beyond.

She slipped through.

There came a heat, a crackling surge, then—

A room.

It looked rather like her cottage in the woods. Larger, taller, but remarkably familiar. And it was old. Very old. Nature had clawed back much, with a thick carpet of mushrooms over the muddy floorboards and skeletal branches poking their elbows through the crumbling walls.

Sunlight filtered through the derelict roof and cast a pool of light on a stone structure in the centre of the room. At first, Gudrun took it for a pedestal, for it stood waist-high and measured no wider than a roundshield. But as she stepped nearer, she saw sunlight dancing on the gleaming surface.

Water.

This was Urd, the Wellspring of Destiny.

And only the Norns of Fate ever drew from its depths.

A motherly voice spoke from the shadows, gentle and tender, startling Gudrun nonetheless. 'What have we here? Oh, don't be afraid. Tell us your story. From whence have you strayed?'

A second voice rasped. 'Uninvited she comes, in our home she appears. A North-born soothsayer with grey eyes that peer.'

A third voice sounded almost childlike, though no less unsettling. 'Oh, hush now, old Crone. Can you not see? Her presence is welcome, as welcome can be.'

Gudrun shifted uncomfortably and tried to sound reassuring. 'No encroachment nor affront was intended, Great Sisters. Please, show yourselves that we may speak.'

They emerged from the shadows.

Instantly, Gudrun wished they had not.

From the waist up, each bore the likeness of a woman. Shawls of twinkling starlight flowed over their shoulders, and their ancient gaze held an otherworldly glow. Yet, as the eye descended, enchantment gave way to nightmare. Instead of human legs, their lower halves were arachnid, supported by the eight sinuous legs of a massive spider, their tips sharp as chisels. Silk strings trailed behind them—sticky, strong, inescapable webs—the threads of Fate.

The first Norn was named Mother. Her face, nurturing and kind, was framed by a cascade of mint-green hair that rustled like leaves in an orchard.

The second was younger with an innocent look. The Maiden. Her locks were white and pure, braided at the sides and shimmering like fresh hope.

The last was the Crone, twisted and bent, her deep purple hair like the bristles of a scarecrow's straw mop. Her face was lined and cruel, and she looked older than Time. Yet, these were the Sisters, the Infinite Norns, each as ancient as the others. The same unknowable age. And, some said, the same person.

'Do I dream?' whispered Gudrun, trying in vain to still her beating heart. 'Or are you real, Sisters?'

The spidery Maiden leaped for joy and clung to the ceiling. 'She asks if we're real, this inquisitive widow! Oh, please may we keep her? She'll live in my shadow.'

The Crone scuttled close, dragging her web-swollen body until her breath blew in Gudrun's face. 'I trust not these Seers, these women of Sight. They drink from our waters, they plunder our light.'

Descending on a web, the Mother ran her fingers through Gudrun's hair, as though inspecting a child for lice. 'Seers are no thieves, Crone, they take what they need. Small slivers of foresight, so small they mislead.'

The Crone ignored her. 'She picks our tomorrows before they are ripe! Divulges them near, divulges them wide! Only to puff up this parasite's pride!'

'Pride?' exclaimed Gudrun, then instantly bit her lip. She had not meant to voice the question. Gudrun had been taught never to question the Wise Ones. But she had not asked to be here and had not expected to be so scrutinised. 'I only ever wished to help my son. To help my people. To warn them of danger. Where is the pride in that?'

The Crone hacked a ragged cough. 'To prove you were gifted, to prove you were right! And where did that lead you, oh daughter of Sight?'

Gudrun kept her tongue. Despite her hostility, the Crone spoke true. For their part, the Norns had shown her the future. However, in Gudrun's haste and through her prejudice she had misinterpreted their vision. And when Erik had resisted her *truth*, she had chosen only to argue, not to listen. The punishment for that one simple mistake had been years of self-imposed isolation.

The Mother waved the Crone away. 'Peace now, sweet Gudrun. We know who you are: the Drum that sounds warnings, the Heart lined with scars. Do you not perceive it? It's not *what* you see. All that bears weight is the *way* that you see.'

Gudrun kept her gaze low. 'It has become difficult to sift meaning from my dreams of late. They're nothing but a muddle of images, too jumbled to piece together. Why must they be so ... cryptic?'

The Mother said, 'Threads can cover or unwrap.'

The Maiden said, 'Threads confuse and overlap.'

The Crone said, 'Threads entangle, bind and trap.'

They had performed this rite from the Beginning, intoning the triad of rhymes known as the Tercet. It was an invisible circle of trust, and of power. Once begun, it needed completing, allowing a life-giving force to flow through the Three. A surge of energy that arced back on itself, like a spoon stirring their essence together. As one, the Norns breathed in deeply. They seemed to grow in size, and their eyes glowed all the brighter.

It was a show of strength.

Though Gudrun could not fathom why.

'I saw a Wolf in the mountains, its fallen foe beheaded. Tell me plainly—is Freya that Wolf? Or will Gorm be victorious?'

The Mother replied. 'Oh, sweet dear, you must not fret. For all will perish before the End.'

Gudrun met her gaze, frustration beginning to simmer beneath the surface. 'Which end? The end of their days? The end of the battle? Or do you speak of the end of all things? Please—no more riddles, no more rhymes. Just tell me what will happen to my people. What will become of Freya and Astrid? If Runolodda is to fall, how may I prevent it?'

'*Prevent it*, she says,' giggled the Maiden. 'Oh, that makes me laugh. No-one can stray from the Norn-chosen path.'

The Crone cackled too. 'We set every choice, every footstep in stone. They can't be undone, they can't be disowned.'

Gudrun bristled, jutting her jaw. 'Nevertheless. I wish to know.'

The Mother sighed. 'See for yourself, look into the Well. Your fears may appear there, they may be dispelled.'

Unsteadily, Gudrun approached the Well of Urd. Ever since she could crawl, she had heard fireside tales of these waters. To personally engage with them was another matter entirely. The Well called to her, drew her near. She stepped to the rim and peered inside.

She saw Astrid struck from her horse, felled by a sword.

Freya, trapped beneath a mountain, drowning in darkness.

The vast Klo army, marching on Runolodda.

The village gates breached.

A field of human heads, rotting on spikes.

A pile of corpses.

She tore herself away, gasping, weeping. Despair gripped her heart. The Well had given her answers, though none were as she had hoped. Falling to her knees, she wiped her eyes and tried to catch her breath.

The Mother loomed over her and stroked her hair. 'Did you see clearly? Saw what you feared? A tangle, a scramble, are the cobwebs of Wyrd.'

'I—I . . .' As Gudrun spoke, a strange sensation stole over her—a crackle, a heat—and her lips vibrated as though whistling a tune. 'That cannot be true. There must be a way. This won't be our ending, won't be our Doomsday.'

The Norns froze.

They cast a discreet glance at one another. Gudrun felt odd. Had she meant to rhyme, or had the words come to her from elsewhere? And was it only her imagination, or had the Crone shrunk a little? Regardless, the bent old woman seemed particularly unsettled by the verse.

'You must be leaving, now you must be gone. We Three have our duties, so hurry along.'

Gudrun felt the words come and turned them over in her mouth.

'I still have my questions. I still have my doubts. Besides, I suspect I won't find my way out.'

The Maiden dropped down from the ceiling, springing joyfully about. 'Now here is a gamble! Now here is a game! Oh, Mother, dear Mother, who'll stake out their claim?'

'Silence, fool Maiden! A danger draws near. There's not been a challenge for ten thousand years.'

The Crone hissed. 'Bite your tongue, Mother, she knows not our ways. Let's tend to our burdens, and send her away.'

Gudrun saw the shape of things, the way this worked. She glared at the Crone. The seemingly all-powerful were, at times, only so because none dared resist them.

'Your rhyming grows lazy, oh Crone of the Norns. Perhaps you grow weary, your power outworn?' Gudrun had overstepped. The Crone lunged, spider-spry, pressing her snarl into Gudrun's face.

'It does not become you, these rhymes on your tongue! The Well has his Sisters, the Three who are One. You are but mortal—bare, blind, and blate. Return to your realm where your ruin awaits!'

But Gudrun would not be cowed.

'I know my shortcomings. They've not been ignored. They call me the Oracle. Perhaps I am more!'

The Crone's eyes grew wide and felt her power dim. To reclaim it, she would need to invoke the Tercet, calling on her Sisters to complete the circle she would begin.

'Threads can cover or unwrap!' yelled the Crone.

Reflexively, the Maiden answered. 'Threads confuse and overlap.'

But before the Mother could complete the loop, Gudrun stepped in, and felt power flow into her as she turned the poem's meaning with a verse of her own.

'Yet threads can fray, unravel or snap!'

'No!' cried the Crone, and the room began to shake. The roots retreated into the walls, the mushrooms sank into the floor, and the vines melted into the air. A gust began to swirl around the room, with Gudrun at its centre.

'What have you done?' roared the Crone, her hands turning slowly to dust before her eyes. The Mother shielded the Maiden from the spinning debris, and Gudrun lifted her chin, hands held high as her hair took on a deep purple hue.

'I am Gudrun of the Woods! My son lies in death! I shall not lose others, not while I have breath!'

Outside, Yggdrasil itself shook, and a Great Horn blew once more.

Gudrun sensed herself ascending, surrounded by an electrifying whirlwind of power. Looking down, she saw her legs had split into eight spidery limbs. Her body swelled and filled with her own silken threads.

'I cannot linger! My family awaits! We claim our own Destiny! We spin our own Fate!'

There was the sound of a mighty rushing wind.

Then, silence.

Gudrun stood alone in the room. It was smaller, squatter, fresher. She glanced around. The Well was gone. The Sisters, distant echoes. This was her own cottage in the woods, the scent of pine on the breeze.

It melted away, and she floated once more in the Dreamspace.

Only now, all was light.

She felt peace at last, and longed to remain here.

But it was time to wake up.

DEADFALL

The sun stood high when the warning drum sounded.

Gorm's fleet appeared on the horizon.

Throughout Runolodda, feet kicked up dust, folk scrambling to don armour, gather weapons, and test all fortifications. Smoke rose from the Great Hall where communal pots of aromatic stew boiled. Vali had ordered a hearty meal prepared for all—they would need their strength today.

He met the anxious gaze of every man and woman he passed, offering encouragement with a nod. Those with children worried most, entrusting a group of the elderly to hide them in the hills. The livestock, too, had been led away, far downriver where the clamour would not startle them. If Runolodda were to fall, the prospects for rebuilding would be meagre.

He rounded a corner and pulled up short. Freya sat by the door of the Great Hall, keeping her gaze from those who entered, focussed on sharpening her sword with a whetstone. She wore full battledress. Leather boots, tightly laced. A chest plate, cinched at the waist with thick leather straps. Articulated leather bracers, studded with polished iron. And finally, Erik's helmet on her head, its nose guard bearing the image of an eagle. The effect was arresting, and those who passed did so in silence.

'Now, this seems more becoming of you,' he said with a soft smile.

'I am pleased to see you satisfied at last, Vali.' She made a face at his protesting look. 'I jest. And . . . about last night. You were right to . . . well . . .' Her eyes thanked him. It was enough, and Vali waved aside the moment like smoke.

'Friends?' he asked.

'Friends.'

He nodded and strode off for the main gate.

A light patter approached from behind, and he rolled his eyes.

'Vali!' It was the Songbird, fretting like a finch.

'I'm quite busy at the moment, Tove.'

'It's just that I heard tell that the cattle have been taken.'

'That's right. For safekeeping.' He reached the stairs to the parapets and took them two at a time, Tove keeping as close as his shadow.

'Well, what about the sacrifice?'

'The what?'

'We need the blessing of Odin. A sacrifice must be made.'

Vali halted at the first battlement and squeezed his eyes shut. Exhaling, he turned to her with a smile. 'I'm afraid it's too late for that, lass. The gates must remain sealed and I can't have you wandering off.'

'I could ask Torsten to accompany me.'

'Torsten is on lookout duty. It was he who sounded the alarm earlier.'

'But there must be a sacrifice if—'

'Quiet!' He raised a finger, cocking his ear. 'What's that noise?'

An odd metallic grating could be heard. Had the drawbridge come loose? No, this was a rhythmic scrape, slow and steady as a heartbeat. It appeared to be coming from within the village walls.

Scrape. Scrape. Scrape.

He pushed past Tove and descended the stairs, running back to the Hall, the sound growing as he neared. Turning the corner, he gaped at what he saw.

Scrape. Scrape. Scrape.

Every one of the villagers—old and young, men and women—sat before Freya, sharpening their blades on whetstones of their own. They covered the square before the Great Hall, gently rocking in unison as Freya kept time.

Scrape. Scrape. Scrape.

She looked like a shieldmaiden of legend, her gaze fierce as a furnace. The people of Runolodda met that gaze, and returned it with equal intensity as each heart caught the fire of her rage like dry grass in the sun.

Freya shifted her gaze to Vali, and an inescapable truth dawned on him.

This was no Chieftain.

This was the Alpha.

*

'Brace yourselves!' cried Astrid.

The keel struck the shoreline, sliced through wet sand, and came to a sudden stop. The ship leant over like a weary traveller. Astrid was first over the rail, feet splashing down into the breakers. She glanced back out to sea.

'Hurry!' she yelled, already racing up Crescent Beach. 'They are upon us!' Only four of the original group of a dozen slaves had survived, and they clung to life as they fled.

Almost within bowshot, Gorm's fleet closed in. Eleven Klo warships bore down at full speed, black sails full, sweaty rowers shouting at the top of their lungs. Gorm gazed steadily ahead from the deck of the flagship. Crescent Bay spread out before him, with the steep switchback footpath looming beyond.

He flexed his neck. Last he was here had been the night of the Full Moon Ritual. The Alpha had defeated him, slain his men. Now, with almost three hundred warriors at his command, he would crush Runolodda beneath his heel and make that She-Wolf beg for the mercy of a swift death.

His ship knifed through the waves, briskly closing the distance. Gorm shielded his eyes from the sun, squinting. There were slaves hurrying up the beach, agitating a flock of crows that pecked at . . . something—an object tall as a man, and glinting brightly. What sort of carcass glinted?

Then Gorm saw what it was.

Coming ashore, he dropped to the sand. He took one step toward the object.

Then another.

'Yah!' He swished the crows away with his axe. The stench compelled him to cover his nose. Blades caught the sun's rays, wickedly puncturing all parts of a dead man's flesh.

'Ulrick . . .' he whispered.

More Klo ships came ashore, men shouting and whooping, scrambling up the beach after the slaves, who had already begun their ascent. Some men slowed to lead horses down wooden ramps. Others slowed to witness Gorm kneel at his friend's feet, touching the brooch at his breast—the Klo salute.

'Come,' urged one warrior to his comrade. 'The King wants the girl. She cannot slip our net.' They dashed off, and by the time they had reached the steep slope, Gorm was back on his feet and running.

High above, Astrid's lungs burned, her legs screamed.

Yet there was no time to catch a breath. The Klo climbed quickly, and once the exhausted women reached the summit, Astrid would still need to lead them across Red Meadow and make it all the way down Two-Mile-Hill before reaching the safety of Runolodda. She heard the Klo shouting close behind— Men of the Wild Hunt. With a resounding cry, she rallied her strength, and clambered up onto the flat.

'Hello, Astrid.'

She almost tumbled back over the edge in shock. 'Torsten!'

'Step aside, please Astrid.' The bull-necked logger smiled as he helped the last women over the ledge. 'I have something special prepared for our visitors.'

He pulled back camouflage branches to expose a tall stack of lumber—tightly bound pines, thick and immensely heavy.

'Back, back,' he urged, then hefted an enormous bearded axe over his head.

And cut the ropes.

Gorm had reached the first bend in the steep path when the ground shook. He looked up. Careening down like the wrath of the gods, massive logs tumbled and crashed, sharp cracks drowning out all cries of desperation. There was no escape. Those close to the summit were squashed like grapes, their cries stifled. Whether the Klo ran, ducked, or pressed against the rock, they were obliterated in the surging turmoil.

Gorm gasped, slid down the slope, and surged into the swarm of warriors fleeing back across the beach. Logs hailed down, bouncing and colliding with deafening thuds and splintering snaps. As he dove forward, they struck the beach, spewing up sand and shuddering like a colossal bundle of kindling.

Gorm rose to his feet, dusting damp sand from his cloak, and glared up the slope. A handful of fortunate souls hurried down.

They dared not face the possibility of a second wave. The path —top to bottom—was smeared with red flesh.

Björn, Captain of the King's Guard, staggered over, blood oozing from a gash on his forehead.

'Curse these farmers! They've cut us off!'

Gorm kept his calm. 'These farmers think like an army. Using the high ground to their advantage. We may lose some time, but the only way forward is around.' He glanced back to see the remaining seven or eight ships reach the shore. 'We will take the coastal trail, then march up through the woods. Send scouts ahead. There may be more traps to follow.'

'Yes, my King.'

'And Björn?'

'Yes, my King?'

'Fetch me a warhorse.'

A RUSHED REUNION

'What's happening?' called Freya.

The horn had sounded. Feet scampered for the main gate from all corners of the village, people yelling. Yet, the atmosphere appeared to hold more excitement than dread.

'It's Astrid, my Lady!' cried an old woman. 'She's come home!'

'Astrid!' Freya ran, shoving through the gathering crowd. She called up to the watchmen. 'Is she alone? Is Gorm here already?'

'No sign of Gorm yet! Though there are women with her!'

'Let them in, by Odin!'

Freya wasted no time and darted through before the drawbridge finished lowering.

There she was.

Her daughter.

Golden hair bobbing as she ran barefoot down the hill. They met on the open gravel, clutching one another in a fervent embrace, tears streaking their cheeks. It had only been days apart, though it felt like years.

'Daughter! Oh, my daughter!' Unbridled joy. A mother's

pride. 'Come inside! Come, all of you!' She beckoned the bedraggled women trailing behind. One look at their grubby white tunics and she knew: these were Klo slaves.

They ran back through the village gates, greeted with an uproarious cheer.

*

Astrid licked her bowl clean.

'You must be famished,' said Freya, scooping a second serving from the pot. 'Have another.'

Astrid suppressed a burp. 'There isn't time, Mother.'

'There is time enough if the Klo have taken the woodland path,' And she handed her daughter the bowl.

Warmed beside the fire, Astrid took it with a weak smile and began gulping down the hot stew. She glanced across at Hedda and her five daughters who occupied nearby tables, inspecting their healing salves and tinctures and tending to the freed slaves. The Great Hall, so often a place of merriment and song, now boasted murder holes for defence, guards at the door, and spikes through the roof. Wholesome on the inside, deadly on the outside.

'So, is this to be our infirmary?' asked Astrid, more for the sake of conversation than a genuine need for confirmation.

'Why? Are you hurt?' asked Freya.

'No, I'm fine. Honestly.' She took another mouthful, hoping her mother would not fill the silence with more of her fussing.

Freya sensed her daughter's tension and quickly changed the subject. 'If only we had time. We might have walked together to your father's resting place. Placed a stone on the cairn in his honour.'

Astrid hesitated. There was that familiar calm before the storm. She turned her gaze back to her meal, not wishing to sour the reunion.

'I don't think so, Mother.'

'Oh? And why not?'

Astrid hesitated. Her father was not *at rest*. He lived in her memory and in every living heart he had touched. And whatever anyone else said or felt, he was certainly *not* a heap of bones, rotting beneath a cairn. But what good would come of such words?

'Perhaps I shouldn't say, Mother.'

'Speak plainly, Astrid. I won't be upset.' Freya truly meant it, surprising herself as much as her daughter.

'Alright,' said Astrid, dropping her eyes. 'To me, a gravesite is simply another sort of cage. We lock the bones away, when in truth, the spirit is finally free.' She paused, took a breath. 'When I die, I want to be burnt on a pyre. All of me. *Bones* and *Being* flying as one to the next world. It is the old way. The way to set the dead free.'

Freya bit her lip.

'For me,' she began, choosing her words with care, 'the thought of visiting Erik brings comfort. Solace endures, even as his physical presence fades. Though I do take your meaning, Daughter. I, too, wish your father freedom.'

Astrid held her gaze, waiting for the inevitable *however*. 'That is . . . good, Mother.'

'However,' said Freya, and she saw her daughter groan inwardly, 'I fear that his freedom will be more hard won than you imagine. For it can only be bought with blood. There shall be no rest for Erik, nor for me, nor for you, until I hold Gorm's head up to the gods and send his screaming soul off to Helheim.'

She had spoken with such casual violence that Astrid had to swallow. 'I see. Well, that would be a fine thing, Mother.' And they shared a smile.

'So,' said Freya, softened by this unexpected closeness, 'your blood transformed Gorm into a Wolf-man?'

'Not exactly. Your bite's venom needed time to spread. Once the wound had blackened, my blood could mix with his to set off The Change.'

'Although his human mind remained unaffected?'

'Precisely. And he's bitten his entire army. All they need now—'

'Is you.' Freya nodded slowly, mulling this over. 'And you could turn me, too?'

'I could. But I'd make an enormous target of you. Gorm will have every arrow, sling, and spear aimed at your heart.'

'Perhaps . . .' said Freya. She knew the power of Wolf-sight, the devastation she could wreak with those claws; more than with a sword. Though Astrid, often possessing her father's ability to see the bigger picture, had a point. Runolodda would lose heart to see their Alpha torn apart. The battle would be lost far sooner than expected.

'And what of the villagers?' she asked, probing the possibilities. 'Transform me now, and I could bite them all.'

'To what end? There would not nearly be enough time for their blood to blacken before Gorm arrives.'

Freya rubbed her knuckles. 'Then we must get you away, Daughter. Go into the hills. Find the elders. They will—'

'No, Mother.' Astrid had hoped to avoid another of their arguments, yet this was too important a point to surrender. 'I won't leave you. Not again.'

'Daughter, you must—'

'I won't lose you too, Mother.' Astrid shut out the image of Scion sinking into the sea; drowning as her father and his father had before him. If she cried now, the floodwaters would never stop flowing. Instead, she gritted her teeth and stared her mother down.

Freya shifted in her seat. 'You would stay and fight?'

'To the death,' said Astrid, resolute.

Freya tried miserably to hide her worry. The battle would be over in a blink if the Klo reached Astrid. She opened her mouth to speak when an inner voice whispered . . .

What did Gudrun see?

Just for a moment, she imagined it to be Erik's voice, faint as a distant sigh, though she could not say for certain. Freya scratched at an eyebrow. Should she trust Gudrun's vision or not? Which would be the lesser evil—to lead Astrid within Gorm's reach, or abandon her to face the Klo army?

Once more, she weighed her words carefully. 'I believe I can defeat Gorm. Though it won't be within the village walls. I must lead him into the mountains. Only there can I lure him to his doom, Alpha against man.'

Astrid frowned. 'You seem so certain he would follow. And of the outcome.'

'There is a prophecy: *The mountains will reveal the Wolf Victorious.*'

'That could mean Gorm,' countered Astrid.

'It could mean me,' insisted Freya.

'Well, then I'm going with you. You can't be the Wolf Victorious without me.'

'Please, Daughter. I cannot lose you either. Bleed me a few droplets so that I can—'

'You may take my blood into the mountains,' interrupted Astrid, 'but I shall carry it there in my living veins. We'll bait

Gorm together. Agreed?' It felt less like a question and more like a door slammed shut.

Freya exhaled. These past days, Astrid had grown. The old fire of compassion and of love was still there. Yet a new flame had emerged—one of defiance, of strength, of an unyielding self-assurance.

'Agreed,' she said at last. 'But keep to my side. Do as I say. Run if I say run. Hide if I say hide. Understood?'

'Understood, Mother,' smiled Astrid. She brought another spoonful to her mouth and paused. '*The mountains will reveal the Wolf Victorious* . . . I've not heard that prophecy before. Who foretold it?'

Freya began to speak when a familiar voice called from the doorway.

'That would be me, Granddaughter.'

'Gudi!' Astrid rushed over, wrapping her grandmother in her arms. 'I thought you were dead!'

'Not yet, my dear. Though I may keel over if I don't get some stew in me.'

It was Freya's turn to tense. Stiffly, she prepared a bowl for Gudrun and set it down before taking a seat opposite the old woman. Astrid shuffled in beside her grandmother, squeezing her wrinkled fingers.

'Gudrun . . .' began Freya.

'Peace, Freya. We have little time and much to discuss, so I will say only what matters.'

Taken aback, Freya simply nodded.

'I have seen much, Freya. And you were right. I have not always seen well. But I say to you now—I have seen you. Seen your spirit. Seen what you were to my son, and what you are to your people.' She saw tears prickle Freya's eyes. 'I have seen the future, yet through a veil. So, regardless of what I *think* I know

… I hope. And that hope rests on what I *do* know—that you are, and ever were, worthy of my trust.'

She allowed the words to settle.

The fire crackled, burning the past and its many hurts to ash.

'Here we are,' Gudrun said at last. '*The Three*.

Mother.

Maiden.

Crone.

Norns of our own Fate. For each of us has chosen our own path.

'Freya, the Mother. Baring her anguish and her wrath before her people. Leading not with her voice but with her actions, inspiring courage in those who gaze upon her fury.

'Astrid, the Maiden. A young witch of her own styling. With her own purpose. To liberate rather than to cage. To summon her people forth rather than hide them away.'

Freya wiped a tear from her cheek.

'And what of you, Gudrun of the Woods? Are you not more than the Crone?'

The old woman hesitated.

Then, tentatively, placed a trembling hand on Freya's, the other on Astrid's.

'I shall be Gudrun of Runolodda once more. I shall be your kin.' She tried to steady those gnarled hands. 'If you would have me.'

Astrid did not hesitate. They called her the Oracle. She called her Grandmother. She leant across and kissed her weathered forehead. 'Of course, Gudi. You are, and ever shall be, one of us. Is that not so, Mother?'

Freya kept silent for an agonising few heartbeats.

She stood, staring down at what remained of her family.

Gudrun tensed, an offender awaiting judgement.

'Well, I suppose that all depends,' said Freya with a wry smile.

'On what?' asked Gudrun.

Freya drew Erik's battle horn from her cloak and handed it over.

'On whether you'll have us in return.'

THE TIPPING POINT

'That's the last of 'em,' beamed Fiske, patting the helmet.

'Quickly, you old goat!' urged Selby. 'Is there too much wax in yer ears? The ground's rumbling! They're almost to the treeline!'

The old men ran across Red Meadow as fast as their aching knees would carry them, and reached the first of the seven pits.

'After you,' offered Selby.

'No, I insist. In you go, old friend,' said Fiske.

'Fine. Where's the rope?'

'What rope?'

'The rope! To get us down there! You were meant to bring it!'

'Well, excuse me! I've been rather busy with the *welcome presentation* for our guests!'

'So have I! Why can't you ever—'

The trees rustled.

'Jump!' hissed Fiske, and the pair dropped into the dark pit.

Gorm was first into the daylight, astride his massive black warhorse. The beast trudged a few paces forward, then stopped short with an agitated neigh. The King's Guard brought their steeds to a halt alongside.

'By the bones of Ymir . . .' gasped Björn.

More Klo emerged. To a man, they fell silent. Red Meadow was a gallery of gore. Maggoty, severed heads on spikes were spread across the grass. Crows pecked at rotting eyeballs. Putrefying skulls dripped muck. Flies buzzed and swarmed. And though decay marred their faces, it was evident to all that these poor wretches were those to encounter the She-Wolf during the Full Moon raid. Presumably, their bodies had washed ashore, where the farmers had butchered their remains.

The display was intended to instil fear. Yet Gorm was pleased to see the opposite effect take hold. His men stood appalled. The farmers had shown no shred of respect to the fallen dead. How dare they? Gorm suppressed a smile. The enemy had performed a great service, for fury spawns brutality, and brutality spawns victory.

Runolodda would regret this gruesome exhibition.

Gorm gestured toward the pits. 'Check them. I want no more surprises.'

Men ran across the meadow, weaving through the festering carnage. They reached the pits and peered down. They seemed satisfied, pausing only momentarily at the first pit, and ran back, one stopping briefly to throw up.

'Empty, my King,' said the foremost scout. Except for that one at the end. It's their bodies, my King. A pile of headless corpses.'

Gorm kicked his horse forward. 'Attend me. We must not slow our march.'

The command was carried down the line, and the force moved on. Grimly, the Klo passed their fallen comrades. Each touched the brooch at their breast, saluting. Once the army had begun their descent down Two-Mile-Hill, and the noise of their tramping boots had faded, Fiske and Selby poked their heads up through the decomposing mass.

'Disgusting!' hissed Selby. 'This is worse than yer breath!'

'Quit yer whining,' grumbled Fiske, wiping putrid slime from his face, 'and find us a way out of here.'

*

'Who permitted the drawbridge to be lowered?' roared Vali.

From the Great Hall, he heard it creak open, and the watchman shout something over the wall. Vali ran toward the sound. Someone was out there, though it could not be the Klo just yet. He had arranged for trained hunting dogs to be positioned at intervals down Two-Mile-Hill as an early warning system. There had not been a single bark yet.

He arrived at the main entrance to hear the watchman's voice call out.

'Foolish girl! How did you get out in the first place?'

As the bridge came down, Vali saw Tove in the distance. She was leading a cow by the collar.

'Foolish, indeed!' he shouted, rushing out to meet her. 'What were you thinking, lass?'

Tove was breathless, having fetched the animal from far downriver. 'I think you know what I was thinking, Vali. There can be no blessing without a sacrifice.'

'Get inside this instant, Tove! You're going to get us all killed!'

Tove heaved on the cow's collar. 'Move your udders, Audumbla!'

Vali yelled, snatching Tove's wrist. 'Leave the beast! Gorm is almost—'

With a swish, a Klo spear skewered through the cow's neck and lodged deep into the gravel. Tove recoiled with a cry, and Vali began dragging her back before the carcass hit the ground.

'Run!' he yelled, as arrows rained down.

The Klo appeared, charging down the hill, shields up. Their scouts had found and disabled Vali's warning system, silencing the dogs from a distance with quick arrows. An iron-tipped arrow streaked past Tove's ear, and she narrowly avoided one in the back as Vali swiftly lifted his shield.

The watchman had been distracted. He fumbled with the warning horn, blowing it desperately, while the village archers released a volley of their own.

'Close it!' yelled Vali as they slipped inside. The bridge closed with a clang, and he saw Freya approach, a hurricane in leather boots.

'So,' she called. 'They are finally here! Man your posts! Defend each other! Kill them all!'

She stopped a few paces away from Vali. He rested his hands on his knees, trying to catch his breath.

'As speeches go, that was downright awful.' There was a twinkle in his eye.

She froze, allowing her stern expression to crumble into a smile. 'Truly? And yet I practised all night.'

'Keep practising, I reckon,' he winked.

'Ha!'

With a smile, Vali strode off, and Freya exhaled deeply, closing her eyes to take mental stock of where her family stood.

Astrid had taken up position near the Great Hall, well-guarded and well-armed, with a spear in her hands and a sword at her side. A bronze helmet matched her blonde hair, which cascaded over her shoulders like a lion's mane. She bore no other armour. Instead, she had chosen to wear Thora's multi-coloured mantle to mark her as Runolodda's new Witch.

Nearer to the front, among a cluster of villagers, Gudrun crouched behind one of the makeshift barricades—a row of carts lashed together with thick rope and bristling with the branches of a thorn tree.

Freya nodded, pleased, and ascended the parapet stairs.

She passed the archers, glaring over the battlements as she walked. The Klo had slowed to interlock shields, forming a protective shield wall. More and more warriors joined. The sun glinted off their iron helmets, their burnished armour, the sharp edges of their many blades. But for the shuffling of their boots, they remained silent, disciplined, alert, and settled into a dragon-scale formation.

Then Björn stepped forward, a black roundshield on his arm. Its iron-plated surface boasted an embossed Valknut, with a ring of vibrant red runes encircling the outermost edge. Slowly, he began to beat his pommel against the shield. Without hesitation, the entire Klo army took up the motion. They seemed to grunt with each strike, a deep *hoom* sound that echoed through the mountains. It took Freya a while to realise they were chanting a single word over and over.

Doom.

Moment by moment, the chant throbbed on, the gleam of malice in every eye, thunder in every voice. The drumming boomed louder, louder, the rhythm quickening, until the noise escalated into a frenzied uproar, cries reaching a fevered pitch.

Then stopped.

The sudden hush was even more ominous than the noise had been. The Klo stood as statues. Their malevolent energy lingered in the air like a pestilence. Björn smirked, then barked a command. At once, the men parted to form a pathway between their ranks through which Gorm approached astride his great steed. Even from a distance of twenty paces, his eyes found Freya's.

Vali came to stand beside her, shield poised to protect her against a surprise volley.

'Is that him? The man who murdered Erik?'

'Leave him to me,' she snarled. 'I want to watch the life drain from his eyes.'

A knot of regret formed in her chest. If only she had a few drops of Astrid's blood. Freya would undergo The Change and draw a million arrows to her shaggy hide if it meant protecting her daughter. Still, wisdom counselled to choose her moment more carefully.

Riding at an idle pace, Gorm made his way to the fore. His horse ambled to a stop, snorting loudly. Its hooves raked at the gravel. Runolodda held its breath. The Klo held formation. At length, Gorm called up, tilting his head to stare at Freya.

'So, we meet again, She-Wolf. Now that I see you in the daylight, I recall your face. You were King Ari's favourite plaything, yes? Well, now your daughter shall be mine. Though she will enjoy *our* games far less.' He raised the tip of his sword. 'Where *is* the half-blood runt? Hiding in that tomb you call a village? She named me Fenrir, you know? The Great Wolf of Ragnarök, the end of all things.' He ran his gloved finger over the sharp edge of the blade. 'Are you ready to face the end, Alpha? Are your people?'

Freya glared down, silent as death.

'Children will whisper tales of this day in dread,' continued Gorm. 'The stench of fear shall linger for generations, a curse upon your lineage. Runolodda might have shared in the glory of the New North, were it not for your insolence. Your relentless defiance.' He waited for a response. When none came, he lifted his sword once more. 'And for that . . . my men shall butcher every man, woman, and suckling babe.'

At first, Freya seemed amused. A gentle ripple of laughter escaped her, growing into a full-bodied, uncontrollable belly-laugh.

'Your *men*, you say? These are no *men*! Men do not raid and slaughter the defenceless! They do not peddle in flesh or prey on the feeble!'

Her thoughts turned to her father. And to her beloved husband. To Vali and Knud and Scion and every man she knew who would die to protect those they loved.

'Men *build* the world,' continued Freya. 'They do not threaten to devour it! You are worms. You are filth. And you will taste death by my hand and the hands of my kin!'

Freya turned to face her people, lifting her sword high with a blood-curdling roar. They roared back, axes rattling against shields, boots stamping, eyes ablaze. Two or three of the archers shook bare buttocks at the fuming enemy, while others spat a torrent of taunts and sordid insults.

'Gudrun!' Freya waved, shouting over the clamour. 'Now!'

The blare of Erik's battle horn split the heavens. It rallied every scattered thought, bringing every mind into sharp focus. It filled the flesh, filled the bones, and the people roared all the more. It blew the fear from every heart. It called forth the warrior spirit. And when Gudrun removed it from her lips—

—Ragnarök began.

RAGNARÖK

'Archers, *loose*!' cried Vali.

The opening volley struck shields and nothing more. Undeterred, the Klo advanced, black round-shields held in front and overhead in a tortoise formation. Again, arrows sprayed down from the parapets, thwarted once more as they bit into the protective shell or ricocheted clear. Bows snapped a third time, some shafts slipping through tiny gaps to pierce flesh. Warriors screamed, some fell, yet still the ranks advanced. From the rear, Gorm called out for cover fire, and the Klo loosed a volley of their own.

Vali raised his shield in time, relieved to see most of his archers do the same. One man was too late, taking an iron point through the chest. He toppled backward, crashing to the ground below.

The Klo absorbed the fourth onslaught, then the forward ranks detached to dash forward. They scrambled to span the encircling trench with ramps brought from their ships.

Crouched beside Vali, Freya saw their overhead defences temporarily break apart while they struggled to shove the boards into position.

'They are open! Fire at will!' she roared.

Arrows rained down, punching through armour and muscle alike. Almost a third of the Klo detachment fell before the ramps were finally wedged into place. The survivors peeled off to make space for a second detachment to rush forward. These men carried a heavy battering ram and ran much faster than the first group.

Vali's archers aimed for chinks between the interlocking shields, firing shaft after shaft, failing more often than not to hit their targets.

The ramming beam struck, shaking the raised drawbridge and rattling its chains.

Thankfully, it made little impact.

Gorm cast his voice across the standing ranks, signalling the foremost division to advance ten paces, drop to their knees, and open fire. The air turned thick with arrows. He called again, deploying twin groups east and west toward the village ramparts. Each group carried ladders—wooden poles with simple blocks nailed on for rungs. They reached the walls under a hail of arrows, and raised the ladders into place, slipping and stumbling in the uneven trench. Gorm shouted a third time, and the four divisions attacked all at once—one ramming, the other shooting, the last two climbing.

'Lady Freya! The ladders! We must protect the flanks!' exclaimed Vali.

'Aid the east side! I'll help the west!' cried Freya.

'Agreed! Good luck!'

They parted, running low around the parapet's curve. Vali could see the villagers trying to dislodge the eastern ladder, struggling as enemy arrows flashed dangerously close past their vision. He reached the ladder in moments and pushed hard. The pole shifted, yet instead of toppling, it slid to the side where it hooked on a battlement.

The first Klo climber kept his grip and his footing to leap nimbly onto the parapet.

'Yah!' Vali was about to bring down his axe when the climber cast his shield aside.

'Wait, old man! It's me!'

The climber lifted his helmet to reveal a dark and sweaty centreline haircut.

'Scion! What are you doing here?' cried Vali, slapping the young man's shoulder.

'Heave now, talk later,' said Scion, taking hold of the ladder even as more warriors came scrambling up.

Vali and Scion pushed the pole free and it fell. One of the Klo shrieked as he landed awkwardly in the trench, snapping his knee backwards. Ignoring him, his comrades lifted the ladder once more. Bows snapped from both sides. Arrows buzzed like wasps, gouging men, splashing blood.

'Where are your friends?' yelled Vali, ducking behind a battlement.

'I don't know!' shouted Scion. 'We were separated when Gorm split his ranks! I think they might be coming up the other ladder!'

Vali had so many questions. Why were the Beastly Boys in the Klo army to begin with? Why had Gorm not killed them? Or had they stowed aboard an enemy ship, disguised themselves, and marched undetected all the way home . . ? Aye, he thought, looking at his crafty-eyed adopted son. The latter was most likely it.

'Then we'd better help them. But you'll be sure to tell me the full tale when all this is over!'

'Done!' yelled Scion, and the pair pelted along the parapets.

Twice, Freya had helped topple the western ladder. Yet the Klo were relentless, raising it again and again, climbing with speed, agile as cats. A woman fought at Freya's side, stabbing ferociously at the first man up. Her blade came back wet with blood. More came. Freya kicked one brute in the nose, hearing the crunch. Incredibly, he held on and swung his shield up to knock her in the chin. The iron rim split the skin as her head snapped back. The brute surmounted the wall in a flash, swinging his sword blindly at the nearest archer who, ducking too late, took the blade halfway through the skull.

Freya wiped blood from her chin, shaking her head to clear the twinkling lights from her vision. The woman by her side swung an axe at the brute, though it glanced off his shield, throwing her off balance. The brute raised his sword and coiled to lunge, when a motion caught his eye. With a roar, Scion barged into him, battering him clean over the wall. The brute tumbled down the ladder, taking all climbers with him.

'Are you alright, Lady Freya?' asked Scion, rising to his feet.

'Scion!' she exclaimed. 'Astrid feared you had drowned!'

'Is she safe? Is she here?'

'Yes, but—'

'Questions later,' wheezed Vali, having caught up. 'For now, keep your eyes out for Birger and Olle. They may be next up the ladder. In fact . . . this could be them now.'

They gazed over the rampart to see a rather round warrior wobbling up the ladder in tight-fitting Klo armour, with an enormous fellow in tow, his black beard poking out from under a *borrowed* helmet.

'Well, that answers that,' said Scion. 'But where's Tyr?'

*

Björn pulled his steed up beside Gorm.

'The front line is almost through the gate, my King!'

'Good!' roared Gorm, his voice carrying over the standing ranks. 'Give no quarter! Show no mercy! Advance!' He spurred his horse ahead, accompanied by the mounted King's Guard. Gorm usually led from the front, yet this battle was far too important to lose. From the rear, he commanded a broader view of the battlefield. No-one would slip his grasp this time.

Tyr slowed, allowing others to pass him by.

So far, his disguise held, though he tightened the helmet's chin strap for the hundredth time. He had a plan. If he could worm his way to the back line there might be a chance to thrust a blade through Gorm's heart. It was a foolish plan and he knew it. Even if the assassination were to succeed, the odds of escape were scant at best. The King's Guard would show no leniency.

And yet, if he could cut off the head of the snake . . .

A soldier shoved him forward. 'Quit dragging yer feet! The King ordered the advance, so step lively!'

Tyr bent over, discreetly forcing his fingers down his throat to trigger an immediate retch. The soldier made a face, sidestepping the vomit, muttering as he marched past. Tyr took another cautious step backward. He was almost to the rear, close enough to hear the tread of the King's warhorse. He licked his lips, watching Gorm's reflection in the flat of his blade.

Nearly there.

Gorm was no more than ten paces away.

Nine. Eight.

Sweat burned Tyr's eyes and he blinked them away.

Seven. Six.

His fingers flexed on the hilt.

Five. Four.

A cheer went up from the front line as the battering ram broke through. The Klo rushed forward in a frenzy, hollering and hooting for joy. Tyr found himself unexpectedly exposed and felt the curious gaze of the King's Guard upon him.

He hesitated, averting his eyes, and did the only thing he could.

He stormed the village of Runolodda.

*

'Three. Two. One. Pull!'

The first soldiers through the shattered drawbridge ran into a thick chain, tugged taut on both ends by the freed slaves of Klo Island.

'For Nala!' they cried.

The Klo stumbled, falling over each other, some dropping their shields. The women descended on their former captors with a furious vengeance. Some hacked with axes, others with sickles. An old farmer joined in, driving his iron pitchfork through a Klo throat, and the archers spat down arrow after arrow. Still, more Klo poured into the village, swiping at anyone in their path. The women fell back even as the villagers rushed past to meet the enemy.

The two forces collided in a clash of steel, bellows of rage and pain resounding through the streets. A formidable foe, the Klo worked in coordinated groups of three and four, strategically locking shields while maintaining the flexibility to strike from any angle. In stark contrast, the warriors of Runolodda charged into the torrent, discarding finesse and opting for wild, chaotic savagery instead.

'Remember your training!' yelled Vali, dodging a sweeping strike. 'Shields up! Keep your balance! Cut and thrust!'

Axes gripped firmly in each hand, he attacked, using one to hook a Klo shield down, swiftly followed by an overhead swipe with the other. His opponent cried out from surprise more than pain, the blow denting his helmet and sending him sprawling. The man tried to rise but Vali lunged, finishing him with a decisive chop to the neck. Blood spattered Vali's face, and he snapped his gaze to see more Klo rush through the gateway.

They flooded in, roaring. For all their military discipline, the Klo were still as vicious and violent as a pack of wild dogs. Men and women were driven back, some trampled underfoot in the stampede. Limbs were severed, bones shattered, bodies run through. Every Klo eye bore a cruel glint, exulting in the slaughter, though the villagers fought back with the valour of the gods.

Vali blinked, his mind racing. The Klo were even stronger than expected. Their tactics, far superior. At a conservative estimate, Runolodda remained outnumbered five to one. And no amount of training would help them survive against those odds.

His heart sank.

Yet before he could shout an evasive order, he caught a peculiar movement from the corner of his eye. A cluster of four or five Klo launched up into the air and crashed down on their comrades. Then another group, then another—like a series of geysers erupting. Through the blur of charging soldiers, Vali made out what was happening. Birger the Bear, joined by his father, Knud the Blacksmith, swung heavy sledgehammers left and right like scythes though wheat. Scion and Olle protected their flanks, shields up, thrusting longswords at those pressing close. Red drops splashed Scion's face and dribbled into his beard, his mouth open in a barbaric roar.

Freya dropped falcon-like from the parapets, her presence lending strength and courage to the villagers. Birger and Knud had created an opening she intended to leverage. A wicked grin tugged at her lips.

'Wheel to the left!' she shouted, waving her arms demonstratively.

As one, her people swung around to drive a wedge through the Klo's flank, cutting off the front runners from the main force. Swiftly, the Runoloddan archers—those on the ramparts as well as those tucked behind the street-level barricades—bent their bows to the newly detached soldiers, whipping iron tips through their chests, their bellies.

It was a small victory. However, none slowed to savour it, turning instead to fend off the relentless onslaught. More and more Klo pressed through, gaining back the ground they had lost, forcing the villagers to reel backward.

Vali saw the enemy's intent to reach the Great Hall. Rightly, Gorm had guessed that Astrid would be positioned there where the most protection could be provided. Vali steadied himself, exhaling some of the tension. First, the Klo would have to breach the many blockades, built high and guarded between every house and workshop. It was Runolodda's last chance to whittle down the enemy.

Vali filled his lungs. 'Fall back to the barricades!'

The villagers retreated, slipping through narrow gaps in the barriers, rolling under carts and squeezing between piles of lumber. Thorns snagged on a few limbs but it was a small price to pay to reach shelter. Runoloddans helped them through, handing fresh weapons to those who had lost theirs in the battle. Any Klo who attempted to slip through the same gaps would be met with a less courteous welcome.

Along the parapets, archers used knotted ropes to haul villagers to safety, including Scion and Birger. In turn, the pair lifted Olle, cutting the rope when soldiers tried to follow.

Together they ran along the shuddering planks to leap down behind the barricades. Scion landed in a roll, diving behind a cart as an arrow whined past his head. Lungs on fire, he peeked over to see the Klo swarm toward every street and alley, slowing to consider these new obstacles.

Most of the barricades stood taller than a man, with slits for the villagers to fire arrows through. One of the Klo shoved his shield up against the solid barrier but jerked back with a howl when a sharp point penetrated through the wood and into his elbow. He cursed, falling back to join his comrades who had formed a compact shield wall. Together they advanced up to the barricade, firing arrows of their own, hearing cries from the other side.

It soon became a war of attrition across the village. Every blocked road became a war zone of its own, with knots of archers clustered around each blockade, sending death both ways.

A group of four Klo found a narrow alley between two houses, the gap piled high with carts and pig troughs. They set to work: two rocking the roadblock back and forth, two defending.

'Topple it, by Thor!' cried one, hearing the thump of an arrowhead in his shield.

'We're trying, curse you! These things must be filled with rocks!'

'I don't give a f—'

The words choked off, and the man collapsed, eyes wild, his mouth frothing white foam. The remaining shieldman glanced down to see a poison dart in his comrade's cheek.

Gudrun loaded her blowpipe once more, smiling to hear voices raised in anger. She stole a glance through the gap. The Klo had not hesitated. While Gudrun's group hurried to fit more arrows, their enemy clambered up the barricade, quick as wildcats, thorn branches digging grooves into their armour, gouging their hands. Arrows snapped through again, though the angle of fire became ineffectual the higher the men climbed.

The first Klo leaped over, landing heavily on a young man who cried out as he dropped his axe. It was the work of a moment for the soldier to slash the young man's throat, swipe a blade across another, and stab a woman through the gut. His movements were so quick that Gudrun's dart missed and she fumbled desperately to load another.

Thankfully, someone threw a rock at the Klo's helmet, dazing him long enough for an older farmer to swing a razor-edged scythe across his belly. The leather split and blood gushed out from the wound even as the second Klo warrior landed nearby. This time, Gudrun's aim was true, striking the base of his skull, unprotected below the helmet. He frothed, dying at an old crone's feet, not living long enough to see what became of his comrades.

*

Tyr entered the village last.

The Runoloddan archers had collapsed the front parapets, closing off that avenue of pursuit for the Klo, and retreated to the rear ramparts. If any had spotted Tyr, they might have sent him into the next world, for he still wore full Klo battledress, his telltale white hair kept hidden beneath a helmet.

Glancing back through the shattered gateway, Tyr could see that Gorm and his cavalry had chosen to keep their distance, no doubt keeping an eye out for anyone attempting to slip through a concealed escape hatch.

Tyr approached the Klo backline, keeping his head down. Up ahead, the Klo had started breaking through the scattered blockades while the rear ranks continued to seethe forward, impatiently straining to see what might be causing the bottleneck.

Tyr singled out the soldier farthest to the back and moved slowly toward him. Quick and quiet, he clapped a hand over the man's mouth and slit his throat. Twitching, the body slumped to the ground, and Tyr was relieved that no witnesses cried out. The main street was littered with the dead, Klo and Runoloddan alike, so it was unlikely that anyone would notice one more corpse at his feet. Still, he moved on to the next soldier with caution, checking that none looked back, before dispatching him in the same manner.

Tyr would need to remain undetected by both Runolodda and the Klo if he was to reach Astrid. One drop of her blood to his lips might turn the tide of this battle.

However, if the Klo reached her first . . .

He shook his head and slit another throat.

THE OFFERING

Astrid fidgeted with her spear.

She could hear the Klo draw near. The barricades were crumbling under the unrelenting bombardment, and many of the villagers had retreated to the next row of defence. The wounded limped or crawled back to the Great Hall, some carried or helped along by others.

Astrid ground her teeth. Where was Mother? Their horses whinnied in wide-eyed agitation, unused to the noise and chaos of battle. Hermod stamped a hoof, his way of warning Astrid of danger.

'Peace, boy,' she soothed, stroking his neck. 'We shall soon ride free.'

'Ride free?' came a voice at her back.

It was Tove the Songbird, looking more nervous than the horses. 'Do you mean to abandon us, Astrid?'

'I mean to draw the enemy away, Tove. Runolodda will soon be overwhelmed, but we can provide a fighting chance.'

'We?'

Astrid sighed. There was a reason leaders did not divulge every plan with those they led. Some folk simply had to question everything, especially when there was no time for answers.

'My mother and I must ride for the mountains. And we must ride alone.' She clutched the Songbird's shoulders. 'Listen carefully, Tove. There is a hatch in the eastern wall. When we go, I need you to help guard it. Can you do that for me?'

Tove hesitated. 'But . . . but why must you ride alone?'

'Can you *do* that for me?' Astrid demanded.

Tove stared open-mouthed at the resolute young witch.

I suppose, she thought, *there will be a sacrifice after all.*

*

The soldier swung a great axe.

Not a moment too soon, Freya dodged and drove her sword upward through his gut. She spat in his face and let the body collapse.

More Klo came and the first worm of doubt crept into Freya's heart. Was it wise to ride off when Runolodda's fate hung by a thread? What if Gudrun's prophecy was wrong? What if victory did not await her in the mountains? She spat again, this time in frustration.

Another barricade broke and the Klo came streaming through.

There was no time for regrets. Heart pounding, Freya sprinted toward the Great Hall, elbowing folk aside. An arrow grazed her leg. Shouts rose at her back. Spattered with blood and out of breath, she reached the horses, relieved to see her daughter still safe and already on Hermod's back, the polished bronze helmet catching the bright sun.

They shared a nod.

Then, with a roar, the Alpha and the Witch rode hard for the eastern wall. Hooves thundering beneath her, Freya saw a figure swing the concealed escape hatch wide open, and Hermod kicked up dust as he bolted through ahead of her.

The landscape opened up before them.

Up ahead lay the Serpent's Tail, a sinuous path up into the Northern mountains. The sprawl of narrow passes there would confuse the Klo, though every Runoloddan played there as a child and knew their twists and turns intimately.

'Here they come!' yelled Freya, glancing back.

Gorm and his King's Guard had spotted them. Bellowing, the men spurred their horses into pursuit, reaching a full gallop in a matter of moments. Freya gripped her reins tightly. The mare she rode was almost as quick as Hermod and if they kept up this pace, Gorm would be hard pressed to catch up before they reached the first bend.

They were halfway up the Serpent's Tail when Hermod was abruptly reined to a halt. He whinnied loudly, rearing on his hind legs. Freya almost collided as she passed, coming dangerously close to losing her balance.

'What are you doing? Don't stop now!' she shouted, reining in a little way ahead.

The rider lifted her helmet, her golden hair wet with perspiration.

'I am sorry, Lady Freya. I could not allow her to sacrifice herself.'

Freya visibly paled. 'Tove! Where is Astrid?'

'Safe. And so must you be. Ride, Lady Freya. I will slow their approach.'

Freya snatched a glance at Gorm's charging horsemen. They were close enough for her to see their gritted teeth, the flash of their swords. 'Tove! No! Get as far away as you—'

'There can be no victory,' whispered Tove, 'without a sacrifice.'

She donned the bronze helmet once more, shutting out Freya's cries.

Then, turning Hermod to face the enemy, she launched ahead.

As the gap closed, Tove tilted her face to the sun, feeling the warmth of the gods' approval. A part of her felt the weight of her decision, the inevitability of her demise. And yet, her eyes reflected not fear but a shieldmaiden's resolve—steadfast and brave as the tales of old.

The Songbird who would soon pass into song.

The King's Guard thundered closer with Gorm at the tip of the spear. His black stallion snorted like a dragon. His battle-axe shone in the low sun.

'Take the girl!' he roared. 'Leave the She-Wolf to me!'

Gorm's stallion dwarfed young Hermod, and as the horses passed, he swung his axe, its sharp edge leaving a gash in Hermod's flank. With a violent crash, Tove and Hermod met the unforgiving ground, and in the chaotic tumble, she felt her collar bone snap. Hermod emitted a high-pitched noise, panicking, scrambling upright to dash away.

The King's Guard let him go, far more interested in encircling their prey.

'Seize her!' shouted Björn, bringing his horse near. Roughly, his men complied, pinning her to the ground. 'Well, well. You've certainly kept us busy. All this trouble you've caused. And to what end?' Björn dismounted with surprising grace for a man of his size. He swaggered up to his prize, kneeling beside her. 'We'll take your blood now, please. Then we can mop up your friends and be on our way.'

He yanked off her helmet . . . and gasped.

Tove smiled, blood in her teeth. 'Expecting someone else, were you?'

Björn glowered up the path. Gorm was too far to call, and the woman he chased had little distance to cover before reaching the foot of the mountains. Without so much as a glance in Tove's direction, Björn stabbed her through the heart and marched back to his horse.

'To the King!' he shouted, and the horsemen charged off again.

Tove lay in her pooling blood, smiling up at the gods.

The sky burned a vivid blue.

And she shut her eyes.

THE BEASTLY BOYS

Astrid opened her eyes.

All at once, the noises came crashing in. It took a terrifying moment to realise where she was, what was happening. She was on her back. She was outside. A battle raged all around. She lifted her head too quickly and the pain lit up like sparks in a forge. Had someone struck her? She could remember speaking with Tove . . . then turning her back . . .

The horses were missing. Freya was missing. Astrid rubbed her eyes. With every other horse and mule led away prior to the battle, how could she reach her mother before Gorm did?

She would need a new plan.

Again.

Lights danced across her vision as she slowly sat up. Easing back, she rested against the rear exterior of the Great Hall. A yell shattered the calm, and two men tumbled into view, grappling and punching. Astrid sprang clear with a cry. The Klo landed heavily on his opponent, shattering the man's teeth with the pommel of his sword. The fog lifting, Astrid sensed the spear still in her hand and whipped the tip forward, missing the Klo by a whisker.

'Astrid!' he cried. 'It's me!'

'W-what? W-who?'

It gradually dawned on Astrid that the Klo's opponent was also a Klo. The victor removed his helmet, allowing his shock-white hair to bounce in the breeze with feline grace.

'Tyr!' cried Astrid, lowering the spear. 'You're alive!'

'As are we,' came a voice from behind.

Scion, Olle, and Birger the Bear stepped close—covered in blood and gore.

It was the loveliest sight Astrid had ever seen.

'Scion!' She lunged into his arms, wrapping him closer than a cloak in winter. 'How? I saw you taken by the waves.'

He pressed into her, enveloping her. 'You can thank Tyr. He fished us out and stowed us away.'

'That's not all he did for us,' said Birger, stepping forward.

He lifted his sleeve to reveal a blackened bite mark.

Olle did the same.

Scion too.

After seven long hours, each bite had turned black as tar.

'Well,' said Astrid, taking a moment to let the truth settle in, 'I imagine you'll want a flint for that *firewood*. Come with me.'

Guards stepped aside as she swiftly led them into the Great Hall, bolting the door behind them. With Scion at her side, she took the spear point to her palm, slicing a deep incision.

Astrid—Witch of Runolodda—held up her palm.

Closed her eyes.

Spoke.

'The ritual moves through three phases. First, *we acknowledge the Wolf within us.*'

The Boys removed their armour.

'Second, *we stand together against the enemy.*'

One by one, they held up their wrists.

'Third, *we yield to the Moon's sway.*'

They felt the Witch touch her blood to theirs.

And the world exploded.

The Boys threw back their heads and roared in unison—a pack of Wolves unleashed at last. In an instant, every fragrance, every colour, every secret nuance of their surroundings opened like flowers. They could hear the swish of distant swords, and the creak of bows from down the street. They saw shapes within shadows—plain as day—and smelled the distinctive leathery sweat of the Klo as if it wafted from a cup held to their noses.

And yet their minds remained keen as knives.

Scion marvelled at the span of his claws, swiping the air to test their range. Birger the *Wolf* was larger than ever, snapping spiked teeth as he flexed his massive neck. Tyr growled, tearing a buckle from his shredded clothes to strap a double-edged axe to his stump. He nodded at the result: Tyr the Wolf-man, the Living Weapon. Olle's transformation was most notable of all. Excess fat had morphed into monstrous muscle. He stood ten feet tall and howled like a hurricane. Disrupting the intensity of the moment, he could not help but salivate at the aroma of a simmering stew, though he shook the temptation from his mind.

There was fighting to be done.

'That's better,' quipped Astrid. 'Though I do wish you boys would refrain from nudity in my presence.' She smiled at each of them in turn. 'Now give those bastards a taste of their own bile.'

Jagged grins spread across the Wolf-men's faces as they turned toward the door. Scion was first into the daylight, roaring, throwing himself into the fray. With terrifying savagery, he slashed and bit and gored, crushing soldiers underfoot, raking them open.

Fear swept through the villagers and they scattered, wide-eyed and screaming.

'It's alright, everyone!' called Scion, wiping blood from his maw. 'It's only us! The Beastly Boys!'

The villagers erupted in cheers. The sight brought back memories of the day Scion and his young friends had returned from a wolf-hunt, draped in its bloody pelt. Fuelled by hope, the villagers plucked up their courage and fought back with newfound ferocity, keeping pace with the Wolf-men as they rampaged through the streets.

Birger cornered a huddle of three Klo who instinctively overlapped their shields. He reached beneath their defences, seizing one soldier by the leg to use him as a makeshift hammer to strike the others.

'They don't make 'em like they used to,' he remarked, tossing aside the battered pulp and grabbing the next shrieking *hammer* from the crowd.

Tyr swung his weaponized stump. 'I wouldn't say that. This thing is coming in quite *handy*,' he winked.

Olle had never felt so alive. He sprang about like a deranged deer, shredding massive claws through the ranks, whooping with delight. Power coursed through him like lightning as he danced clear of every attack, Klo blades stabbing at smoke. He skipped. He ripped. He twirled on his talons, basking in the soft spray of red droplets that twinkled in the sun like fireflies.

It was a good day.

Astrid stood beneath the eaves of the Great Hall and watched. If the Beastly Boys could not win victory for the village, no-one could. She would need to entrust Runolodda's fate to them. Her fight lay in the mountains. Freya needed her. Needed her blood. Without it, Gorm would surely triumph.

'You must not delay, Granddaughter. It's a long way up the

Serpent's Tail.'

Astrid whirled to face Gudrun, the old woman limping, a gash on her wrinkled cheek. 'Gudi! You're hurt!' She rushed to her side, helping her to sit. 'What happened?'

'War happened, my dear. But I'll be alright. Your mother, on the other hand, won't be. Not unless you hurry.'

Astrid tried to speak, but the words caught in her throat. Tears spilled over and kept on spilling. She flushed with shame, knowing full well that this was not the time for fragility, yet seeing Gudrun hurt dredged up everything she had been holding back. All the fear. All the uncertainty. Every squandered moment. Every unspoken word.

'There is one thing I must ask of you, Gudi. One thing I need you to tell Scion.'

She whispered the words into her grandmother's ear.

Her message, her wish.

The old woman nodded, wincing with pain. 'I will tell him. You have my word.' She shoved Astrid away. 'Now go! There may be time for fussing later. Save your mother! Save the *Alpha*!'

Wiping her nose on her sleeve, Astrid nodded, hiked up her dress, and ran.

On the far side of the village, the battle raged on.

Scion moved through the right flank, bloody claws reaching far. The Klo fought back frantically, with the villagers frustrating their every effort, swarming at their backs. Only a few Klo blades managed to find Scion's hide, though the wounds healed quickly enough not to slow his momentum. His claws were a blur of violence, his jaws thick with blood, and he approached the centre in a vicious barrage of speed and raw power.

The Klo rallied, surging toward the villagers, roaring, hacking. Runolodda responded with a shout, standing their ground against the incoming tide. Vali stood among them, bracing his shield with his shoulder to push them back.

The Beastly Boys swept in like owls on mice to tear sizable gaps in the thinning Klo ranks. Their line crumbled and Runolodda advanced, cheering all the louder.

Desperate, the Klo sent arrow after arrow from their dwindling supply. But the villagers locked shields like scales, with some braving personal risk to defend the Boys, others sending every last arrow of their own in an answering volley.

At that moment, the battle was over.

It became a massacre.

With their blades bristling like the hairs of a great boar, Runolodda charged as one. The Klo—raiders and ravishers all—fell to the sword and the axe, the tooth and the claw. Their last thoughts were not of conquest or plunder. They no longer imagined their exploits immortalised in song or in saga. In their final moments, they knew only fear and torment and despair as the men and women of Runoloddaa cut a swathe through their midst.

And drowned them in a wave of blood.

JÖRMUNGANDR

Gorm peered into the shadows.

He had followed hard on the Alpha's heels, weaving up the Serpent's Tail until patches of snow and ice appeared on the stony ground. Yet as Freya entered the mountain passes with its labyrinth of ragged pinnacles, Gorm sensed a trap. The tall, thin pillars towered like guardians of the shadowy maze. He did not believe in omens, but the overhead screech of a raven only added to his disquiet. Eventually, Gorm decided to throw caution to the wind. He took a step to enter . . . when the sound of hoofbeats caught his ear.

'It was not the half-blood, my King,' fumed Björn, reining in with the King's Guard. 'Just another ruse staged by these infernal swineherds.' He spat on the ground, wiping Tove's blood from his blade. 'Should we return to the village, my King? Or pursue the She-Wolf?'

Gorm stroked his tapered beard, rage simmering beneath the surface. Of course, retrieving Astrid was the primary objective. Yet it gnawed at his pride to abandon his hunt for the Alpha. He felt both torn and cheated.

Then, something quite curious crossed his mind.

An overlooked possibility.

Uncharacteristically, his mouth broke into a wide grin. 'Why settle for one half-blood runt when the She-Wolf could be forced to produce more?' The King's Guard caught his meaning and their eyes filled with cruel delight. Gorm shifted in his saddle, gazing back down toward the village. 'Let our foot soldiers capture the runt, while we go after the mother.'

The horsemen roared in agreement and lifted their swords high. Dismounting, they entered the maze, greeted by a sudden chill as the enormous spires cast shadows, obstructing the daylight. With the sun already low, the night's cold would soon take hold. This pleased Gorm. Cold, he found, had a sharpening effect on the senses. And they would need their wits about them, now more than ever.

'Flush out the She-Wolf,' he ordered. 'But she must be kept alive. Constrain her, club her, cripple her if you must. But do not kill her. Forfeit your own life before forfeiting hers. Understood?'

'Understood!' they replied in accord, punching their chests.

'Good. Now spread out.'

Gorm fastened the iron sheath over his sword and held it before him like a truncheon. He tested the added weight with a swipe, satisfied he could knock the Alpha senseless if necessary. Raising his iron-plated shield, he advanced, taking the centre trail while his men fanned out to form a net.

Spiders converging on a solitary fly.

*

Freya shivered in the shadows.

She cursed. Every misstep had led to another, and now she hid in the rocks with no way to become the *Wolf Victorious* of Gudrun's blasted prophecy! But what other course could she have taken? The King's Guard had cut her off from Astrid and the path back to the village. There had been no choice but to ride for the mountains. The decision, she knew, could spell her doom.

Freya pushed the thought away and shifted on her haunches. The alcove was cold, very cold, though it provided two advantages. First, the shadows were deep indeed. Deep enough to conceal the glint of her sword. Second, she was perched a little above the narrow pathway, high enough to swoop down on passers-by.

It seemed an age before the crunch of a footstep announced her first victim. Freya swallowed. Held her breath. As the soldier came into view she could smell the oil on his armour and wondered if he could smell the blood on hers.

The Klo paused, gazing carefully about.

He took another tentative step, peering around a rock.

Keeping steady in such a low crouch, Freya could feel her ankles and knees pleading for relief. The soldier was almost near enough now. She squeezed the hilt, knuckles whitening.

Waiting, waiting.

Then the man turned back, choosing a different path. Freya hesitated. If she was quick, she could drop down and reach him in just two strides. However, on this loose gravel the soldier would likely hear her and cry out before the blade struck. This had to be a silent kill, quick and quiet.

Startlingly, a second Klo emerged. His presence clearly annoyed the first, who reprimanded him in code through a series of clipped hand signals. *Spread out*, he seemed to say. *I'll head left. Don't follow me!*

These passages all look the same! signed the second, ending his communication with a patently rude gesture.

The first man rolled his eyes and disappeared from view. The second glanced around, selecting a path that would take him directly beneath Freya's hiding spot.

Quick and quiet, she thought, muscles coiling once more.

Her leap was silent, her strike was swift. The blade slipped through the crevice between the soldier's helmet and shoulder guard, piercing flesh, artery, and spine. Death was instant, and Freya landed as lightly as she could, easing the man quietly down to the ground.

She heard the first soldier hiss with irritation and turn back in her direction. Soft on her feet, she pressed her back to the rock and raised her sword as though drawing back an arrow. She would need to time this perfectly if she hoped to keep things quiet. Freya saw the Klo's shadow, then his boot, and she lunged. The blade flashed forward, slicing through his windpipe, and she caught his weight in both arms while his blood gushed over her chest plate.

'Here!' came a cry, and Freya spun to see a third soldier rush toward her.

By Thor! Did the Klo not grasp the concept of *spreading out*? She ran, twisting this way and that through the spires. The shadows were heavier now, yet she knew her way well enough. That, at least, would give her the advantage of speed. She pictured a similar hideout nearby. Hopefully, she could reach it before—

An iron sheath whipped out, smashing into her face.

Freya flipped feet over head to crash hard on her belly. Nose broken, she gasped, shocked, in sudden anguish. She tried to crawl away, but her limbs shook weakly. Her ears rang over muted sobs and gurgling breath, and the last thing she saw before darkness took her was a pair of heavy boots approaching.

Gorm stared down at the Alpha.

And spat.

*

Astrid picked her way carefully between the grey spires.

As a small child, she had played hide-and-seek among these winding passageways, naming them *Jörmungandr's Fangs*, after the Midgard Serpent who would aid the wicked Fenrir, Wolf of Ragnarök. She had always thought it a fitting name. After all, the jagged network began above the Serpent's Tail and looked very much like the upturned teeth of a great snake. Yet as evening fell, that name sent a shiver down her spine. No child's play would echo through *Jörmungandr's Fangs* tonight.

Spear-tip pointed ahead, she stepped forward. The cold bit through the haunting silence. She passed pockets of shadow that never saw the light, where rock hoarded ice like treasure.

Astrid's breath steamed out.

Her thoughts floated back to finding Hermod on the trail, blood weeping from his side. The poor colt had been in too much pain to carry her and she had sent him away with soft words and a ruffle of his mane. Finding Tove had been a shock. The dead girl still stared up at the sky, ants crawling across her open eyes.

Astrid shivered, returning her thoughts to the present danger.

How would the King's Guard treat Mother if they reached her first?

As though summoned, Freya shouted a distant warning, her voice cut off by an angry, deeper yell. Astrid hissed. She was too late! Mother was captured! Perhaps the Klo had been unable to prevent Freya from crying out. Or, perhaps Gorm had allowed the outburst, hoping to lure Astrid near. Knowing first-hand how Gorm treated his prisoners, the latter seemed more likely.

Astrid swung the spear westward.

'I'm coming, Mother,' she whispered. 'Hold onto hope.'

She quickened her step, keeping low and quiet. If memory served, the paths converged into a wide recess up ahead. Chances were, this was where the Klo waited. Astrid wove through a circle in order to reach the site from an angle. By slipping through a narrow tunnel, she might be able to subtly draw her mother's attention.

Subtlety vanished when an involuntary yelp escaped her lips. She had stepped on an upturned blade, the bloody point poking up through her instep. Astrid cursed her carelessness, despite the trap being impossible to see in the shadows. Even as she tugged the knife free—the motion almost causing her to cry out once more—she heard the rustle of footsteps to her left and to her right.

Clutching her spear and the bloodied knife, Astrid ran. The footsteps grew louder, with shouts rising and echoing off the rocks. Astrid did not look back. She wove in a limping run, leaving a trail of blood like breadcrumbs along the winding path. How many times had the Klo cut her, struck her, bled her? She wanted to break them. Make them pay. The rage pushed her on even as the fear and the pain pulled her back. She ran, ran, ran.

—And skidded to a halt.

She found herself out in the open again, trapped on a frozen river that cut through the tall cliffs of a narrow canyon. She could see a river rushing beneath the thick, blue ice that reflected the stars like jewels.

'Here! I have her!' called a soldier, emerging from the passage. He was soon joined by another, then another, kicking up frosted shards as they ran. In moments, the King's Guard had taken up positions to block Astrid from moving either upstream or downstream.

Astrid backed away until she felt the rugged cliff touch her spine. Warm blood ran from her wound, steaming as it melted into the pillowed snowdrifts at her feet.

'Stay back!' she warned, holding the knife to her throat. 'Stay back or you will never taste my blood again!'

A deep voice called from the passageway. 'I think not, young Astrid.'

Her eyes widened as Gorm stepped into the moonlight, holding Freya by the arm. She was bound at the wrists, with a thick smear of blood across her face.

Astrid glared into Gorm's icy gaze. 'You filth!' she growled, pressing the sharp edge to her throat. 'Let her go this instant! Do it or I shall cut!'

Gorm smiled. 'Go ahead. The Alpha's womb can soon yield an entire litter of your kind.' He stepped out onto the crystalline surface, dragging Freya with him. 'Naturally, she will be compelled to comply. You, on the other hand, have a choice. Either share in the glory of the New North or die here today. It matters not. Your death will delay my campaign by no more than a year.'

Gorm passed Freya over to Björn, who squeezed her shoulders so hard that she gasped. From across the ice, mother and daughter locked eyes, sharing a gaze of both love and sorrow. Gorm stepped in between them. He knelt on the frozen surface to run his fingers through the streak of Astrid's blood.

'Stubbed your toe again, young Astrid? You really should mind your step.'

He stood, letting the blood trickle down his glove. Then, approaching his men with the aura of a dark sorcerer, he recited an old verse like an incantation.

In shadows deep, where twilight meets the roar,
Fenrir awakens, a tempest's core.
Ragnarök's herald, with fangs aglow,
the Great Wolf rises, laying worlds low.

He touched Astrid's blood to their lips.

Instantly, bones contorted, sinews stretched, and one by one the King's Guard mutated into nightmare creatures.

'So, which will it be, young Astrid?' asked Gorm. 'Your mother has lost her husband. Will you see her lose her daughter, too?'

'You don't need her,' murmured Freya weakly, and the Wolves grinned madly at the pathetic display. 'I'll come with you. Please, Gorm. Release her.'

Ignoring her, Gorm took a step toward Astrid.

'Never,' he said.

Licking the blood from his fingertips, he lifted his chin to the sky. With an ear-splitting roar, his body convulsed and Gorm became the Great Wolf—the Doom-Hound, the World-Eater, the Slayer of Men—Fenrir made flesh.

Astrid should have screamed.

She should have run.

Instead, she shoved the spear's tip into a crack in the cliff behind her.

'I am sorry, mother!' she called. 'But I must set Father free now!'

Freya swayed on her feet, frowning at her. 'What are you talking about, Daughter?' Then her eyes widened, realising where they stood. 'Astrid. What have you done?'

'Return to the Midgard Serpent, Mother! Return to *Jörmungandr's Fangs*!'

'Astrid, no!'

'What are you blabbering about?' growled Gorm. 'Seize her!'

'Now!' screamed Astrid and clung to the lodged spear like the branch of a tree.

Gorm heard a rumble . . .

The earth shook.

A mighty roar filled the canyon.

Seizing on the Klo's distraction, Freya dropped, rolled backward between Björn's legs, and leaped into a run.

Gorm snapped his gaze up, gripped by a sudden rush of fear.

Silhouetted against the bright moon, a great shape bloomed —a shadow filling the sky. Diving like a whale, it plummeted from the high clifftop toward the Klo. Too late, Gorm saw what it was—an enormous longship, heavy with stones. A falling cairn for a fallen Chieftain.

Erik's burial ship.

There was a deafening crash, an explosion of cracked ice and smashed timber as the ship rammed through the surface. Released from its glacial prison, rushing water burst up in a great fountain, swallowing the Klo. They screamed, drowning, sinking in the vortex of icy terror. The splash soaked Astrid as she hung above the churning water, feet dangling, grip slipping. She saw the ship begin to sink, cairn stones tumbling and spilling over as the prow reared up like a startled horse.

On the opposite side of the river, Freya dove for the stony bank, scrabbling to find purchase as the freezing water spewed and spat against the rocks. The river had come alive, a wild and angry monster set free, and panic jolted through her as she swallowed water, coughing and gasping.

Her bonds caught on a rock, then sheared clean off. She grabbed frantically for the next handhold, ignoring the agony as her fingers twisted to hold on. At last she was able to lift her torso up onto the bank. But before her legs cleared, she felt an immense pressure around her ankle.

And a great claw dragged her under.

THE WOLF VICTORIOUS

Scion sped sinuously through the spires.

Wolfsight made a blue streak of Astrid's scent, and he chased it on all fours with the zeal of a hunter. Somewhere up ahead, the sound of the Beastly Boys' roar echoed as they pushed Erik's ship over the ledge. Scion heard it smash through the ice, and he bolted, straining his neck forward with every stride.

Rounding the final bend, he caught sight of the river, and Astrid clinging to the spear on the far side. She was struggling against the river's pull, wriggling to find a better grip. Scion saw her fingers slipping.

It was happening again.

Memories of his mother and father flashed before him. He saw their pale faces beneath the ice. Their fists pounding against the pitiless surface. Their mouths open in a silent scream as they sank into the gloom.

Never again!

Scion roared, taking the final few strides to launch into the open. He soared over the raging water, his body stretched out like a wildcat in full leap. He saw Astrid slip, then fall. In a heartbeat, she sank beneath the surface. Landing on the cliffside, Scion drove his claws into the sheer rock, plunging one into the water. He felt something resembling seaweed and tugged.

Astrid emerged with a gasp, wincing as Scion hauled her up by the hair to hug her to his chest.

'One should really *ascertain* the depth before diving into unknown waters.' Once again, Scion had chosen a poor moment for a jest. And yet, Astrid smiled, slapping his chest.

'You certainly took your time!' She held him tight, coughing water on his tawny fur.

Scion smiled awkwardly. 'We came as soon as Gudrun delivered your message. Are you alright?'

'Mother!' cried Astrid, darting her gaze around. 'Where is Mother?'

*

Freya thrashed in the surging current.

More crucial than the numbing cold needling her skin was her desperate need to breathe. The river ran black as ink beneath the mountains, concealing any elusive air pockets from her sight. She choked on the frigid water, convulsing, screaming at the back of her throat.

Something struck her boot and she flinched. A submerged rock? A drowning Wolf-man? What did it matter? Air. She needed air! It crossed Freya's mind that the river could run for miles underground before spilling out into the valley. Still, she stretched her limbs out wide, hoping to grasp something, anything.

There was a lurch, and then . . . air!

She filled her lungs, thrashing to keep head and shoulders above the surface. The darkness remained absolute, yet Freya was glad at least to know which way was up. The tunnel ceiling must have risen, though it could dip again at any moment, so she stretched her hands protectively ahead.

Her knee hit something solid and she spun, gulping water. Then, another lurch came, and she fell, her chest plate taking most of the impact from whatever it was she landed on. Rapids! Drawing in a deep breath, Freya curled up into a ball right as the current swept her into the rocks, first striking her hip, then her elbow. She embraced the pain, only daring to uncurl when the water eventually slowed.

Perhaps her eyes had grown accustomed to the shadows, for she saw a pillar loom ahead, splitting the watercourse in two. Swimming to the left, she soon felt the crunch of a riverbed underfoot. Her outstretched fingers slapped against the slimy root of a tree. She grasped again, catching a thicker root, and hauled herself onto solid ground.

She lay on her back in the dark, listening to the pulse surge in her ears, a percussive beat over the music of rushing water. Groaning, she rolled over onto her side. At least the chill numbed her battered body, dulling some of the pain. Freya stood in a stupor. A pinprick of light beaconed to her from a distance, and she lumbered toward it. Slowly, she caught her breath, dragging one foot feebly in front of the other.

There came a growl from behind.

Freya froze.

She took one careful step and heard it again.

Without looking back, Freya hurtled forward. Her left leg lacked any bounce, suggesting her kneecap must have cracked. She blew the pain away, eyes fixed on the growing point of light. The growl swelled into a roar, and the creature began to move up the tunnel after her. Freya shouted back in defiance, daring to glance back, though it was still too dark to see. The light ahead was all she knew now, all she lived for.

Reach the light, Freya, reach the light.

She tripped, scrabbled back up, hobbled on. Paws bounded closer, accompanied by another roar, this one louder, fiercer. For one mad moment, Freya hoped it was nothing more than a bear. She gasped, realising where she was. This was the same path she had taken the day she met Erik. The day she fought the Runoloddan hunters in the *Battle of the Bear Cave*. Fate had brought her back to the place where it all began. Whether for good or ill, she could not yet say.

The tunnel became the cave, its mouth framing the night sky, and she rushed out into the crisp air. The roar followed her, saturated her, and before she could reach the trees, heavy claws raked her back. Her leather armour tore and she was knocked to the ground, cracking a few ribs on the hard earth. Freya screamed, trying to scramble away, when a claw flipped her over onto her back.

Gorm the Wolf-man loomed over his prey, panting plumes of white cloud. Foam bubbled and dripped from his jaws, and he howled in exhilaration. There was nowhere for the Alpha to run. He knew this, and so did she.

'At last,' he growled.

Gorm had managed to dive partially clear of Erik's ship, though not far enough to escape unscathed. His left hand had been torn off, with Wolf-flesh already grown back over the severed bone, though the bone itself racked him with pain. His broken jaw and ribs had mended crookedly, protruding at odd angles from his twisted form. And yet he had survived. Navigating the underground by Wolfsight, he had followed Freya. And caught her.

Freya glared up at Gorm, refusing to show any sign of the

terror that writhed in her gut. The moon shone bright and clear, and she could see his mad, red eyes, and razor-sharp claws. If there was ever a time for the gods to intervene, it was now.

'You will never—' she began.

'Enough! No more threats!' Gorm pressed his muzzle in her face. 'You are mine now, do you understand? Freya of Runolodda is no longer the Alpha. *I* am! You're nothing more than my shadow, an instrument for my machinations. That is all you are worth!' He stepped back, making room for her to rise. 'On your feet! It's a long walk back, *slave*.'

Freya felt dizzy. Gudrun had seen the end, and this was not the way it was meant to be. Wincing, she came to her knees, taking a moment to steady herself.

Freya noticed something on her wrist.

Something tucked beneath her bracers.

She pulled it out.

It was what Gudrun had brought from her cottage.

Astrid's blood-stained bandage—wet as waves though still stained red.

'I told you to *move*, slave!' barked Gorm.

'We are the Norns of our own Fate,' whispered Freya.

Gorm shook his head. 'More yammering. More procrastination.'

Could it work? thought Freya. *Could my daughter's light have survived the battle? Survived the floodwaters? Could her light shine on even after so much darkness? So much violence and death?*

Of course it could.

Astrid is the Moonlight.

And Freya of Runolodda is the Alpha.

She took the sodden cloth to her lips and licked.

'What is that?' muttered Gorm, taking a step back.

Power crackled through Freya's veins. The flint had been struck. The oil had been lit. And the volcano in her flesh erupted. Muscles bulged all at once, snapping buckles, tearing leather. She slumped forward on her hands, roaring as they stretched into hooked talons. All that was battered, all that had bruised, was made whole once more. Freya stood to her full height and threw back her head, teeth glinting like knives in the starlight.

'No . . .' murmured Gorm, taking another step back. 'It cannot be.'

Freya met his gaze, amber eyes to his red, and spoke for the first time as a self-aware Wolf-woman. 'You slew my husband. You took my daughter. You invaded my people. Your reckoning is due, Gorm of the Klo.' She advanced, stretching her arms wide. 'And know this: here in the mountains, it is I who shall emerge as the Wolf Victorious.'

The hair on Gorm's back bristled, and he gritted his teeth, coiling to pounce.

'I said . . . no more threats, She-Wolf!'

They lunged simultaneously, the sound of impact like the slap of meat on a butcher's table. Caught in a deadly dance, they grappled, neither able to topple the other, their clawed feet gouging thick grooves in the soil. With an audible chomp, Gorm sank his teeth into Freya's shoulder, biting through to the bone. Pain exploded through her and out in a great howl. She flung her arms around him, digging her claws into his back. Gorm drew in an agonised breath, and his bloody jaws roared apart, lifting the pressure from Freya's shoulder.

She held on tightly and sank her claws deeper into his shoulder blades. Gorm arched back to make room for a killing sweep to the throat, though Freya anticipated the move, aware that his severed hand meant he could only attack from the right.

She ducked out of reach, breaking the deadlock, and they sprang clear of one another.

Panting, Gorm spat a globule of Freya's blood. 'Luck will not bring triumph tonight, She-Wolf. I have trained since I could walk. I have won more battles and spilled more blood than memory can hold. I am Gorm, King and Champion of the Klo army!'

Freya grinned. 'I recall defeating you once before, *Champion*. And my sweet daughter obliterated your guards. I am not nearly as impressed as you think.'

Gorm's lips stretched back into a crimson snarl.

Claws flashed in the moonlight, and he lunged with a sweeping crescent strike. He might have split open her gut if luck had favoured him. But Freya dodged again, countering swiftly by punching her claws like daggers in a series of lightning-fast strikes to his side. Blood gushed out as though Freya were a dog digging up dirt. Gorm howled, ribs broken, lung burst. He dropped to one knee, exhaling ragged, whistling breaths.

He glared up at the She-Wolf. She paced back and forth like a hungry lion. The delight in witnessing her enemy's pain was unmistakable. And for the first time in years, Gorm felt a creeping doubt run up his spine. Already, the She-Wolf's shoulder had mended, though his own, more serious wounds would take frustratingly longer to heal. Freya now stood as the stronger, faster rival, and he needed some way to balance the scales.

Contingencies upon contingencies.

Crouched, he seized a handful of soil, discreetly crushing it into a fine powder. 'Do you suppose Valhalla is as glorious as the songs describe?' Slowly, he stood upright. Freya circled him warily. 'Quite honestly,' he continued, 'I've often wondered if it exists at all. Perhaps the dead simply rot. Or perhaps their souls linger with no-one to hear their lonely cries. What is your feeling, She-Wolf? Will you ever see your dear, departed husband again? Or is he destined to forever wander the listless shadows?'

Without hesitation, the She-Wolf pounced.

Gorm was ready, hurling the powder as he leaped aside. Freya landed in a roll, blinking rapidly in a vain attempt to clear her vision. Spinning blindly, she swiped her claws in all directions.

'Snake!' she roared. 'I do not fear you!'

A howl ripped through the haze, and Gorm struck. A sudden heat bloomed across Freya's chest and she reeled. Gorm pressed the attack, cutting her again and again as he ran unseen— orbiting, passing, darting in and out.

Fear found Freya and sank into her bones. How could she fight what she could not see? There was that copper tang of blood in her mouth, and her knees gave way under the ceaseless assault. Swinging madly, she cursed the blurred world around her.

Then—a revelation dawned.

She possessed the *Wolfsight*.

Freya stopped. Breathed. Listened. Wolfsight went beyond the senses, making colours of smells, images of sound. She needed only to focus. Relaxing, she closed her eyes and absorbed her surroundings afresh.

Time slowed.

Through the veil of obscurity, shapes emerged with startling clarity. The landscape unfolded, every outline defined by the subtle interplay of scents that danced upon the night air. Light became music, and she perceived the stars, the moon, the ethereal symphony of the aurora. Trees, rocks, earth, and sky. All came alive in vibrant detail.

And she perceived Gorm.

His scent, a potent mixture of sweat and fur, painted a clear portrait in her mind's eye. He was moving toward her, claws pointed like speartips, the sharp smell of blood betraying his precise position. Freya waited until the final moment. Gorm leaped, claws outstretched, his teeth bared in a malicious display of overconfidence.

He missed.

In a blink, the predator became the prey. Pivoting, Freya ducked beneath Gorm's torso and vaulted upward, mouth wide, teeth flashing. Like a spring trap, her jaws snapped shut over Gorm's exposed throat, cutting off his cry before it could fully form. Gorm was lifted high and brought down with a savage slam, and Freya thrashed him by the neck in a frenzy like a wild dog with a rabbit. His blood gushed like a fountain, and no amount of clawing did him any good. He was pinned down, dying, staring into the savage eyes of the Alpha.

Freya chewed through the flesh, snarling, snuffling. At last, her razor teeth found the ridges of Gorm's spine. She held him there, watching the life fade from his eyes.

And bit.

Gorm's head came free. It rolled a little way away, leaking dark fluid. Freya watched as though in a trance. The life spilled from Gorm's body, crowning the Klo King's severed head in a puddle of his own blood. She felt his body start to shrink beneath her, claws and fur retracting, the last traces of his tyranny disappearing from the world like smoke from a ruin.

Freya lingered momentarily, drinking in the stillness and the bracing cold. She breathed out, exhaling years of fear. Of shame. She closed her eyes. Kissed her father on his stubbled cheek. Skipped stones with Maisie on the loch beside their childhood home. Danced with Erik on a pebble beach beneath the bright summer sun.

Her eyes opened slowly, and she peered down. Gorm's face had already paled, his icy blue eyes dilated to black and staring up at nothing. She lifted it by the ears. Held it to her face. Stared at it, turning it this way and that.

'Perhaps you are mistaken, Gorm. Perhaps Valhalla is real after all. I hear they continue to fight and feast, day in, day out. Perhaps Erik awaits you there, yet I doubt you will find him in a feasting mood.'

She stood, taking Gorm's head to the edge of a cliff. The valley spread out before her. Runolodda stood in the distance beside the starlit river, framed by the grey snow-capped mountains. She would wait here until the sun rose. She would lift Gorm's head high and roar into the new day. Then all the North would hear who she truly was.

Not a slave.

Not a shadow.

She was the Wolf Victorious.

MARIGOLDS

They strode hand in hand across Red Meadow.

It was in the heart of summer, amidst the crimson sea of poppies, that Scion and Astrid pledged their bond. The meadow, adorned with garlands of vibrant blooms and fluttering banners, encompassed the entire village, gathered to bear witness to the union.

Less than a year had passed since the Battle of Runolodda. Wounds, both of the flesh and of the heart, were yet to fully mend. Still, village life had largely returned to normal. It helped to keep busy, some said, and to find happiness in the warmth of shared kinship.

And shared mead.

Olle raised his drinking horn with a cheer as the couple exchanged vows and gifts, among them swords embellished with delicate patterns carved by Birger the Bear.

Scion, garbed in fine furs and a polished helmet, smiled at his beautiful bride, radiant wildflowers in her golden hair. 'Whether home or far afield, I pledge to you my sword and shield.' Scion passed Astrid his sword, his intense gaze causing her to giggle.

'My, my,' she whispered. 'Now that was a promise as steadfast as the mountain's hold.'

Scion relaxed. 'You can be sure of it,' he winked.

'And I make this vow to you, Scion of Runolodda—' she said, lifting her voice for the village to hear. 'I bind my fate to yours, in solemn troth. As in love, as in oath.' She offered him her sword, and he sheathed it with a flourish, eliciting another raucous cheer from the people.

Vali stepped forward, taking the couple by their wrists. 'Let us bless these two with gifts, with music, and with good luck in the bedchamber!' The village roared with laughter, and the crowd rushed off to begin the festivities.

A great feast awaited, tables groaning under the weight of roasted boar, mead flowing freely from horns passed hand to hand. The summer air filled with the sounds of laughter and song that mingled with the beat of drums and the strumming of strings. Torsten banged out a rhythm, leading all in one of Tove's songs. His voice rang out, and even with the weight of her absence on his heart, it did not crack.

Not even once.

Gudrun strode up to the happy couple and presented them with a decorated ram's horn.

'I am elated for you both,' she beamed, enveloping the pair in a hug that only a grandmother could give. 'There will always be a pot of rabbit stew on the boil should you ever wish to visit.'

'Well,' said Astrid, struggling to breathe in the old woman's embrace, 'Since we're now neighbours, I'm sure that can be arranged.'

Gudrun let them go, smiling as she looked them up and down. 'Ah, it is good to be home.' Withdrawing, she caught both Fiske and Selby staring her way. They began to squabble as she passed, muttering something about *sharing*.

A bonfire blazed at the heart of the celebration, its flames leaping into the heavens, casting a warm glow that held deep into the night. Around it, dancers swirled, holding hands in a great ring. One of the slave women, now forever free, laughed with Tyr as he swung her around by his artificial limb.

The smoke rose higher and higher through the night.

Until the darkness gave way to a new day.

*

The Beastly Boys soaked in the hot spring.

Steam wisped from the bubbling surface into the crisp autumn air, and Scion sighed to feel his bones warmed after another successful hunt.

'Do you remember the time Chief Lennärt caught us stealing honey cakes? We must have been four, maybe five summers old.'

'Aye,' grinned Birger. 'Seven lashes each! I can still feel the sting of his switch.'

'But do you remember our sweet revenge?' asked Scion.

'I do,' chuckled Tyr. 'We hid on a rooftop, throwing stones at his door all night. I don't think the poor sap slept a wink until morning.'

'I think the real reason he left the village was to escape the likes of us!' quipped Scion, and the roar of their laughter startled a robin from a nearby branch.

Birger lowered his gaze. 'Regarding Lennärt . . . I have something of an announcement to make.'

'Oh?' said Scion.

'After seeing his library in Hvalvik, and his many beautiful scrolls . . .'

'Out with it, Birger,' urged Tyr.

Birger sighed. 'I want to learn letters. How to read them and how to write them. I hope to find Lennärt, wherever he and the Brotherhood have fled to. I shall ask him to teach me. I'll read as many of those beautiful scrolls as possible.' He paused, allowing his friends to absorb the news. 'My days in the smoky forge are over. There is a world of wonder out there and I intend to learn all I can of it.'

'When will you go?' asked Tyr.

'In the spring. No sooner.' He looked them both in the eyes. 'Fear not, my friends. There will be plenty of time for drunken goodbyes until then. And I shall return before too long. You have my word.'

Scion shared a look with Tyr. 'What does Knud make of this?'

'Father seemed rather pleased for me, though I suspect he puts on a brave face for my sake.' Birger splashed the warm water into his face and through his hair. 'I shall miss you, brothers. Try not to get into too much mischief while I'm gone.'

'Well,' said Tyr, pointing to their kill for the day. 'You can't leave before I get my new knife. That was our deal: an elk for a seax. Remember?'

'Ha! I do. Alright. You will have your blade before the winter ends. But I want the meat cut thin and cured for my journey. Agreed?'

'Agreed!' said Tyr, and they clasped wrists in a mock-serious pledge.

'Well, brothers,' said Scion. 'The full moon rises tonight. I trust you are prepared.'

'Of course,' said Tyr, 'I never leave home without it.' He lifted his stunted arm, adorned with a fitted leather covering that hid the stump beneath. Birger and Scion watched in fascination as Tyr unbuckled the strap holding it in place to reveal an insulated leather pouch nestled within. Carefully, he untied the string and poured a tiny amount of sparkling powder into the palm of his hand, careful not to spill a grain.

Scion smiled.

This had been his wife's idea.

Learning from Scion that silver could annul the moonlight's effect, Astrid had swiftly gathered every last scrap of silver in the village. She had instructed Knud to grind them into a consumable compound, and soon the Beastly Boys—and her mother—had enough of the glittering dust to last for years to come. The Full Moon Ritual was abandoned, and the pits were filled in. The Wolf-kind need never be caged again.

'Can't say I enjoy the taste,' mumbled Birger, taking a pinch to his mouth.

Scion swallowed his portion too. 'I wonder if it could be mixed with a little mead?'

'Aye,' said Tyr. 'A fine idea, brother.'

'Best pack the silver away,' warned Birger, pointing up at the prow-like cliff where their portly friend hurtled toward the edge, naked as the day he was born. The Boys scrambled out of the way, and Olle soared in a magnificent arc through the air.

And landed belly first in the warm water.

*

Freya stepped out onto the ice.

Winter had come once again, and the river had frozen over. It shone like a crystal ribbon beneath the steel-blue sky.

Freya stopped halfway across and lowered herself on one knee to peer through the glassy surface. Erik's ship lay on the deep riverbed like a submerged dream. And though the hull had cracked, the overall shape of the ship remained fairly intact.

A broken heart settling into rest.

'Hello, husband. I've brought you these.' She reached into her cloak and drew out a fresh bouquet of yellow marigolds.

Never one for eloquence, Freya knew her actions had always spoken louder to Erik's heart than words ever could. Now, after all was said and done, she hoped it was enough.

'Be free, Erik.' Those were the only words that came to her. He would know what she meant—that he had been avenged. That she would look now to the future, as he would have wished. That she and Astrid would be well. That the village would flourish once more.

The tears came, though this time they came to heal.

To wash over her like a river.

'Where I go, you will go. Into tomorrow and tomorrow until we meet again.'

With care, she laid the golden flowers on the ice.

Then, turning, she wiped her eyes and set off for home.

THE END

Printed in Great Britain
by Amazon